touching the surface

willow

touching
the
surface

KIMBERLY SABATINI

SIMON PULSE
NEW YORK   LONDON   TORONTO   SYDNEY   NEW DELHI

SIMON PULSE

An imprint of Simon & Schuster Children's Publishing Division
1230 Avenue of the Americas, New York, NY 10020
First Simon Pulse paperback edition October 2013
Copyright © 2012 by Kimberly Sabatini
Also available in a Simon Pulse hardcover edition.
For information about special discounts for bulk purchases, please contact Simon & Schuster
Special Sales at 1-866-506-1949 or business@simonandschuster.com.
The Simon & Schuster Speakers Bureau can bring authors to your live event. For more
information or to book an event contact the Simon & Schuster Speakers Bureau at
1-866-248-3049 or visit our website at www.simonspeakers.com.
Designed by Hilary Zarycky
The text of this book was set in Centaur.
Manufactured in the United States of America
2 4 6 8 10 9 7 5 3 1
The Library of Congress has cataloged the hardcover edition as follows:
Sabatini, Kim.
Touching the surface / by Kim Sabatini. — 1st Simon Pulse hardcover ed.
p. cm.
Summary: In the afterlife for the fourth time, seventeen-year-old Elliot
knows she has one last chance, but before she can begin her fourth life
she must delve into her past, earn the forgiveness of her best friend, reconnect with
her soul mate, and set things right for the future.
[1. Conduct of life—Fiction. 2. Future life—Fiction.
3. Reincarnation—Fiction. 4. Death—Fiction.] I. Title.
PZ7.S1154Tou 2012 [Fic]—dc23 2011041854
ISBN 978-1-4424-4002-9 (hc)
ISBN 978-1-4424-4003-6 (pbk)
ISBN 978-1-4424-4004-3 (eBook)

"Little Bird"
Words and music by Annie Lennox
Copyright © 1992 by La Lennoxa Ltd. and Universal Music Publishing MGB Ltd.
All Rights Administered in the U.S. by Universal Music – MGB Songs
International Copyright Secured   All Rights Reserved
Reprinted by permission of Hal Leonard Corporation

This book is dedicated to my dad.
Can you hear me? I have a voice now.
It's big enough for the both of us.
Love's divine . . .
Your beautiful baby

the other side

of

the surface

My body smacked the water. Thoughts scattered like a handful of beads dropped on a bare wood floor. I gasped for air and the current rushed in. My throat burned. Panic, thrashing, spots of light exploding in my head. Surrender. I sank softly down . . . until . . . fingers wrapped around my wrist, yanking me out of the water. As my head broke the surface it all became clear. I had died . . . again.

I stood on the end of the dock that jutted out toward the middle of the lake, fingering the silver eagle feather charm that hung in the hollow below my neck. The chain tangled in the short hairs below my ponytail. I was stunned and spots bounced in front of my eyes. Memories of Mel and my previous visits to the Obmil were rushing at me, but when it came to knowing who I was in my last life, all I could pull from the murky haze was the fact that I was a girl. A girl and a failure.

"Samantha? Is that really you?" Mel inhaled deeply and smiled, confirming that she knew exactly who I was.

It was starting to come back to me now. Everything around me looked the same as it had on my last two visits. I, on the other hand, was guaranteed to appear completely different. But that wasn't unusual or problematic. A soul in the afterlife is recognizable. When you arrive at the Obmil in the last body you inhabited, it really isn't much different than showing up at a family reunion in a different outfit. Everyone has a scent, a personal pheromone that overrides the optical illusion of the body they're wearing. I'm told my soul smells a little like freshly cut wood and dark chocolate.

Mel took another deep breath and smiled at me, her face warm and welcoming. Slowly, the knot of information in my head was unraveling. It was Mel's familiar hand that had pulled me from the water, out of my third life. That made sense. After all, she'd greeted me on my last two arrivals at the Obmil Center for Progression. Crappity, crap, crap—this meant I was here for the third time. I was stuck.

Mel studied me for a moment, then dropped her gaze and focused on recording my arrival in her notebook. She was big into journaling, but I also suspected she was giving me time to get my bearings. Her pen flew across the page as she wrote down tidbits of information. I could imagine her comments about my future. *Lost soul—going nowhere fast.*

I thought about it for a moment, realizing that I wasn't Samantha anymore. That had been my name in my second life, the last time I'd taken a detour through the Obmil. I could feel the skin between my eyes crinkle up as I searched my memory. Who was I now?

On my first visit to the Obmil, my memories of life had been like Swiss cheese: baby Swiss, to be exact. There was more information present than missing. As a Second Timer the gaps were larger. It took a little longer for the memories to return, but with time, all the voids were filled. Honestly, it had almost been easy. No Delving was necessary for First and Second Timers. But I could still hear Mel's voice warning me last time that *remembering* my past wasn't my primary goal, I was supposed to be learning something deeper about myself during the process, to avoid ending up at the Obmil again. Why hadn't I done it then? Being a Third Timer was humiliating. It was like failing gym because you refused to change for class. But as stupid as I felt for being in the afterlife again, I also knew I would have to find out what had led me here.

Last time, I'd tried doing what Mel suggested, letting one

of my memories go deeper, but it had been like rubbing my heart against a cheese grater. In my second life, my husband had cheated on me. Repeatedly. Remembering that was painful enough, but then I discovered my response to his philandering. I'd thought I could fix it. I thought it was me. I was convinced that if I put my mind to it, I could be whatever it was that he needed. I stayed—in an all-star show of pathetic behavior—and then he dumped me. I'd wanted to kill myself and maybe would have, if it hadn't been for my best friend. She'd saved me from doing something unforgivable.

What I'd learned from the exercise was that self-examination hurts. It had taken my breath away. I never wanted to do that again. Things were better on the surface.

Standing on the dock now, the memories from my previous life as Samantha raced past me like a train passing through the station. I was so engrossed in the slide show in my head that I sucked in my breath when the recollections suddenly stopped short at the end of my second life. Who was I *now*?

Mel's hand steadied my elbow and I knew without a doubt that this time around, things were different. I was empty. There weren't any significant memories from my third life for my mind to grasp. The whole thing was one big, blank hole. I didn't know my own story. It was the Obmil's way of forcing my hand, upping the ante.

"Samantha?" Mel waved her hand in front of my face.

I felt a small ping. Like the wink of a firefly, one small memory shot across my mind. "It's Elliot. Elliot Turner," I answered.

"Elliot . . ." She rolled the name around on her tongue, looking me over from head to toe. "You're younger than you were on your last visit. Not as curvy, either."

I hugged myself, trying to make my own acquaintance, more small details starting to emerge. I squeezed tighter, attempting to reconcile the changes between my body as Samantha and the new me—Elliot. My hands and arms crushed my chest and sides. My new shape wasn't a roller-coaster ride, that was for sure. Leaning over, I found my reflection in the smooth water of the lake. Seventeen was a lot younger than forty. I studied my face. It was plain compared to Samantha's. The new me appeared forgettable. I turned away from the water.

Mel tilted her head to the side. "How was your trip in?"

"Wet."

Sarcasm? I wasn't sure where that came from. Maybe it was my first clue to my new personality.

Mel paused for a second, maneuvered her mane of frizzy red hair out of the way and gave a chuckle. Everyone who came to the Obmil through a waterway was dry as a bone when they exited. It was one of the perks of being dead. There were others. The last time I'd been here I'd dropped in from the sky. Cause of death: plane crash due to mechanical failure. Luckily, high-impact landings were about as painful as water entries were wet.

Searching Mel's sympathetic eyes, the full realization of being a Third Timer crashed over me like a wave. Without thinking, I flew into her arms.

"I don't remember anything at all this time." Small hiccups bounced my shoulders up and down. I remembered my first two lives, but my life as Elliot felt as if it was tucked away, someplace long forgotten, and no one had given me a map to find it. I buried my face in the crook of Mel's neck where she always smelled the strongest of lavender and peppermint.

"Sshh . . ." Mel crooned in my ear. "It's okay. There's nothing to feel embarrassed about. I know you thought you'd figured it out last time, but I did try to warn you. It takes more than just touching the surface." She squeezed my shoulder and smiled. "It's fine, it wasn't meant to be. Besides, if you'd gotten it right, I wouldn't have the chance to see you again."

I sniffed once or twice, allowing myself to feel safe for a moment, wrapped in her arms and her confidence.

"Enlightenment is highly overrated," I said, pulling back and shrugging my shoulders. I thought about the cheese grater pain of recollected memories and deeper emotions. I shuddered.

"I'm not in a rush anyway. Staying here isn't so bad—I'll just hang around with you for a while."

"You don't want to do that," Mel snapped.

I looked up in surprise. She was usually as even-tempered as they come.

"Listen, Elliot, I'm not really supposed to interfere too much with a soul's personal journey. I'm simply a guide. But you should know that there are consequences for lingering too long at the Obmil. It's okay to take all the time that you need if you're actively working toward your growth plan, but eternal avoidance isn't an option."

"What kind of consequences?" I asked, noticing how her mouth was a thin hard line.

"It's—let's just say the consequences can be hellish." She shifted her gaze away from mine.

"So, what you're saying is that there really is a he—" Mel cut me off with a sharp stare before I could finish. Everyone at the Obmil was always speculating. Do all souls move forward after their time here, or are there other options—less pleasant options?

Mel cleared her throat. "I'm just saying that the best way to handle being a Third Timer is to take Julia's approach."

"Who's Julia?"

Mel gave herself a light thunk on the head. "Sorry. Julia is Emma."

Emma. My best friend in life and the afterlife. During my first life she'd also been a *he*. In fact, we were eighty-year-old twin bachelor brothers named Arty and Jim. We'd both died in our sleep and woke up in "twin" beds at the Obmil.

During my second life as Samantha, Emma was my best friend. We'd met at a divorce support group. She'd found me when I was at the end of my rope. We were on our way back from a retreat when our plane went down. Twice we'd been in the same life and afterlife together.

"When did she get here? Is she my age? What does she look like? Does she remember her last life? Has she started Workshop yet?" I would've kept going but Mel had a funny expression on her face, like she was sucking on something sour.

"What? What's going on?" I dug my nails into the palm of my hand, but nothing happened. I glanced down, realizing I no longer had Samantha's perfectly manicured fingers. I fought the urge to yank at a hangnail with my teeth.

"Going—Julia Going." Mel stumbled over her words. "That's her last name. And, well, she isn't in my Workshop this time." The corners of Mel's mouth turned down ever so slightly.

"What do you mean? Why didn't you take her?" My voice was louder than I expected and it echoed off the rock walls.

"I tried to take her." Mel folded her arms and then unfolded them. "She didn't want to be in my Workshop."

"What?"

"Come sit with me." Mel patted a sun-warmed spot at the end of the dock. The warm cedar smell lured me closer.

I sat down next to her and she put her finger up and touched it to my lips, stopping the next question that was sitting on the edge of my tongue. "Elliot . . ." She removed her finger and began tapping it on the wood. "She didn't want to be in the same Workshop as you."

I was sure I hadn't heard her correctly. My jaw hurt from grinding my teeth together. I was not going to cry again.

"Before you ask, I want you to know that I don't know the answer. She wouldn't tell me why she didn't want to be with you. You're going to have to ask her yourself." She waited, but I was suddenly out of questions.

"Can I be selfish for a moment?" Mel asked, reaching for my hand.

I nodded, unable to say anything.

"I missed you. I love everyone who walks into my life at the Obmil. I'm where I am today because I'm good at connecting with lost souls, but you and I have a special bond, Elliot." My name already slid off her tongue like it was the only one I'd ever had.

I felt just as strongly about her. I wanted to tell Mel how special she was, not selfish at all, but I felt like a leaf floating haphazardly downstream. I couldn't stop thinking about Emma. Wait, she was Julia now. Unfurling my clenched fingers, I wiped them against my pants. I could feel Mel's gaze as I picked at the cuticle of my thumb.

"Is she a lot older than me or something?" I needed to find a reasonable explanation.

Mel winced. "She's nineteen."

"Oh."

Mel stood up and dusted off her wildly colorful peasant skirt. "Come on," she said. The two inches of silver bangles on either wrist jingled. I glanced at her untamed hair, down to her toes painted in a rainbow of colors. Even if Julia was mad at me for some strange reason, how could she not want to be with Mel?

"Let's go up to the Haven and get you settled in your room." Mel tilted her head toward the path. "We should get out of here. David's on his way down to the lake. Looks like he's meeting someone who's arriving in a little bit." She peeked back at me with one eyebrow raised. I didn't like David and I wasn't fond of Mel's eyebrow at that moment either. Not wanting to get cornered on the dock with David, I double-timed it to solid ground with Mel. Now that I was paying attention, I could feel the subtle vibration in the air that gives advance warning of a new arrival. Follow the quivering and you'd have a pretty good idea where the next dead soul was going to pop up. Even though the vibrations were stronger facing the lake, I turned and watched David make his way toward us.

David also worked at the Obmil, but he was nothing like Mel. He oozed arrogance. I opened my mouth to say something unpleasant about him, but Mel put her finger to her lips. I wasn't sure if this was because David was striding toward us or because she didn't want to hear me bad-mouth another "dedicated" soul at the Obmil. Before I could find out, David was standing four inches too close. I could smell his overpowering cologne as his bulk towered over me, blocking out the sun. He leaned over and gave a big mucous-filled sniff.

"Samantha." His voice boomed. "You're back so soon." He plucked at his bushy mustache, then started counting on his fingers.

"It's Elliot Turner now," Mel said.

He shrugged and continued like he'd never been interrupted. "Miss Turner, doesn't that make this your third visit? Time for you to step up. When you're a Third Timer, you have to truly resolve your issues before you get to move on. Unfortunately, you don't seem like the type who's very self-motivated." I gasped. He cocked his head to the side. "Or maybe, you have a reason for avoiding the truth."

Everything he said was too loud. His smile was overly

big and bright. Even though he was an overfed, overdressed windbag—more like a caricature of a powerful man than an actual one—I still stepped behind Mel like I was seven instead of seventeen.

I opened my mouth, but nothing came out. He dismissed me with a wave of his hand and sauntered past us, speaking over his shoulder. "Must be going. I've got to hurry and register this new arrival because it's almost time for Workshop. I don't want to keep my prize pupil waiting." He stopped walking for just a moment and winked. "I suspect that unlike you, Miss Turner, Julia Going is going places. She's very motivated and can't wait to leave the Obmil."

circles

in

the sky

My right temple pulsed. Anger rushed through my veins. It wasn't just me who felt like this. Emma—I mean Julia—hated David too. He was kind of a creep to everyone, but he really didn't like us. It had started when we'd first arrived as the twins and obviously it had escalated. There was no way that Julia would want to be in his Workshop. As soon as I talked to her I knew I could straighten this out. Since I couldn't take my frustrations out on David, I kicked at the rocks on my way up the path. After I almost blasted one into Mel's back, I kept my eyes glued to the Haven, stomping my feet as I stalked after her.

The Haven sat above the lake, a grand mountain lodge perched on a foundation of rock. It wouldn't have surprised me if it had grown there, wood, glass, and stone nesting on the curve of the water, the turrets and towers of the roofline rising above the trees that blanketed the mountains in every direction.

The closer I moved to the building, the safer I felt. At least something here was comfortingly predictable. The Haven and its lake never changed. Life everywhere else at the Obmil School of Progression was constantly shifting like a busy mind. When you stepped out of the Haven and looked around, you never knew what you were going to see. The landscape, weather, and other buildings were as unpredictable as the emotionally charged people who were stuck in the afterlife.

In the distance I could see a couple having an argument, a pocket of dark storm clouds hovering above their heads. Nearby, a woman was tucked beneath a tree, reading a book. The arc of a rainbow framed her face, completing the upturned curve of her smile.

There were advantages to this physical disclosure of emotional temperament. I knew to maneuver away from people with thunder in their vicinity, and I knew who to seek out for a good laugh. With concentration and awareness, people could control their feelings and hide the display, but honestly, you'd be surprised at how often emotions get the better of people.

My eye returned to the couple with the storm clouds and I had to laugh. Bursts of bright fireworks were going off above them now as they moved into a blush-inducing embrace. Wearing your heart on your sleeve for everyone to see had its ups and downs.

As I climbed the flagstone steps to the Haven, I felt a thrill of anticipation, knowing I would be seeing Julia any minute now. While there were hundreds of people moving in and out of this particular Obmil on any given day, somehow we'd always managed to be in the same place at the same time. Mel had said it wasn't unusual for a group of souls to travel together. She'd said Julia and I were traveling in a kind of spiritual Gulf Stream that was keeping us in close proximity to each other. Was it possible that Julia's soul was trying to swim as far away from mine as the current could carry her?

What worried me now was the unknown. I had no freaking idea what I was supposed to discover about myself. With all the magic that happens around here, you would think it wouldn't be so hard to come up with a manual or something—*What to Expect When Confronted with the Unexpected: A Failure's Guide to the Afterlife.* And what would happen after Julia and I figured out our growth plans? There were no guarantees we'd follow the same current after moving on from the Obmil this time. The whole thing was too vague for my taste. I figured that if we at least left the Obmil at the same time again, we'd have a much better chance of staying together. David made it sound as if Julia was well on her way to enlightenment and leaving, but that didn't make any sense. In fact, it made me want to start kicking rocks all over again. I needed to calm down and remember that he was probably just trying to use her to upset me.

Once again I looked around, hoping to spot Julia, which was stupid since I wouldn't be able to figure out who she was until I was close enough to smell her. Still, I eyed a dozen teenagers sitting at a cluster of picnic tables. I wanted to move in close to everyone until I found someone who smelled like vanilla and warm sand, but I figured that if one of them was Julia, Mel would have let me know. I stopped lagging behind and hurried up the steps and into the lobby. The first person I saw was Freddie, the caretaker of the Haven. He was right where I'd left him at the front desk.

He breathed in deeply. "Samantha, good to see you, rascal. I've missed you." He edged closer, carrying an ornate brass key on a burgundy velvet ribbon.

"It's Elliot now," Mel chimed in.

"Hi, Freddie," I mumbled. I was pressed tightly into the bib of his overalls and plaid flannel shirt. He smelled of root beer and motor oil.

"Let me look at you, sweetheart," Freddie said. He cupped the charm around my neck with his paw of a hand. "Still love your eagles, I see."

"I'm a Third Timer, Freddie," I said, feeling like a squirrel darting out into traffic.

His eyes shifted to Mel. "Then you'll be needing a place to stay."

"You're going to put me with Julia, right?" I asked. "Any chance our room is overlooking the water?" I shuffled my foot back and forth across the worn wood floor. I always felt a little claustrophobic if I couldn't see the lake or the cliffs. I'd whiled away a lot of hours here observing two eagles, far across the lake, circling their territory. I'd started watching them on my first visit to the Obmil. It was beyond fascination. It was a magnetic pull. Watching them circle the sky was meditative. That's why I'd been so confused the day they violently locked together, talon-to-talon, free-falling toward the lake.

I'd thought they were attacking each other and were willing to crash to the surface before either would admit defeat. But right before cartwheeling to certain death, they broke apart and each flew lazy spirals in the vast expanse of blue sky. It had been romance. . . . I hadn't realized it until months later, when there were three instead of two.

I repeated the question. "I'm rooming with Julia, right?" My stomach clenched when I saw the look that passed between Freddie and Mel.

"Listen, honey, you are going to be rooming with Julia, but

she's not necessarily thrilled about it." Freddie patted my hand. "She's agreed to do it because we're so crowded, but she surrendered under protest. Thinks it will be too hard for both of you."

"Too hard?"

"What he means, Elliot, is that Julia has chosen to put some distance between you two and she thinks that this might send a mixed message—be confusing for everyone," Mel said.

I didn't know what to say.

Mel straightened her peasant top. "I think it will be fine. It'll give you a chance to talk it out." She smiled bright as the sun, and it was just enough to remind me that Julia and I were best friends. Of course we would work this out.

"Well then, follow me." Freddie gestured to the left, his hand calloused and tough on the palm, yet paper-thin and blue-veined on top. "I've got just the thing for you, Elliot." He moved slowly, reminding me that he hadn't been a young man when he arrived at the Obmil. Mel and I followed him up to the seventh floor, the roof of the south side. At the end of the hall was an arched wooden door. Freddie tugged it open, revealing a spiraling stone staircase. Silently I followed him up to a lofty tower room. The windows were propped open in every direction and a soft breeze blew through the space.

I spun around, trying to take it all in. It was a little hideaway, a unique perch above the crooked mob of hallways below.

"I never knew this was here! I thought that door was a closet."
I danced a little jig. Julia and I wouldn't be fighting over a bed
with a view. Everything in the room was by a window.

Freddie cleared his throat. "Well, I usually save it for my
special souls. The ones that need a little less chatter and a bit
more sky. Although in your case, I imagine you'll just chat at
the sky." He gave a little grunt. "Just thought you might like it."

I glanced at Mel. "You knew about this?"

She smiled. "Nope, I found out about it when he brought
Julia up. Freddie is really good at keeping secrets." She waggled
her finger at him, making her bangles tinkle softly. He clutched
his hat and looked down at the floor, a faint blush on his
cheeks.

"Enjoy it, Elliot." He handed me the fancy key, warm from
the heat of his hand. I placed it on the window ledge, doubt-
ing that I'd be carrying around something five inches long with
decorative curlicues and a velvet ribbon. Nobody locked his or
her doors at the Obmil anyway.

Freddy glanced at his pocket watch and then stuffed it
back into his overalls as he turned to leave. "I'll see you later
for lunch," he said, moving slowly down the stairs, one foot
meeting the other at every landing.

"I'm going to head out also," Mel said. She paused.
"Elliot?"

I turned to look at her.

"I know you're scared to be a Third Timer, the focus of Workshop. You're afraid to be vulnerable in front of everyone, but I'll be there. I'm going to guide you through this. It's the way things are supposed to be." Her focus shifted to something over my shoulder. "It won't be long before you're ready to leave here, get a new growth plan, and start all over again."

I opened my mouth to protest, but she cut me off.

"I know you think you don't want to leave, but trust me, you don't want to linger here with me. No good can come from wasting time. Especially Obmil time: It's a gift."

I nodded, frustrated at my inability to seem enthusiastic. Honestly, it was scary. My stomach twisted into knots just thinking about it. There's nothing easy about moving to the next level, jumping streams. It's a huge transition. Something small and dark nudged at my insides, making me wonder if there were any real guarantees. What if there was the possibility that I wouldn't be moving on at all? Maybe you could screw up a life so bad that they didn't give you another one. Then where the hell would you go?

Mel deposited a reassuring kiss on my forehead. When she stepped back, someone was in the doorway staring at me.

3

reunions

Tendrils of vanilla and beach sand danced around me, confirming who this girl was, but it seemed so unlikely. The last time I'd seen her she'd been tall and raven-haired with warm brown tones. Now her skin was pale, almost translucent. Before she'd had the body of a volleyball player. Now the biggest thing about her was the mop of blond ringlets that corkscrewed in every direction.

I rushed past Mel and threw my arms around Julia. Her head tucked itself under my chin.

"Ouch, Samantha. Think you could ease off on the bone-crushing enthusiasm?"

I loosened my grip and felt her skinny little toothpick arms wrap around my waist. Her lungs inflated as she sucked in my scent. I buried myself in the nest of her hair.

Mel cleared her throat. "Ladies, I've got things to do and no time to waste witnessing sappy reunions." I thought I heard her sniffle and smiled to myself. I knew everything would be all right. "You two catch up. By the way—she's Elliot now, not Samantha, and don't forget she won't be attending Workshop today. Today's arrivals start tomorrow. You, on the other hand, need to be on your way in just a few minutes. See you later, girls."

Julia wiggled out of my arms like Houdini. Then she sat down on her bed, pulled up her knees, and wrapped herself up into a tiny ball punctuated by blond fluff. "So you know?" Her voice was a squeak.

I plopped down on the remaining bed and peeked out the window. "I was told you didn't want to room with me. If that's what you're referring to. I also heard that you aren't in Mel's Workshop, that you're in David's." I tried, but I couldn't keep the disgust from leaking into my voice. "Is it true that you picked David to be your guide?" I turned and inspected Julia, who appeared to be getting smaller as I examined her.

"Is it because you didn't want to be in Workshop with me?" I couldn't help it, I got teary. "What's going on, Jules?" I began to pace, unable to sit still any longer.

"Don't call me that. My name is Julia." She vaulted off the bed. "You always do that."

"Do what?"

"You decide things. You make choices and you never ask me how I feel about them." She grabbed an indigo hoodie off the end of her bed and put it on. The color brought out her eyes and made them take up all the space on her face. "I don't want you giving me a nickname."

I threw up my hands. "Okay. Sorry. I didn't mean to upset you. I just missed you. I'm trying to figure out what's going on here."

"I missed you too." Julia walked over and hooked her arm through mine. It was a familiar gesture, something that she'd done before as Jim and Emma. It stopped the out-of-control feeling that battered me from all sides.

"Jule-ia," I stopped myself. I could hear her sigh as if she knew it had been too much to ask. It was like I couldn't be counted on to get the simplest things right. That sigh was another nail being pounded into my coffin of failure. Yet, even though I knew what an utter screwup I was—back here for the third time—it seemed ridiculous to feel bad about wanting to call my best friend by a term of endearment. I just wanted to make her feel special, but my rationalization of the situation wasn't stopping the sick feeling in my stomach. I hated the sensation of not doing things the right way, or, should I say, the expected way.

"Sorry. I promise I won't do it again."

"I know." She rolled her eyes and smiled—major mixed message. "Listen, Elliot, about the whole David thing." She flipped her wrist and took a look at her watch. "Oh crap, I've gotta go. Listen, we'll talk later. I do love you, Elliot—I just don't think I can stand to be in the same room with you for too long." Before I could react, she'd darted down the stairs, her feet moving over the steps so quietly, it was like she was flying.

I didn't need a clock to know that it was lunchtime. My stomach growled loudly. I racked my brain to remember when I'd last eaten. Like everything from my previous life, it was a mystery. I headed down the stairs, my shoes tapping a staccato rhythm on the stone beneath my feet. Instantly I was surrounded by the smell of brick oven pizza. Closing my eyes, I inhaled, filling my lungs with the perfect combination of cheese, tomato, and spices. I must've loved pizza in my earlier life. It smelled so delicious right now.

I opened my eyes, ready to follow my nose all the way down to the dining room. My mouth watered in anticipation, but I couldn't resist one last peek up the curved staircase. I was in love with my room—our room. I felt a tap on my shoulder. Julia must have forgotten something important (like the fact that we *were* best friends forever). I turned quickly, ready to accept her apology—the one that wouldn't have been necessary if she hadn't gone all looney to start with. No one was there. I felt a double tap on my other shoulder—the old tap-the-opposite-shoulder trick. She was notorious for that when we were a very young Arty and Jim. I whipped around, ready to make her beg for forgiveness, and almost choked on my own tongue. The guy standing in front of me was . . . was . . . radiant. Guys can be radiant, right? 'Cause this guy was beautiful. But it was more than just the blond waves in his hair and the earnest green eyes. It was like he glowed—from the inside.

"Hi, Elliot." He appeared to be about my age, but he came off like a little boy waiting in line to sit on Santa's lap and give his wish list. He bounced lightly up and down on his toes as he watched me intently. He almost vibrated. How the heck did he know my name? I stared at him. Nothing about him was familiar. Despite his youthful exuberance, he seemed weirdly worldly, like Yoda trapped in the body of a sun-kissed teenage heartbreaker. Bizarre. He gave a soft laugh.

"Do or do not . . . there is no try." He sounded just like the pint-size Jedi Master. My jaw sagged open and Radiant Guy raised an eyebrow at me and waited.

I glanced up, wondering if I'd managed to somehow project a cartoon bubble with my Yoda thoughts for him to read. That's when I saw it: I'd created a recording of the introductory roll-up that starts the *Star Wars* movie. The familiar theme music was playing softly near my left shoulder, words scrolling over my head—*in a galaxy far, far away.* . . .

For exactly ten seconds I was completely weirded out, but then he hunched over and said, "Good relations with the Wookies, I have." I couldn't help it, I cracked up, which made him chuckle, leading me to laugh harder than before. I think we would have stayed there forever, entertaining each other, if Mel hadn't shown up.

"There you are, Oliver." She pointed a finger at him. "I seem to recall asking you to let Elliot get her bearings before you inundated her with your relentless enthusiasm." The scowl she flashed was a complete fake.

Oliver grinned. "I tried—couldn't wait."

"You've been waiting for me?" I asked. My mind was jumping around like water on a hot skillet. I twirled a loose strand of hair around my finger. His name was Oliver. So, I knew that, and the fact that he was a *Star Wars* fan; but that wasn't really enough to explain why standing next to him made me feel like coming home after a really long vacation. How could someone be utterly familiar and completely unrecognizable at the same time?

"Yes, I've been waiting." He said it with confidence. The magnetic pull between us made me want to reach out and touch him, lay my head on his shoulder. I was being lured in by the subtle scent of freshly mowed grass and shampoo. I shivered, but managed to curb the odd impulse. I was flooded by the most unexplainable connection with this boy. In all my lifetimes, I'd never experienced anything like this before.

Mel cleared her throat, reminding me she was still there.

"Is he like this with everyone?" I asked.

"He's lovable."

"But is he . . ." I was having trouble explaining the deep connection that had sprung up so quickly. I needed confirmation. "I've come here over and over again with my best friend and up until"—I swallowed—"this visit, I would have considered us to have a special bond. But this isn't like that. This feels different. Am I wrong?"

"Nope. This is a bit unusual," she said.

"I'm standing right here." Oliver's finger made a circling gesture. "Girls," he muttered under his breath.

We ignored him.

"Have you ever seen this happen before?" I asked.

"Just once," Mel said, making little frown lines over her nose. "But we really should be going, kids. Elliot, I can hear your stomach growling from here." She turned and headed down the twisting corridor. I turned back to Oliver and at that exact moment my stomach gurgled like something volatile in a science lab beaker. We were standing so close I wondered if he could feel the rumbling.

I extended my palm and Oliver took it. His hand fit perfectly in mine and within a few strides we'd found a comfortable rhythm, stomachs rumbling in unison.

Crossing the threshold of the dining room, I was blissfully happy to zero in on a steaming pie sitting there for the taking. I made a beeline for it, dragging Oliver behind me. I looked at the pizza and then down at our still connected hands, not really sure how I was going to pull this one off. Oliver gave me a very Zen smile and said, "It's pizza—we must." I cracked up and wiggled my fingers loose. I loaded up a plate with enough pizza for a small army. Oliver got some too.

We found an empty table and plopped down. I picked up a steaming slice and leaned over my plate, knowing it would probably burn the roof of my mouth but willing to take that chance. When the first bite of hot gooey cheese was grafted to my insides, I glanced up.

I didn't know who the guy at the table across from us was, but he was staring at me with a dark scowl. At first I thought I'd violated some weird afterlife pizza-eating etiquette, but his pale blue eyes were too cold for that. He was dressed in black boots, black jeans, and an equally black T-shirt that read I DON'T DISCRIMINATE. I HATE EVERYONE. I flinched. I'd never seen this guy before—the murderous stare had to be coincidental. Still, I found I couldn't keep myself from peeking up at him. Before I could ask who he was, Oliver leaned over and whispered in my ear.

"That's Trevor. Appears to have anger issues."

"Yeah, I got that," I said.

Trevor pushed back his chair and stood up. He must've been over six feet. "Is he always angry like this?" I wondered aloud.

"Not completely sure. He just got here. He came right after you." Oliver ripped off one third of a new slice and chased it down with a few chugs of whatever was in his glass.

"How do you know who he is, then?" I asked, already feeling a wave of dread washing over me.

"I overheard Mel talking. He's going to be in our Workshop." Oliver paused. "But that's not all. I think I knew him in my last life." His eyebrows scrunched up. "I can't quite figure it out. There's something about the guy I don't like. He just annoys me."

Happiness sloshed around my insides hearing that Oliver and I would be together for Workshop. I watched as Trevor stalked off, hitting the exit door hard enough that it banged into the wall on his way out. Some of my excitement lost its fizz. There were dozens of different Workshops at the Obmil. Why did Angry Boy have to be in mine? But I knew the answer to that—Mel. She couldn't pass up a stray.

"Anything else I should know?" I asked.

Oliver's face lit up. "Plenty, but I'll start with the important thing first—there's dessert on the table."

A big plate of chocolate chip cookies appeared on the buffet. In my mind, exchanging a hostile guy for warm cookies was a good trade. Maybe we could talk Mel into bringing dessert to Workshop tomorrow and leaving Trevor at the Haven.

After lunch I was strangely concerned that separating from Oliver would be traumatic, but as we said good-bye, I still felt relaxed. Perhaps it was the side effects of the pizza and cookies. I stood on the Haven porch, watching as he walked backward toward the trail that led to Workshop.

"It's not so bad," I shouted out. "The separation, I mean." I felt dumb after I said it, but Oliver nodded his head in agreement.

"It's because I'm full," he called back.

"Of pizza?"

"No—full of you."

"Huh?"

"When I first saw you, I felt like I was running on empty.

As if I'd been away from you for far too long. I needed an Elliot fix." He grinned. "But now I'm feeling fully charged again. I've got a full tank." He patted his heart twice. "Now I can venture out, safe in the knowledge that I know where to find you should I need to replenish my reserves."

I blushed. Who was this guy? Granted, I couldn't remember my last life, but I was pretty sure that no one could have ever made me feel this special before. I grinned, completely embarrassed, but sort of wanting him to say more.

I waved, sending him off, but a small sigh escaped as he disappeared from view. I could feel the effects of him wearing off and the reality of being a miserable Third Timer setting back in. I was happy that he was content and running on full, but the truth was, I already felt like there was a cloud blocking out the sun.

I went back to my room, and spent the afternoon reliving everything that had happened so far. I was hoping that Julia might show up so we could hash out all this nonsense between us, but she either had a full dance card or she was avoiding me. I thought about exploring the grounds but it didn't seem nearly as fun as it would be with Oliver and I was afraid I might run into Trevor. He'd just arrived too, so he also had the day off to get his bearings.

I finally saw Julia at dinner, but she walked in with David

and the rest of her Workshop. Not an optimal situation. But I cheered up when I spotted Oliver. The sight of him made me feel lighthearted and optimistic for the first time in hours. But as he passed by Julia's table, some guy yelled out for Oliver to join them. I held my breath. I couldn't believe it as I watched him squeeze right between Julia and David. Julia's face lit up and David clapped him on the back. Everybody adored him, not just me.

What if this whole deep connection we shared was just the way Oliver was with everyone? My stomach twisted into a knot of a million different emotions. I couldn't join them and I certainly couldn't watch. My heart hammered inside my chest as I leaned up against a wall. Everything had me feeling off balance, even Oliver, so I decided to hide in my room again. It was foolish to be so insanely wrapped up in this guy—I'd known him all of a couple hours. I didn't understand this whole magnetic attraction thing, but Delving was going to be tough enough, I didn't need additional complications making things harder. I already had plenty of problems.

I figured if I waited in our room, Julia would have to show up eventually so we could really straighten things out. I knew I couldn't possibly survive the Obmil feeling so lonely. Oliver was great. He was like a life jacket keeping me afloat, but no boy can ever take the place of your best friend.

The sun was just about down when I heard her soft voice in our doorway. "Where'd you take off to during dinner?"

"I didn't feel like watching you with your new guide." The bitterness in my voice was like black coffee. Ironically, David smelled like black coffee underneath the Old Spice.

She lifted her chin. "I have my reasons, you know."

"Are you going to explain them to me? Because I can't seem to make sense of them by myself."

Julia plopped down on a pile of pillows on the floor, folding in her spindly limbs like a doe curling up for the night. "I need space, Elliot."

"Space? Space from what? From me?"

"I don't want to hurt your feelings." It appeared that she meant it, but that didn't make it better.

"Why do you need space from me? We've always done everything together. It's worked out perfectly up until now." I hated the whiny pleading sound to my voice.

"That's it right there." She snapped her fingers. "We've done everything together. Life and afterlife and every single time, you've led the way. Forgive me . . . but I want to be in charge of myself for a change. Oh, wait—forgiveness isn't your strong suit, is it? You have to have the control—better to run the show and not let anyone make any mistakes. This way you don't have to be judgmental at all."

"Excuse me? If I remember correctly, in my Samantha life, you pulled me out of the depths of depression and saved me. You took charge then." I crossed my arms and gave her a look.

"You were still running that show though. Everything that was happening—all about you."

"I—that's so not . . ." I didn't even know where to start. I threw up my hands. "So, take the lead. Nobody's stopping you."

"Aw, come on, Elliot. You know I can't be in charge with you around. We've got a pattern. I've got to break that routine. This is something that I have to do."

"You can be the one calling all the shots." I pointed at her. "I don't care. I'll support you. I'm not a bully, you know."

Julia blew a curl up off her face but it settled down right in front of her eye and she had to sweep it away. "I know that you don't mean to do it, but you have a tendency to need things to be the way you think they should be. That doesn't leave a lot of room for the rest of us to have an opinion."

It felt like a slap. "What are you going to do, then? Just discover everything without me? Avoid me and move on? What's going to happen if you make sense of everything before I do and then you leave? We might not be able to get into a new stream together if we don't leave here at the same time."

"I know."

She said it quietly.

So quietly it was like a knife sliding in between my ribs and severing my heart into two pieces, halves that would never be whole again.

"Well—now I guess I know too." I rolled over, putting my back to her. Now that I'd badgered her for the truth, I wanted to put it back where it'd come from. Neither one of us said anything, but I felt her hand perch upon my shoulder like a bird ready to take flight.

"Elliot?"

I didn't answer.

"There's one more thing you should know. I figured it out once you showed up at the Obmil and I could see what you looked like in your last life. We weren't together the way we've always been. We've already gone our separate ways."

4

creation

variation

The next morning Julia was gone when I awoke. I was stiff and uncomfortable from sleeping in my clothes and staying on my right side in order to avoid looking at her. She'd snuck out early but left an origami crane sitting on my pillow. Cranes are supposed to be extremely loyal. Legend says that if you fold a thousand cranes you'll be granted a wonderful wish, like a long life. Since I was already dead at the age of seventeen and the closest soul I'd ever known wanted to get away from me as fast as possible, it was too depressing to think about.

I placed the crane on the shelf over Julia's bed, but then changed my mind. I didn't need a constant visual reminder of everything wrong between us. I held the tips of the wings between my fingers and gave a test pull. It wouldn't take much.

I bit down on my lip. I couldn't bring myself to cause harm, even to a little paper crane. Compromising, I moved it to the corner of the shelf above my bed where I couldn't see it.

I glanced at my watch. Although I'd had the periodic urge to escape from the dark loneliness of our room last night, now I was finding it hard to leave the Nest, my nickname for the place. I headed out anyway, feeling as if I was traveling down the path of other people's choices.

Despite my reluctance to get to Workshop, I found I was actually enjoying my walk to the Delving School. I was torn between avoiding my past and enjoying the rush that came from playing with my surroundings. I knew the novelty of creating would soon wear off and become second nature, like breathing, but for the moment I greedily envisioned my two favorite seasons at the same time. I sighed as I watched beloved characteristics from autumn and spring jump to life in front of me. I was having so much fun tromping through crunchy leaves and smelling flowers that my steps became a little quicker, despite the fact that I wanted to avoid my destination. Thinking about it, I realized that the last thing I wanted to do right now was to engage in an emotional excavation of my last life. It wasn't like I was going to discover something good—how well could my last life have gone if I'd ended up here? But on the other hand—I'd be spending more time with Oliver since he would be in my Workshop.

When I reached the doors of the school, no one else seemed to be around. This was evident because the school appeared exactly as I would imagine the perfect school to be. Unlike the stability and continuity of the Haven, this building was subject to personal interpretation. It had a designated location in the clearing at the top of the western trail, but that was about as much consistency as this part of the Obmil offered. When no one was around I imagined the space was like wavy heat dancing over hot pavement, but I was only guessing. Whenever I got close enough, my vision filled the gap.

With my imagination unimpeded, the main section of the building was stone and brick with large windows and ivy crawling any place it could get a hold. There were large majestic oaks, maples, and willows keeping guard around the edges while smaller, bud-laden trees held court in the front entrance. Over to the side there was an addition to the building, a seamless connection that was glass and light, beams and angles, a modern contrast to the ancient history of the brick and stone. It was the equivalent of the glass pyramid that announced the Louvre in Paris. It was wrong in such a way that it wouldn't be right if it were any other way, at least for me.

Resigning myself to my fate at Workshop, I headed toward the towering dark wood doors. Suddenly they disappeared. I found myself standing in front of a drab gray urban warehouse of a building. Where there once was ivy and gently warmed stone, now stood graffitied concrete and dirty chicken-wired windows that blocked me from seeing inside. A mere two inches from my face, a vent belched moist, dank air straight at my nose.

My gut told me exactly who had done this. Somewhere nearby was the sullen-looking Trevor with the piercing blue eyes. Only he would create something like this. Instinct suggested I move out of his way, but I was not going to give him the satisfaction of seeing me flinch again.

I had two options. One was to stand there and fight it out with Trevor, to try and override his pathetic preference in architecture. Or I could partially suspend belief and share the design. If we had a creative confrontation I couldn't imagine how long we'd be standing there flipping architecture back and forth, but it killed me to have to cocreate with Trevor. I felt a twinge of guilt. Hadn't this been what Julia was suggesting— that I had to always have things my own way? I shrugged it off, because that couldn't possibly apply here. No one in their right mind picked rusty chicken wire as a decor choice. He had an agenda.

It was so silent I could hear the soft ticks of the minute hand of my watch. I released the tension in my clenched fists, realizing that I'd have to at least give it a try. I hated feeling vulnerable, but if I didn't make the attempt, Trevor and I would find ourselves spending half the day ping-ponging between my creative vision and his dark and nasty view. Besides, I'd sworn to Mel that I wouldn't be late and I wasn't planning to break my promise, even to irritate someone so rude.

I closed my eyes and opened them again. A soft sigh of relief escaped me. He'd cooperated.

If I was honest with myself, the result of the cocreation wasn't that bad. The corners of my mouth turned up slightly. The outcome of blending our two visions was a modern version of my building, merged with a clean, almost architectural version of his.

A clock tower chimed and I reached for the handle of the sleek but elegant glass doors. My fingertips had just grazed the smooth metal when the whole door disappeared.

unguided

Out of the corner of my eye, I saw Trevor dash into the building through a dinged and scratched windowless steel door that hadn't been there seconds before.

"Jerk!" I kicked the grungy brick wall. I didn't even have time to rub my throbbing toes as I darted into the building, heading for Workshop.

My toes were fine in seconds, but running like a startled rabbit down the hall left me frazzled and breathless by the time I reached Mel's door. I paused outside her classroom to steady my breathing and collect my thoughts. I wanted to walk into the room seeming completely unruffled, but Trevor's antics had left me flustered. I needed to be calm and prepared. I knew once everyone was settled, I would have to step up to the Swing and Delve for my memories. My hands were sweating just thinking about it. I planted my face in my palms, trying to erase the sudden vision of myself in the Swing, everyone judging me. Things would be so much easier if Julia was here.

I'd never Delved before, but we'd witnessed other Delves during our last two visits to the Obmil. I'd learned a lot from watching other Third Timers dissect their pasts. But obviously I hadn't learned enough to avoid becoming a Third Timer myself. I should've listened to Mel more carefully; she was always dropping little hints about how easily *anyone* could find themselves being a Third Timer. But I'd never really thought it could happen to me. Now I was standing here with knots in my stomach, worried about being dropped like a rock into my own unenlightened past.

I felt a small sting as the taste of blood hit my tongue. I'd gnawed too voraciously on my cuticle. I sucked on the fresh wound, then stuffed my bloodied finger in my pocket, pushing the door open with my hip. Turning to face the class, I instantly realized I was the last one to arrive. I scanned the faces but stopped abruptly when I saw Oliver and Trevor glaring at each other with blatant hostility, sparks practically flying between the two.

Before I could break away from the sight of them, a low

humming noise filled my ears. Everything was fading. My legs began to go numb. My knees sank to the floor. As Oliver and Trevor disappeared from view, I noticed a tiny pinprick of light and heard the faintest sound of music in my ears. I'd never heard of anyone making a Delve unguided before, but my memories crashed over me before I could stop them.

The applause no longer rang in my ears but the memory of it vibrated through my heart, causing me to feel more alive than I ever had before. Onstage I was someone special.

I opened the windows in the car and the wind whipped my hair around. I was glad I'd taken the extra minutes to remove my stage makeup before I met up with everyone at the cast party. It was the end of the school year and there wouldn't be many opportunities to get together with friends before we all went our separate directions. It always felt like the summer would be loaded with extra time, but jobs and vacations seemed to fill up all the potential empty spaces.

Dad had offered to drive over with me, which was sweet, but I kind of wanted a few minutes to myself. I only needed to go a couple miles down the road to hook up with the cast and all my adoring fans. Elliot Turner having fans——who would have thought? I felt lit from within.

I turned up the song that Mom had left in the car. I'd always been a music mutt, pulling inspiration from whatever was around. "Little Bird" by Annie Lennox was pumping like a heartbeat and I felt as if I was flying. I was alive, belting it out with Annie. It was just me on the road, except for a silver minivan up ahead. I was singing so loud I wondered if they could hear me.

"They always said that you knew best,
But this little bird's fallen out of that nest now.
I've got a feeling that it might have been blessed,
So I've just got to put these wings to test."

"Damn it!" My cell phone was ringing and my bag was on the floor. I hooked the strap with my finger and tugged. It didn't budge. I swiped the hair out of my face again and gave another tug as I glanced back up at the road. The bag flew up onto my lap, tipping over the morning's coffee remains.

"For I am just a troubled soul,
Who's weighted . . .
Weighted to the ground.
Give me the strength to carry on,
Till I can lay this burden down.
Give me the strength to lay this burden down . . ."

I could still hear the ring of the phone wandering off into the wind as I flipped it open and squeezed it against my ear. I blotted up the coffee. Oh shit! I was leaving a trail of damp tissue paper on my skirt and I didn't have another change of clothes for the party.

"Hello?"

The airbag responded first, exploding into me. The seat belt bit into my chest, trying to hold me back from the metal and glass that had silenced Annie Lennox's voice. Something wasn't right, but I couldn't quite figure out what it was. I felt as if my brain was moving at a fraction of its normal pace.

Oddly, I was now holding the phone clutched between my fingers. A panicked far-off voice kept screaming "Ellie!"

I tried to open the car door, but it didn't seem to work when I tugged at the handle. I used my shoulder to shove it. When I stepped out, a cascade of glass fragments leapt to the pavement and scattered like stars across the night sky.

I glanced up and saw the silver minivan with its front end wrapped around a tree, like a bun around a hot dog. The rear of the van was similar to an accordion. The sweet bite of gasoline crept into my nose. Unbidden, my feet began to move. I couldn't look at my car. Instead I walked in a wide circle to the front of the minivan. I was afraid to get too close, but I was magnetically drawn to the wreck.

The woman in the front seat was screaming. Blood streamed down her forehead and into her eyes. Her hands were flying everywhere. She was ripping at herself. Her seat belt finally released her and she was free. Stumbling out of the vehicle she practically tore the sliding door off its track. Her animalistic howl almost knocked me over. That's when I saw her: a little girl, maybe three or four years old, buckled into her car seat. My heart stopped as the mom grasped the little girl's head in her hands, smearing a bloody trickle across the side of her face. As if the woman's hands contained the spark of life, the little girl, ponytails crooked, reached for her, returning from horrific silence. The harder she strained against the car seat, wanting to be in her mother's arms, the louder her cries became. I took a step forward thinking I could help, somehow fix things, but I stopped cold when I realized that the woman was tearing through the van like a hurricane. It didn't make sense— why was she ignoring her daughter? What was she looking for? She whipped around, wild-eyed, searching. I froze, thinking that maybe it was me she was searching for, retribution her focus. She went as still as I. We waited— the only noise from the backseat, an endless "mommymommymommy" . . . thumping against my head like a heartbeat. Then I realized the woman was staring at the missing windshield. As if a switch were flipped, her face twisted into waves of panic and frenetic energy. Her whole body contorted with pain and then I understood, even though I pushed it away, trying to slam shut the doors to my awareness.

No.

No.

No.

I still couldn't move. I watched the mother as she gazed beyond me, desperate. Then her face changed and I knew. I turned around as she flew past. She was headed to the crumpled pile of bloody blond curls in the leaves. She was running to Oliver.

the

distribution

of guilt

Waves of fear and horror washed over me. I was drowning. If I screamed long and loud, maybe I would disappear from the inside out. I wanted to die, but that really wasn't an option anymore.

That's when I felt fingers gently brushing against my forehead, almost as if they were trying to sweep away the ugliness that was imprinted there. I quieted, staying fetal on the floor, eyes closed, heart beating like a trapped hummingbird inside my chest. I could feel Oliver sitting inches from my head.

"Why are you crying, Elliot?"

"I am so, so sorry, Oliver." Each word was ripped from my gut. Tears streamed down my face.

"Why are you sorry?"

I heard the scraping of a chair and feet pounding against the wooden floor. The contents of someone's stomach emptied into a nearby garbage can. I cringed. My own stomach lurched wildly. Maybe if I'd reacted so strongly to someone else's Delves when I was a First or Second Timer, I wouldn't be lying here on the floor right now.

"Elliot, why are you sorry?"

The heaving had stopped and everyone in the room was deathly silent. I couldn't hear another sound besides the velvet lilt of Oliver's words. I craved the sight of his face, was desperate to see the same kindness that was in his voice, but the urge to hide from the rest of the room was stronger. I could feel dozens of eyes boring into me. I didn't want to know who was hunched over a dirty trashcan. I pictured the looks of disgust on everyone's faces. Everyone would have seen what had happened in my Delve.

With lids shut tight, I pulled my limbs in tighter. The silence was palpable. What do you say to the guy that you murdered? Are there words that could reach past the surface? I had ripped him away from his life. I opened my eyes and searched his face. We were nose to nose—he'd tipped over, mirroring my position on the floor. Oh God, he was smiling at me.

He nodded matter-of-factly and said, "It's okay."

What was he thinking? It could never be okay. Never. I'd killed him.

I had two options. I could close my eyes again and spend all of eternity right where I was or I could lift up my head and meet the eyes of everyone else in the room. I could face the people who weren't delusional like Oliver. I wasn't fond of either option.

"You're all right, Elliot," Mel said.

It sounded like she was talking me down off the edge of a cliff. I wanted to believe her, but there was no way that anything could ever be all right again. Obviously there wasn't a hell or I would've been magically transported there instantaneously. Or maybe this was hell. Maybe heaven was innocence, limbo was ignorance, and hell was fiery illumination.

"Look at me, sweetheart," Mel said. "Please."

I lifted my chin, letting her gaze at the disappointment of me. I was waiting for the ugliness I was feeling to make itself visible in the windows of her eyes. Beat after beat, my heart ticked off the seconds, and yet there was no disgust or hatred in her face. I didn't deserve it, but I was grateful.

"I'm bad, Mel. I'm really, really bad." My voice quivered.

"You're not bad," she said.

"Okay—whatever—but what I did was horrible. Thoughtless." Once again I could hear Julia talking about how I was self-absorbed. I shook my hand like there was still a cell phone in it I needed desperately to get rid of. "Did you—did you see his mother? Oliver's mom? Oh, I can't . . ." I sat up but started to hyperventilate. Oliver gently tucked my head between my knees.

"Elliot, you're not bad, you've just been blindsided by your memories," Mel said.

"I can't turn it off—the pictures in my head—it's all I see now." The acid from my stomach was rising up into my throat again. Everything was bitter and raw.

I could feel Oliver's hand resting lightly on my back. Part of me wanted to shake off the unbearable weight of him, but he was the only anchor I had. Without Oliver to ground me, I suspected that the rational part of me would take flight and disappear. It was tempting to fall apart, but something wouldn't let me go there. Some primal defense mechanism kicked in. Wasn't it human nature to blame someone else when things go wrong? Suddenly I felt pissed. Where was Julia? She should've been here. Friends shouldn't be around for just the fun stuff. Best friends are supposed to be there for you when ugliness seeps out of your soul. I jumped to my feet.

Fired up, I dared Mel to really examine me.

She spoke softly. "You're not the first person to be overwhelmed by such strong memories. In fact, I've been here awhile and you know that Obmil time is a lot longer than regular time. I've seen my share. Shocking revelations are par for the course. That's what happens here, although I will admit, you're the first soul I've met whose memories couldn't wait until you were settled in the Swing. So, while you may be a bit hasty in your approach," she gave a tiny smile, "you're not alone. I promise you won't feel like this forever if you continue to Delve and try to see. The point isn't just to learn about our past, it's to learn from it."

I wanted to believe her. I could feel myself swaying, wanting to be convinced of an eternal fairy-tale ending. I allowed myself to look around the room. I was met with pair after pair of scrutinizing eyes. They didn't appear angry or disgusted, but there was something there. It felt like curiosity, or maybe even fear. Perhaps they were remembering their own ugly secrets and fearing exposure. Maybe they were happy not to be me right now. I couldn't blame them for that. I didn't want to be me either.

I felt a chill dance along my spine. That's when I saw Trevor.

He was standing with one leg thrown over a loft railing, acting as if he might spring down upon me. He had created his Workshop space in the form of a catwalk that ran all the way around the room. It was both disconcerting, having him patrolling the area above everyone, and a relief, because he'd moved away from Oliver.

He tapped his chest twice, driving my line of sight to his

T-shirt. It now read IT'S NOT PARANOIA IF THEY REALLY ARE AFTER YOU. Great. He already had a strong instinctual hatred for me, and now I'd just proven that maybe his gut instincts were right.

I forced myself to stare at him and then I knew why there was no hatred in the faces below. Trevor owned all of it. There was nothing left for anyone else. The last thing he did before hopping down over the rail was mouth one single word.

Bitch.

the walls

between

us

The word seared me, like a brand upon my soul. I scuttled backward, shielding myself from the coming attack. I let out a gush of air when I saw that Trevor wasn't headed toward me, but to the Swing. Crap. The truth was that I didn't want him to Delve, either. I was afraid of seeing inside the mind of someone so completely hostile.

I fiddled with my ponytail as Trevor tinkered with the Swing. Talk about someone who had to have things a certain way. Ironically, I found myself feeling impatient. It was time to suck it up and let this Delve happen. Maybe it would be better to let someone else be in the hot seat.

I headed to my chair with Oliver right behind me. To be honest, Trevor wasn't the only one making me jumpy. It just wasn't natural to be so calm about having your life mowed down. No one was that perfect, were they?

"Umm, which spot is your space?" I asked, taking a step back from Oliver.

He grinned. "Right here, next to yours." He pointed to a gigantic tree. Well, what would have been a gigantic tree if you could see all of it. The top half of the tree emerged straight from the floor as if the rest of it continued downward into the room below. A multicolored hammock was suspended from a sturdy branch, on which sat a tree house that any kid would die for. Or any guy who was a kid at heart. As someone who'd always longed for a leafy hideaway but also got squeamish about heights if they weren't safely enclosed, I could appreciate the advantages of such a layout. Oliver bounded up the ladder into his branches, then turned and held out a hand for me. I was tempted but shook my head. For some reason I couldn't follow him while feeling Trevor bore holes into my back. I kept my back to Trevor, deliberately postponing my need to turn around and face him.

My creative space was nestled in the shade of Oliver's tree. Behind me was a glass wall, overlooking the far end of the lake. Across from me the First and Second Timer senior citizens were arranged around a bingo table. Just down from them were three middle-aged businessmen in suits. They held disposable coffee cups in their hands, paced the floor, and gesticulated wildly while they talked. I figured the odds were pretty good that at least one of them would be coming back as a Third Timer. A few women were comfortably ensconced in a variety of chairs and love seats, nestled up against a stone fireplace. They seemed relaxed, as only First and Second Timers can.

Stepping into my space, I flopped down on my plush purple armchair with matching ottoman. It wasn't the fluffy couch that Julia and I had always shared, but I was flying alone now. Might as well get used to it.

Unable to avoid it anymore, I glanced up to meet Trevor's gaze. There was clearly a challenge there. I gulped, still marked and tender from his earlier attack. I could sense Oliver above me, moving around like he might come back down from his tree, but then Mel hooted and jumped up, no longer rooting through the epic pile of stuff on her desk. "I found it!" She waved her notebook over her head, looking like the winner in capture the flag.

I scrutinized Mel's organizationally challenged creative space. Her area reminded me of an eagle's nest, an aerie. It was bigger every time I visited the Obmil. Two eagles begin by building a nest that meets their basic needs. Every year they add onto their place of residence, and the pile of sticks and fluff that they started with becomes a home of epic proportions.

It was rumored that Mel had originally started with one extremely heavy oak desk. She'd added on quite a bit since. Eagles have been known to work on a nest for their lifespan of thirty years, with some nests reaching up to two or three tons. I wondered how long Mel had been building her nest here at the Obmil.

"Trevor, you ready to go?" Mel interrupted my runaway thoughts about her domain. Trevor hopped back up, giving the Swing a kick with his boot before sitting back down and slipping on his headset. The Swing reminded me of a suspended recliner. It sort of resembled a float you might see in a swimming pool. When you climb aboard, it works like a giant air hockey game. You never really touched the recliner, because a powerful layer of air suspends you above it. If that wasn't enough to place you in a state of hypnotic relaxation, the swing also gently rocks back and forth. If I weren't so afraid of what would happen in the chair, I'd be dying to lie down and relax.

All of the other twenty plus people in the room already had on their headsets, which look like the offspring of earmuffs and a sleep mask. No one needs them to observe the Delved memories of another soul, but they block out distractions, making the process quicker and easier for everyone. I pulled mine on, eager to block out the sight of Trevor's dark scowl.

"Trevor?" Mel repeated.

He grunted some kind of affirmation of readiness. Despite the tensions of the day, I could feel myself begin to relax as we slipped quietly into his past.

The summer rain was warm, but it fell with an unrelenting intensity. As Trevor drew closer to the memory, I could see waves of people standing under a flock of black umbrellas. It reminded me of an endless sea of raven wings.

Everyone was staring at something, and as Trevor drew closer to his memory, I realized it was a coffin, encrusted with flowers. Next to the coffin was a crumpled-up figure, kneeling in the mud, bareheaded and out of the reach of the umbrellas' protection.

At that moment, the perspective changed. All I could see was the mud and the rain pelting the petals of the flowers. I was seeing through Trevor's eyes. He was the figure on the ground.

I sucked in my breath. In my past visits to the Obmil, I'd always felt like a pure observer when watching someone else Delve. Julia and I often joked about "going to the movies." This was a different experience. I wasn't privy to Trevor's thoughts or feelings, but I couldn't escape the weight of the water pounding on my head, the chill that seemed to penetrate deep into my heart. I felt closer to this memory than I should feel in someone else's Delve. If this is what it felt like, simply touching the surface of Trevor's intense emotions, I was grateful that I didn't have to handle it from his perspective.

Trevor's gaze shifted to his hands and I could see his fingers clutching a clump of grass whose roots were torn from the mud. His fist was crushing the fragile shoots so tightly that his knuckles were white. Under his breath I could hear him chanting, "Wrong. Wrong. Wrong."

Trevor lifted his eyes away from the muddy streams traveling between his fingers and settled on a heart made of white roses. A deep blue ribbon lay draped across the heart and it was scripted with the word BROTHER. I tried frantically to look around, searching for more information. It was hopeless. I could see only what Trevor chose to focus on. He stared endlessly at that one word, and then as if he had mustered up the courage, he focused on a bigger heart of roses. It read OUR BELOVED SON, OLIVER.

silhouettes

I felt hollow, like a gourd. As I trembled, the dried-up, shriveled seeds of who I thought I was danced around in all my empty spaces.

Trevor shot up out of the swing, ripping off his headset, flying through the air. I wanted to cringe as he came at me like a bird of prey, talons ready to rip me to shreds, but that was a luxury my guilt didn't allow. I stood there needing his absolution but ready to accept punishment. It was only fair.

Right before he would have found his mark, a Plexiglas wall sprung up between us. I flinched as he slammed into it and flew backward onto his back on the floor. As he shook off the disorientation of the impact, all I could picture were the black avian silhouettes that are used to keep birds from hitting windows and glass partitions. Hysterical laughter bubbled up in my throat as I pictured black shadows of Trevor placed on the glass. Would Trevor silhouettes have obnoxious sayings across the fronts of their T-shirts?

"Son of a—" Trevor thundered. He didn't finish his sentence. Instead his leg shot out and his boot made contact with the Plexiglas. A web of cracks radiated from the point of impact.

Mel was now by his side, trying to help him up off the floor. He pushed her away.

"Relax. Calm down. I'm sorry, Trevor. I didn't mean for you to hit that hard. It was all I could come up with before you did something you'd regret." I couldn't tell if Mel was trying to hug or restrain him.

"Regret?" Trevor shoved against Mel with his shoulder. "I regret you saving Elliot. Now we know for sure where your loyalty lies," he said with a sneer. "It isn't like I could kill her anyway. I can't do to her what she did to my little brother." He spit out the words as if he had battery acid on his tongue.

"You may not believe this, Trevor, but I did what I did for Elliot *and* you. I care about you, too. I've been around here long enough to know that things are never as simple as they first appear."

"You think what she did was simple?" His voice was layered in icy darkness.

"No, Trevor. You'd be surprised how utterly complex I know things to be." She gave a tired little sigh and brushed a tangle of hair off her face.

"This is the first big memory you've acquired by Delving; it won't be your last. Remember, this is about you, not Elliot." She reached for him, but he shrugged her off. "We've now established that you, Elliot, and Oliver are linked. While I respect your initial emotions, I'm hoping you can see that this is an opportunity to heal and grow—together."

"Little brother . . ." The remembrance was barely audible. Trevor whipped his head around, searching frantically, and then locked on to Oliver. Moving away from me, he reached his hand out. "Ollie?" The uncertainty in his face was in stark contrast to his previous waves of hostility, but it was oddly as intense.

Mel eliminated the Plexiglas wall protecting me, but I stayed where I was, fascinated by the electric sparks of emotion that seemed to bounce back and forth between the two brothers. Suddenly, without warning, Oliver strode past Trevor and firmly planted himself shoulder to shoulder with me. My ears heard Trevor's guttural moan, but the rawness of it registered deeper, causing me to take a step backward. Swamped by a red-hot tide of guilt, I pulled Oliver toward me, burying my face against his shoulder.

I whispered into his shirt, "Oliver? He's your brother." I had to see his face. "You're here because of me. Trevor didn't do anything."

This time there was no Yoda wisdom. He bit his lip, confusion darting across his face before it returned to its usual level of boisterous confidence. "Everybody does something, Elliot. I'm here because I made you a promise."

"You made me a promise? What does that mean?" I wanted to sneak a peek at Trevor, to see his reaction, but I was afraid. It felt twisted to still have Oliver's attention and loyalty.

Oliver shrugged. "I'm not a Third Timer like you and Trevor. I'm a Passenger. The only thing I remember is that I came here to help you, Elliot. I don't remember anything about him." He nodded in Trevor's direction. "From the vibes he's been giving off, I really can't imagine how we ended up being brothers."

I'd heard talk about Passengers. The phenomenon is rumored to happen at the Basin, the Grand Central Station of the afterlife, where souls travel between one life and the next. When a soul decides to become a Passenger, he makes the choice to journey with another soul, a Tandem, into a third life, to be a catalyst for their growth. The idea is to have an impact on that person—to make the Tandem look at things *differently*. The Passenger tries to help the Tandem avoid returning to the Obmil as a Third Timer. It's very altruistic. By being present in someone else's life, the Passenger is passing up an opportunity to work toward a new growth plan of their own. I'd never actually run into a Passenger or a Tandem on my visits at the Obmil. Obviously, they weren't very common. I groaned. Knowing that I'd failed at my third life even with special assistance only made me feel like a bigger loser.

"You're my Passenger? Are you sure?" I asked.

"I'm sure. I came here to help you because—well—I love you."

Oliver's words were a vacuum, sucking all the noise out of the room. My skin began to prickle. I could feel everyone focused on me.

"How do you know that you don't have your own growth plan to figure out?" Mel asked.

Everyone else in the room leaned forward in unison. It surprised me that Mel seemed to have never met a Passenger either. She'd worked here a long time, but was clearly seeking information.

Oliver gave me one of his enchanting little smiles. "I know because—I just feel it." He crossed his arms, satisfied as a cat with a feather sticking out of its mouth.

"So we're supposed to bow to your expertise based on what? Warm and fuzzy feelings?" Trevor grunted for a finishing touch.

Oliver took a step in his direction. "Oh, and I suppose immature, violent tantrums are the true pathway to enlightenment." He let his gaze drift to where the Plexiglas had been.

"Boys, boys." Mel put up one palm in each direction. "This isn't helping—"

"You love me?" I interrupted, then clasped my hand over my mouth. I hadn't meant to say that out loud.

"Of course he doesn't love you." Trevor sneered. "That whole soul mate, deep-connection sappiness is a bunch of crap."

"Don't get all freaked out about the *L* word. I didn't say I was *in* love with her, just that I love her." Oliver stared pointedly at Trevor. "But maybe someone is protesting a little too aggressively. Maybe someone is a little bit"—Oliver brought his thumb and finger together—"jealous?"

"What?" Trevor and I shouted in unison.

"That's bullshit," Trevor responded.

"You're an ass," I shot off, staring at Trevor. *Grrrr*—he brought out the very worst in me, every time.

"Ladies and gentlemen!" Mel's voice was getting louder. Despite the noise, I heard the door open. I wondered if someone was fleeing the chaos.

"Sorry to interrupt, Mel." I knew that voice. Julia's head peeked into the room. "David wanted to know—"

Like we needed this right now. Not that Oliver or Trevor had even noticed Julia's arrival.

"Hey, Elliot, are you okay? What's going on in here?"

I ignored her, irritated by her god-awful timing. She never managed to show up when I needed her. Now I had other things to worry about. Sparks were flying between the two brothers again.

"Guys, what's the matter?" Julia's soft little voice didn't even penetrate the thick wall of hostility between the brothers.

"Now is *not* a good time." I glared at her.

"I can see that. Despite what you think, I'm not an idiot." Julia's eyes welled up.

I looked from her to the guys. Both brothers were waving their arms and shouting. "Sorry, I'm just a little stressed right now." I shoved my hands in my pockets. "I had my first Delve and it was—it was unpleasant." That was putting it mildly.

Julia wrapped her fingers around my wrist, anchoring me to her. "You can tell me anything. . . ." Julia's voice was just a whisper, but it came in the only pocket of silence the room had seen since this fiasco started. Everyone stopped, but I couldn't be sure if it was because they were listening to Julia or it was because everything was beginning to fade and we were all dropping into a Delve . . .

• • •

My first reaction to the Delve was that I felt small. Minuscule, in fact. I was in the Basin. I felt certain of it. There just aren't many rooms that are a cross between the Roman Coliseum and New York's Grand Central Station. I tried to turn my head and nothing happened. Wasn't my Delve. Trevor's again? Suddenly I was looking at myself—sort of. It was me, but back when I was Samantha. Whoever's Delve this was had fixated on me. Despite the fact that I was all grown up, I appeared nervous. I guess change had never been my thing.

"God, this place is huge. I don't remember being here last time, do you?" Emma's voice sounded just as nervous as I looked.

We were in Julia's Delve. I mean, she wasn't Julia yet, she was Emma, but I'd know that soul anywhere.

"It's epic," Samantha said.

Weird. Being in Julia's Delve meant that I was now watching myself. The Samantha version of me kept right on talking. "I think they don't want you remembering this part. Actually, I think we aren't supposed to remember Basin stuff at all. Isn't it supposed to be deep, emotional internalization or something?"

"Yeah, I heard something like that too," Emma said. Her gaze began to wander around the room. In the center of the marble floor was a placid pool. The water was so blue, it seemed as if the tile below it was a vibrant cerulean. Yet, that couldn't be the case—there couldn't possibly be a shallow bottom because a head was slowly breaking the surface and a body was rising upward through the pool like it was on a platform elevator. This was the doorway into

the Basin and the elegant gentleman with the silver hair and tailored vest who emerged was dry. His feet glided ankle deep through the water as he strolled to the edge of the pool. Then he righted his already straight bow tie and stepped out onto the floor.

"I don't think I'll ever get tired of watching that," I listened to Samantha say.

"Yeah, me either, but . . ." Emma's voice trailed off. Her eyes searched the outer walls of the round room. The whole place was ringed with archways, one floor stacked on top of the other. There was a pinprick glow of light at the top, but I wasn't able to see the upper floors. Layer after layer of arches: these were the exits.

"Samantha?"

Emma was watching Samantha again, but Sam's focus was on the room. I wondered what she was thinking.

"Sam, there's kinda something that I wanted to talk to you about," Emma said, focusing on nothing but me.

"Yeah, sure," Samantha said. "What's up? Oh, wow. It looks like the guy who just came out of the water is set to leave already. That's kind of a quick turnover, don't you think?"

"I guess. But that's kind of what I wanted to ask you about. I need to talk to you before we step onto the ring."

"That's right, I forgot about the ring. Oh, check it out—he's stepping on it now."

Emma finally turned her head away from Samantha and focused her

67

attention on the dapper guy getting ready to jump streams. He placed his toes right up to the hairline break that separated the largest part of the room from the last ten feet of space near the archways: the outer ring. No sooner did his toes make their intentions clear, than the outside loop began to glow. Dapper Guy crossed the line, stepping over onto the ring. That's when the wind picked up. A rush of air came from both above and below us at the same time. The two forces counterbalanced each other, making it feel as if we were in zero gravity, but gently incapacitated. We couldn't move. I mean, Emma could turn her head and move her arms, but it was like being in slow motion or encased in clear jelly. It was pleasant enough, but that wasn't its purpose. It was a safety measure designed to keep other souls off the ring when someone else was in transit. No last-minute, highly emotional, snap decisions could be made as you watched someone else pick a life choice. You were only supposed to move forward when you felt the pull.

"Seems like he figured out his growth plan pretty easily," Samantha said, as the ring rose like an elevator.

He traveled at least fifteen levels before the upward momentum stopped. It was replaced by a slow spin, like a geriatric roulette wheel.

"How long do you think it will take us to get to that level?" Samantha asked, nudging her chin upward.

"That's exactly what I wanted to talk to you about. Do you think that maybe this time around you could do me a favor?" Emma's voice wavered, shaking like a child who'd spent a little too long in the swimming pool.

"Hey, you okay?" Samantha directed her attention back on Emma. She very slowly moved her arm through the column of air and draped it around Emma's shoulder, pulling her in close and rubbing her hand up and down Emma's arm—mistaking the moment for a real chill instead of an emotional one. "Look! He's getting ready to go."

"I'm not cold—" Emma's voice was low, more like an mumble from under her breath, but while it may have been hard for Samantha to hear, being in Julia's Delve made her words distinct to everyone who was a witness in her head. "I want you to be my Passenger."

I felt topsy-turvy. It was like I'd taken a swig of sugared coffee, expecting it to be light and sweet, only to find out I'd grabbed the salt by mistake. She'd wanted me to be her Passenger? No, this couldn't have been how it happened . . . could it?

Oblivious, Samantha pointed up to Dapper Guy. My stomach coiled, tightening around this ugly piece of information.

The ring had stopped moving and Dapper Guy was standing in front of an archway glowing with light. "He's getting ready to jump streams," Samantha said. "I love this part—particularly when it's someone else making the leap into the unknown."

Without glancing back, Dapper Guy walked into the light and disappeared. The ring dropped back down into place and the wind died away.

Emma took a deep breath, but it was Samantha who jumped in first. "Emma, I think I need your help. I mean—I think I need your help again. You were amazing in our last life and so supportive at the Obmil. I hate to think about the choices I might have made if you hadn't been nudging me in the right direction." Emma started to interject, but Samantha held up her hand. "Please, just listen. I know how much you've helped me and I think I was close—really close—to figuring out my growth plan. Don't make that face. You can't blame yourself, you did everything you could. I'm so lucky to have you, but now there's something else you can do that might really make a difference . . ." Emma leaned backward as if she was trying to get out of the trajectory of Samantha's words. I could feel myself leaning with her, wanting to get as far away from my own self-absorption as I could. There was nowhere to run.

"Emma, I know it's crazy to ask you this, and I haven't really thought it through, but there isn't time. This is my last chance. I don't want to be stuck back at the Obmil or worse. You know what they say, that some people don't get to come back." Samantha's voice dropped several octaves but her face was puppy-dog eager, like she was waiting for someone to throw her a tennis ball or scratch her behind the ears. Like she knew that the answer to something was just within reach. I could feel Emma shrinking in on herself and I wanted to switch the channel. I didn't want to watch this stupid show anymore.

"I—I don't know what to—" Emma paused and took a deep breath.

Before Emma could continue, Samantha's head shot up and whipped to the side, like she was privy to the frequency of a dog whistle. Emma's attention tore off in the same direction, wondering what had caused the reaction.

I would have rubbed my eyes if I could have made Emma's arms do my bidding. Coming out of the water were two identical guys. Mid-forties, salt and pepper hair, the kind of guys you'd see walking the red carpet at the

Oscars. Oh, this was double trouble. As they stepped out of the pool, they were shoulder bumping each other and bantering back and forth. Mid-jab they froze, as if they'd heard the same dog whistle as Samantha. Emma rubbed her eyes after all, but it didn't make my double vision disappear. The twins were headed our way and I could feel my own displaced heart racing faster as they drew closer. They stopped directly in front of Sam, watching her like she was the sun, the moon, and the stars—all rolled up into one little universe. Both of their hands reached out to touch her at the very same moment. All I could think was that they had long fingers, nimble like a pianist and then— BOOM! The moment they made contact with Samantha, my head exploded like a firecracker in a tin can.

I don't know how I knew it so instantaneously, but I did—we'd switched Delves. These were my memories now. It was as if the magnetic surge of energy from the twins' touch had to be experienced firsthand. My head throbbed from the sudden jolt of switching roles. I felt like a time traveler. I was in Samantha's head, but now that I'd watched her, I didn't know if I wanted to be.

The twins had dropped their hands but both stood, focused on Samantha— on me. Waves of emotion flowed off of them, landing on me as if I was the shore. The brother on the left was sending off a vibe that made me want to hug him. He was the tide when it gently meets the beach, hypnotic, slowly washing away the rough edges of life. There was a rhythmic ebb and flow of energy between us. To my right, it was a different story. This brother was a force that made my heart race. He was the uncontainable ocean that inundates the rocky cliffs where it isn't safe. And while the water was icy cold, the sheer will of it, forcing itself into every crack and crevice, created its own kind of heat. How could two people who appeared identical be so insanely different?

"I don't mean to interrupt, but . . ." Emma turned to the twins. "We were sort of having an important conversation when you guys arrived. I need to ask Samantha something."

I shook my head, clearing the fog.

Emma finally had my attention, for the first time since the guys had shown up. I examined her closely, trying to see if the twins had the same weird effect on her as they had on me. It didn't appear to be the case, and now in retrospect, the whole thing seemed bizarre. Who were these guys and why did I feel this way? What was I doing? Yes, she was right, we needed to finish up this Passenger conversation. "I'm sorry, Emma, I didn't mean to lose track of what we were talking about." I looked back at the twins, trying to explain. "I know it's a big thing to put out there, but I'm asking Emma if she would be my Passenger for my third time around."

"But . . ." Emma sputtered.

I held up my hand to stop her and looked at the twins. "She's my best friend. There's no one else I'd ask. No one else I could trust."

"But I said that——"

Emma seemed as if she was going to crumble. My stomach felt sick because I could see the train wreck coming even though Samantha didn't have a clue. Or maybe I felt nauseous because I knew I should've seen it and I hadn't.

"So, what do you say, Em?" Samantha asked.

Emma took a deep breath. "No. I'm sorry, but I say no." Two tears plopped down on the smooth marble. I wasn't sure if they were hers or mine.

"Why?" Samantha asked, her voice shaking.

"You really have to ask?"

"Are—are you mad at me?" Samantha stuttered. "Did I do something?"

Emma bit her lip hard. "I'm not mad at you. I mean, maybe I am. But—no—I just wanted— Does it matter, Sam? I just can't."

"I'll be your Passenger." Both of the twins said it at the same exact time.

"What?" Emma and I replied in unison, making it slightly creepier.

The twin on the left, the gentle one, reached out and grabbed my hands. "I know you don't know me, but I have this feeling, this strong feeling that this is right. I'd be more than happy to be your Passenger." His eyes twinkled with sincerity and I felt mesmerized by him all over again.

"Hey—" The other twin, intense and edgy, took a step forward and grasped me by the shoulders, commanding my attention. "I don't think you want to do that." He raised his eyebrows and waited, making me feel as if there was an answer I should provide.

"Okay. I mean—why not?" I was suddenly very confused.

"I should be your Passenger." The intense twin was staring me down.

"Don't listen to him." The gentle twin butted back in, pulling my gaze. "He's got a competitive streak. Can't you feel the connection between us?"

I felt like a Ping-Pong ball, bouncing back and forth between the two.

Now the intense twin was back, cupping my chin in his hand and bringing my attention back to him. He leaned forward and whispered in my ear. "I'm the one who's supposed to be important in your life. I can feel it."

The warm air from his mouth sent icy hot ripples down my spine, but then I felt a yanking sensation coming from the pit of my stomach. The pull of the ring had started and it was strong. I gave a little involuntary yelp of surprise. I wasn't prepared for this yet. I didn't have enough time to think. My eyes rocketed back and forth between the twins. I couldn't tell if either of them was experiencing the pull. That would have been an easy way to decide if one of them was really supposed to go with me. I glanced around, trying to find a clue to help make the decision. Emma! She was still standing there, a weird expression plastered to her face. I sighed. It was obvious that Emma's expression meant she was feeling the pull too. My feet were moving toward the ring. It was making me dizzy not to honor the pull.

"Samantha, you have to choose." I wasn't sure which brother said it. My mind was reeling. I needed a Passenger. I couldn't be a failure again.

"Okay, I'll pick, but I need to move over here." I motioned toward the ring and both guys moved with me. "Come on, Emma," I called over my shoulder. She walked over and all four of us placed our toes up to the line. The floor started to glow.

"You have to make a decision." Both twins spoke at the same time again. The sweet twin was still on my left and the intense one on my right.

"I know," I said, my heart racing. But I was sure I'd never know the right answer. My hand shot out and the brother on the left grasped it tightly in his. His sweetness rolled over me and he practically glowed with delight. I felt sure I'd made the right decision—until I turned to peek at the other brother. He looked like a puppy who'd been kicked—hard. How could I explain? There wasn't time. I had no idea if he felt the pull; if he was going to step forward too, even though he couldn't be my Passenger. The wind would be coming soon and I couldn't take that chance. I grabbed the other brother and pulled both of them onto the ring with me. I needed them both.

I never even noticed that Emma had taken a step backward . . .

suspending

disbelief

It was eerily quiet when we all returned from the Delve. But Trevor didn't stay speechless very long. "This is bullshit!"

"You should be glad she even wanted you along," Oliver said.

But Trevor wasn't watching his brother. He was locked on to me. I could feel red heat flooding my cheeks, despite the penetrating chill emanating from him. He looked volatile. I wasn't feeling the magical magnetic pull anymore—it was more like repulsion. I turned my head away from him and caught Julia staring. She seemed shocked; wounded. I groaned—things had just gone from bad to worse in the friendship department. Now that she remembered what had happened at the Basin, she had new ammunition. This new incident was just icing on the Elliott-screwed-up-again cake. I opened my mouth, wanting to say the right thing, but before two neurons could get together and at least attempt a plan, Julia burst into tears and dashed from the room.

"She'll be okay." Oliver put an arm around my shoulder. The sweetness of it was baffling.

"Doesn't seem that way." Trevor's voice had a sarcastic bite. And he was correct. There was no reason for Julia to be all right. It hurt me to admit it, but she had bad taste in friends.

Oliver interrupted my thoughts. "Seriously, don't worry. We'll get it all sorted out. Julia is going to be fine." He glared at Trevor. "My brother is the king of misguided emotion. He's just sore because you picked me to be your Passenger. He seems to think that you're his soul mate."

Mt. Saint Trevor looked as if it were about to erupt. Up until now he'd been so cold, but it appeared that Oliver knew how to cause friction. Acrid smoke rose all around him as if something had ignited inside and was eating all the oxygen in the room. I noticed that he'd reengaged his billboard T-Shirt. It now said GO TO HELL! I wrapped my arms around myself, the slogan giving me the shivers. It felt too much like a premonition. Trevor stood there long enough to make his commentary known and then turned and strode out the door.

"Are we done, Mel?" Oliver asked.

Mel glanced over at Lily, the other Third Timer in our group. "You interested in Delving today?"

Lily ran a hand over her silky scarf and sighed. "I Delved yesterday and, honestly, I'm feeling tired from reliving the chemo. Maybe I could skip it today?" She gave Mel a subtle nod and I knew she must have been a mother in her last life. She had that I'm-going-to-do-whatever-is-best-for-the-kids expression on her face. I felt torn between being appreciative and feeling manipulated. Unable to decide, I figured I'd just ignore the whole situation.

"Wanna walk back to the Haven, Elliot?" Oliver said.

"You sure you want to go with me?" I asked, my heart skipping little beats of surprise and hope.

"Yup." His curls bobbed up and down.

I nudged him with my hip. "If you're sure you want to go slumming." I said it with a light, airy tone in my voice, but I knew I meant it.

"Don't say that." Oliver's brow furrowed.

"But it's the truth. You were there. You saw what I did to you. The way I treated Julia when she was Emma." I tipped my head and hid behind a curtain of hair, trying to buffer myself against the truth.

"Look—maybe it makes you feel better to say that kind of stuff, but it makes me feel bad." He rubbed his temples like he could smooth away the headache I was giving him. "If you can't do it for yourself, do it for me."

"Do what?" Now I was confused.

"Give yourself a break."

I stared at him, trying to gauge his level of sincerity even though I somehow knew that he was honest to a fault.

"If you can't believe it, fake it. Okay?"

I couldn't help it, a sigh escaped. I had a feeling that fooling myself was something I might be really, really good at. I shrugged my shoulders, sensing that Oliver had me wrapped around his little finger. "Sure," I replied, shaking my head but smiling.

As we walked out of the classroom, Oliver launched into a description of a project he was working on with Freddie. They were building a greenhouse with a retractable roof for Freddie's vegetable garden. Although it would be easy enough to create the food, just like most things here, we all tended to want to do things the familiar way. Even if it was ridiculously time-consuming, everyone had certain stuff they were nostalgic for. And of course, some people just liked the challenge. Or maybe they wanted to avoid thinking about other things. Oliver stopped short and tapped his fist into his palm. "Damn."

"What's the matter?" I was immediately on guard.

"I just remembered—I was supposed to check with Mel about what materials we should use. We were thinking about having the roof open and close automatically depending on the temperature. You never know what the weather is going to be like around here, with so many people and their different moods. A lot of tomatoes could be ruined by one of Trevor's frosty outbursts." Oliver's face crinkled up in laughter.

"Well, why don't you go talk with her now?"

"I promised I'd walk back with you."

"Because you want to or because you're worried that I'll go fetal again if left alone?"

He blushed. "Would it be so bad to say a little bit of both?"

"Nah," I replied. "It would just make you truthful. How about I wait for you outside? I'll sit under one of the trees out front and work on giving myself a break." I mimed giving myself a big hug.

"That would be awesome." He gave me a quick squeeze and turned back toward the classroom, calling over his shoulder, "I won't be long at all."

I waved him off and headed toward the main lobby. Immediately my mind buzzed, busily replaying everything that'd just happened. I couldn't help it, my thoughts drifted from one random idea about Trevor to another. Something was surfacing in response to my memories, but I couldn't put a finger on it. The harder I tried to focus on it, the more obscure the thought became.

Deep in my own mental gymnastics, I rounded the corner and caught a glimpse of Trevor at the end of the hall. His back was to me and his arm was propped up against the main door. I immediately braced myself for another bout of Trevor hostility before I realized he didn't even know I was there. Then it hit me: Trevor wasn't alone. All his attention was focused on someone else. His other arm was cradling a dizzying array of wild blond curls.

OMG! He was kissing Julia.

10

tilt

I shouldn't have cared one bit about who that idiot was kissing, yet Oliver's words jumped into my head and repeated like a ticker tape in Times Square: *He seems to think that you're his soul mate.*

Thinking about it was causing a disorienting, warm flutter in my lower gut. *Really?* I visualized a fisted hand thumping me on the noggin. The ridiculous words rattled around momentarily like a shiny orb in a pinball machine and then dropped out of sight. Tilt.

My temples throbbed. Julia and Trevor were still attached at the lips. "Oh, for God's sake, get a room." I instantly pictured walking in on a tangled pile of Trevor and Julia, and quickly added, "And I don't mean mine."

Julia stiffened and peeked out from under Trevor's arm. She looked like Dorothy after being blown into Oz. No clue as to how her little house had migrated from Kansas.

Trevor turned around with calculated ease. He kept his grip on Julia, who seemed like she wanted to bolt.

"Elliot, um, I . . ." Julia sputtered.

I couldn't stop staring at her mouth, puffy from being kissed. Without making eye contact I barked at her. "Spit it out—you're in charge now. Remember?"

Trevor released Julia and sauntered up to me. "I'm sorry"— his sarcasm had extra bite—"but is there some reason why this is your business?"

I could feel the color drop from my face like an elevator with its cable severed. Why was it so hard for me to think things through before barbs started flying out of my mouth?

"I asked you a question." Trevor's voice tightened.

I stared at him, realization crawling over me like mold. The kind that you see in fast-forward on a *National Geographic* special. I was being invaded by the nasty green knowledge that possibly, maybe, I could be slightly, just a bit—jealous. *What the hell?*

"Leave her alone," Oliver said. He must've snuck up behind me.

Leaving me alone seemed like the last thing that Trevor wanted to do. His face was anything but inviting, yet he was looking at me like I had something that belonged to him and he wasn't leaving without it.

I dropped my gaze. "I'm sorry."

"It isn't true." His voice was low, the words slicing the air with the precision of a blade.

"What isn't true?"

"What he said." He shoved his hands deep in his pockets and nudged his chin in Oliver's direction. "You know—about the stupid *soul mate* thing." He said the words "soul mate" like a toddler might say "lima beans."

"Oh, I never thought it was true," I said. I could feel Oliver tense, ready to protest, but I squeezed his hand and whispered, "Just let it go."

So there it was. Well, I didn't want him as my soul mate either. Julia could have him. Too bad he wasn't interested in being in David's Workshop too. What a relief that Oliver, sweet and funny Oliver, was my Passenger.

Why was I wasting my time here? As if Oliver knew what I was thinking, he grabbed me by the hand and we skirted around Julia and Trevor. I'd almost made it to safety when I felt Trevor's fingers grip my arm. My pulse sped up and I could hear my heart thundering in my ears. I had to remind myself that I was already dead. What could he actually do to me?

11

revelations

I braced myself, expecting to be swept away in his anger and hatred, waiting for the vise to tighten.

"He's my brother."

It was a quiet and simple statement and I couldn't get a lock on the motivation behind it. Then I remembered Trevor's despair at Oliver's funeral, his crumpled form.

Oliver tugged at my hand, but I let my fingers slip from his grasp. For the first time, I tried to see everything from Trevor's point of view. I didn't want to admit it, but his new memories must've been as shocking to him as mine were to me. It didn't matter how big of an ass he was, his Delve to the gravesite had been heart wrenching.

I decided to extend the olive branch. It was obvious that he'd been hurt too. Like Mel had suggested, maybe we were in this together. Besides, he didn't have a Passenger watching out for him.

I glanced up at Trevor. Correction. I obviously wasn't in anything with anyone. Julia moved forward and entwined her fingers with his. The placement of each finger was like the tumblers of a lock falling into place. She was on one side and I was on the other, separated by a wall of Trevor. I focused on the newest slogan printed in neon across his chest.

HOW CAN I MISS YOU IF YOU WON'T GO AWAY?

He was hateful! I was trying and he was so—

I scrolled through my mental list of nasty phrases and they all seemed to apply.

Arrogant.

Destructive.

Cocky.

Insensitive.

Rude.

Conniving.

Manipulative.

Ugly—I threw that one in just because I felt like it. Finally, convinced I had enough anger in me to hold my ground, I faced him. His jaw was clenched so tight it pulsed, and I felt myself wilting under his gaze. All my bravado melted into puddles at my feet.

My weakness made me hate him more. The fact that he had Julia and I didn't was unbearable. I rushed past Oliver and out the door.

I skipped lunch and snuck up to my room. I had one ear tuned toward the door, listening for the delicate dance of Julia's footsteps. This was the first time I was hoping she wouldn't show up. If I heard her coming, I might seriously consider hiding under the bed.

I'd expected to feel safe up here, but I couldn't get out of my own head. I couldn't block out the vision of Julia sucking face with Trevor or stop remembering Oliver bloodied and broken.

I broke him.

I flipped back and forth between self-loathing and confusion. I winced as a fresh strip of cuticle was torn from my ring finger, a hapless victim of my emotions. I started picking at the next finger while I paced. I couldn't remember her, but I so wanted my mom right now.

What about Oliver's mom? She must be devastated. She wasn't aware that he was safe and happy, here with me. She couldn't comprehend that he loved the girl who'd taken him away. She might be struggling to believe there even *was* an afterlife. Did she have moments where she wondered if her baby had been erased?

I flashed back to the look on her face, when she knew without a doubt that Oliver was gone. The raw, visceral noises that poured out of her soul as she ran to him.

I could hear the hum and feel my legs quivering. The lights were going out again. This memory was the last place I ever wanted to return to but it seemed like my intense emotions were the trigger for these unexpected Delves. I threw out my hands in protest but . . .

I couldn't watch anymore. I couldn't move. Horror anchored my feet to the earth. I could hear sirens in the distance, but they were too late.

Too late to save Oliver.

Too late to save me.

Too damn late.

Staring at my feet, I noticed my hand. It had blood on it. Curled between my fingers was a cell phone filled to capacity with the indescribable cries of my mom.

I flipped the phone shut. It slid from my fingers and clattered to my feet. I was alone, wishing for my mother and realizing that I didn't deserve to have her comfort me.

The little girl in the car seat wailed and I could hear the sirens coming closer in the moments when Oliver's mom quieted, pressing her lips to his dirt-streaked face. Her silence only lasted as long as it took for her mind to rewrap itself around the trunk of that tree. It was agonizing to watch. Then her head shot up and she blazed with accusation. She burned from the inside out and all her fire was directed at me. She knew what I'd done.

I woke up sprawled across my bed, with the sun peeking up over the trees. I must have staggered over before falling into that Delve. I didn't know if my exhaustion was from the heart-wrenching memories or if it was a shut-off valve for having taken in too much information. Either way I'd slept through the night. I was grateful. Sleep had been a reprieve from the problems that were never going to go away.

Looking around, I realized Julia wasn't here, but she had been. Two more paper cranes lay on my pillow. Now I had three of them.

There was a persistent tap at the door. "Elliot, open up." The voice was male and authoritative. I must've processed the words a little too slowly, because as I glanced up he was coming through the door.

"David?"

What was he doing in my room? I didn't see a hospitality basket with muffins.

David stood in the middle of my sanctuary and slowly rotated 360 degrees. My fingers reached up and clutched a lock of my hair, trying to find something tangible to hold on to while my space was being invaded.

"So, this is where Mel stashed you." He sniffed and a plug of phlegm shifted and rattled. "I suppose Freddie had something to do with it too."

Was I supposed to say something? This guy was utter kryptonite—rendering all my best snarky retorts useless in his presence. My brain rattled around like a squeaky hamster wheel. I closed my mouth for fear of drooling and giving him more ammunition.

"I imagine you're wondering what I'm doing up here," he said, as his fat fingers molested the fuzzy blanket tossed over the end of my bed. He plucked one of Julia's cranes, sending it flying into the limbo space between my bed and the wall. I could feel cold sweat pooling in very unattractive places.

"Mel asked me to check on you since she's busy spending time with Trevor. You remember Trevor?"

"Trevor and Mel are together?" I choked out the words.

When I looked up, David's bushy mustache could barely disguise a smirk. The twinkle in his eyes showed how much he enjoyed my distress.

I stared at him but found myself sliding backward toward the headboard of my bed, bracing myself for his next verbal attack. I didn't have to wait long.

"You seem confused, Miss Turner. Did you expect her to come and comfort you after your big day of revelations?" He twisted the chunky ring on his pinky finger. "She isn't really your mother, even though you act like she is." He leaned down and lowered his voice. "Mothers don't always come to the rescue. Sometimes . . . they've got nothing to give."

Unshed tears pressed hotly against my eyeballs. My scalp hurt, as my finger twirled my hair tighter and tighter with his every comment.

David took it all in and then dropped the bomb. "Mel's probably helping him privately Delve for more memories. I imagine he is dying to know how else you've destroyed his life."

That's why David was here. He was gloating, rubbing salt into my wounds. What had I ever done to him?

The room was spinning and I couldn't think. I slammed down the feelings of betrayal. I didn't have the right to expect other people to be there for me, not after what I'd done. But I'd assumed that Mel was still in my corner. I wanted her to be on my side since Julia had abandoned me. I ached with need.

I tucked my head between my knees, feeling dizzy from the thoughts swirling around between my ears, like flotsam in a whirlpool. I was ashamed of what kept circling back for self-examination. For once I agreed with David—I was the stuff that should be washed away.

12

still

waters

run deep

I'd killed Oliver. But then there was Trevor. I hadn't made the connection until now: *two* boys were dead from one family. Thinking about it caused my stomach to twist and knot.

I pinched myself, forcing my mind to focus on something else besides the horror film in my head. Taking a deep breath I glanced around once more. David had disappeared, but the overpowering scent of his cologne lingered, polluting my safe haven. It didn't really matter. The truth was that no place was safe anymore. I hightailed it to the stairs.

Common sense dictated that I couldn't hide from any of this, but my feet seemed to have other ideas. I walked down to the water and followed the shoreline away from the Haven, Mel's Workshop, and the smell of David.

I was gagging on my guilt as I headed for the lake. I needed to escape, get out of my own head. I seriously thought about taking up drinking, but I was already too aware of how revealing my sober bursts of emotional creativity could be. Drinking at the Obmil could cause quite a show. I didn't want to be a sloppy mess. As it was, I could barely meet the eyes of the people who'd Delved with me.

I plodded forward. The soft, sandy beach was getting progressively rockier. Before I knew it, I was climbing boulders and hugging sheer rock walls. Sweat dripped from my brow, and my thoughts narrowed to a pinpoint of focus. My palm stung from gripping a knife-sharp handhold.

I tried to increase my speed and slammed my knee into the wall of granite. I could feel a bruise rising to the surface. I let out a hiss and rubbed the tender spot. I'd have to concentrate more in order to move forward safely. A chuckle escaped at the thought. "Hello, dummy, you're dead and can't be injured." I said it aloud to myself. Old habits die hard. The living are wired for self-preservation and I'd never been able to shake those instincts over the course of my visits.

Once when I'd been eighty-year-old Arty, I was goofing around, trying to make silly faces at a child who wasn't interested in eating her dinner. In the middle of my theatrics, I tipped over my glass and it shattered on the floor. In the scramble to pick up the broken pieces, I'd sliced open the palm of my hand. Blood oozed through my fingers. Spots danced across my vision. Just as I began to panic, Mel asked me to stop for a moment and picture the wound healed. The image was in my head no more than a few seconds before the cut and the blood were gone. I asked her what would have happened if I hadn't pictured myself fixed. Would I have sat there bleeding and suffering forever?

She'd laughed, assuring me that the process was automatic and would kick in by itself. We simply had the capacity to hasten our own ability to be healed.

A sigh escaped from my lips. I could create weather and buildings. I could make the world around me appear just like I envisioned it. I could make myself whole, too. Well, at least physically whole. Mel also seemed to think that if I tried hard enough, spiritual and emotional wellness could be mine for the asking. It sounded nice, but I had my doubts.

The rocky terrain leveled off as I moved away from the lake. I found myself walking through a shady forest of old growth trees. There was no path. This was clearly a manifestation of my own state of mind, proof that I had no idea what direction my life should be taking. I squinted. I'd stepped out of the cool and quiet darkness of the woods into the sunlight. The sudden movement from dark to light blinded me, so I took a step back and shaded my eyes with my hand.

In front of me was a pond. I could smell its earthiness now that I was paying attention to my senses. The outer edges were decorated with a filigree of lily pads and blossoms. On one side, across from where I stood, there was an army of reeds and cattails fencing in the perimeter. The bull's-eye ripples on the face of the water gave away the last location of a small frog. Directly across from me was a small peninsula of land that jutted out into the placid water. A tiny, cedar-roofed gazebo—really just an awning over a bench—caught my eye. I exhaled, not realizing until then that I'd been holding my breath.

The whole scene was beautiful, but I hadn't created it, so who had? This place was so achingly lovely and relaxing. It had to be someone's creation, but I'd never heard about it, so I must have stumbled across someplace private. There were some legendary places at the Obmil that souls passed down. If I left here and told Julia about the pond, and later she came searching for it, she might actually find something that was pretty darn similar because my vision had become her vision. Not like that would actually happen, the way things were between us.

I scanned the banks of the pond. No one was here. I moved to the left and circled around. I felt as if I should be cautious, but the calmness of the place balanced out the strangeness of not knowing where the mysterious creator was.

That's when I saw him. Trevor was sprawled out on the very tip of the peninsula. He'd been hidden from view by a clump of wild grasses growing by the water's edge. His eyes were closed and he was soaking up the sun. He appeared relaxed, and obviously he was, if he could create such a tranquil place to rest. His chest was free of his usual taunts and it rose and fell slowly as he breathed. What was he doing out here? David had told me that he was off Delving with Mel. I wondered who'd been lying.

I edged closer, crouching down and moving like a ninja from one form of cover to another. I felt silly, but I couldn't resist seeing his face relaxed, devoid of its usual hostility.

When I reached the gazebo bench I stood on the seat and threw one foot up on the railing. Wrapping my arms around the side support I pulled myself upward and peered down at Trevor, not knowing how I would explain my awkward behavior if he woke up.

The sensation of wrongness hit me immediately. At this height I could see the other side of his languid pose. His arm was tucked underneath him in an awkward position. He wasn't sleeping—something wasn't right.

I leapt off the railing, reaching for him as I dashed down

to the water's edge. As I moved closer I could feel my vision starting to disappear and my legs dissolving into fizzy tingles. Before I could reverse my forward momentum I realized that he was deep in a Delve and I was being pulled in by my proximity to him. As I tumbled into Trevor's memory, I felt my body fall against his. Great.

I dropped into Trevor's memories like a cartoon anvil. He'd already settled into himself, and catching up with him so rapidly knocked the wind out of me.

He was back in the cemetery. He was alone this time, in the warm golden light of the morning sun that reflected off the jet-black marble bench that served as a headstone.

Trevor straddled the bench, one leg thrown over each edge as if he were riding a horse. His finger traced the words carved in the cool stone and then hypnotically moved around and around the O in Oliver.

Without warning his hand stopped. I could feel the tension as he sat rigid, barely breathing. His eyes remained on the O but his focus was elsewhere. What was it? I felt a small knot of fear as I wondered if he knew I'd dropped into his Delve and was spying on him. I didn't think it was possible, but I didn't really know for sure.

Just when I thought the anticipation would drive me crazy, his gaze inched to the right. Now I could see that we were at the top of the hill, where a smattering of newer graves butted up against the tree line. This was where Oliver was located.

Trevor glanced into the woods. The rest of him never moved an inch.

I gasped as the object of his attention came into focus. Large brown eyes were visible in the shadows. They stood out against the deathly paleness of a face—my face. Before I could digest that I was the broken-looking creature in the woods, Trevor tore off at a run, hurtling toward me. His voice thundered.

"Who the hell are you?"

13

questions

We were back at the pond and I was no longer sprawled on top of Trevor as I'd expected. Instead his heavy torso had me pinned to the ground. I could feel his rapid heartbeat through his chest, movement and adrenaline rushing back into his body. My own heart was already racing from the Delve, but it was becoming faster. I wondered if I could've escaped undetected if Trevor hadn't somehow rolled onto me.

I didn't have time to speculate as he roared back to awareness. "Why are you spying on me?"

Did he mean here or in the cemetery or both? It didn't matter because I couldn't answer him anyway. I could barely breathe with him crushing my ribs like twigs, and when I tried to suck in air, the weight of him compressed my lungs even further.

"Gahhhhh . . ."

"Oh, sorry," he mumbled, pushing off the ground next to me and rolling to the side. He sprung to his feet, agile like a cat. I, on the other hand, was trying to reinflate my lungs before I made any sudden movements. It occurred to me that I would require air to deal with Trevor.

I was less than graceful as I moved into an upright position, nearly tipping back over as I tried to free a stick from my tangle of hair. Trevor paced back and forth between where I sat and the gazebo. His feet were surprisingly stealthy considering the intensity of his movements.

He stopped abruptly and studied me. "Can you answer me now?" His voice was calmer but still had an edge to it. His face was all kinds of serious.

I wasn't sure how to answer. Like it would matter, anyway. My existence alone was enough to tick him off. I gave a seriously unattractive snort thinking about it. Realizing that there was nothing I could do to make him happy had released all the pressure that was building up inside me.

"All right, Trevor," I said, flying to my feet and dusting off the butt of my pants. I felt a small quiver of power, as his eyes grew large at my unexpectedly confident response. Feeling braver, I strode toward him. Giddily I watched him take a step backward, then two.

What would he do when his legs pressed up against the wood of the gazebo? The thrill of dominance prickled the hairs on the nape of my neck. *Let's see how he likes being the prey for a change.*

"First of all, no one is spying on you." With my arms crossed, I threw my hip out to emphasize the point. "It's called hiking. It's what I do to blow off steam and get my thoughts together. I accidentally came across the pond and . . ." How could I say it without giving him an even bigger ego? "Well, I was searching to see who'd created it. It was just so surprisingly beautiful." My eyes were slits, making sure he didn't mock my honesty. If he laughed even a little bit I'd throttle him. But his gaze stayed steady and he remained quiet so I continued. "That's when I found you and at first I thought you were sleeping. Then I noticed your arm was twisted and . . ."

He was easily swiveling the appendage around with the tiniest of smirks on his face. "Good as new," he said.

"Oh. Well, good. I'm glad to hear it." I unfolded my arms.

"Anyway," I continued, "I ran to help you and—" I was interrupted by a much louder snort than my own. I ignored it and continued. "So as I got close to you, I mean near you, I fell into your Delve and that's how I landed on . . . This really could be seen as your fault."

I found myself taking a step back at the same exact moment that Trevor took one in my direction.

There was a slight drawl in his voice as he asked, "So you were trying to save me?"

He was drawing closer and if I moved back too much farther I'd be standing in the pond. Maybe it wouldn't be such a bad thing; I could feel the heat flaring up in my cheeks.

"Well, I appreciate your worry."

I couldn't tell if he was being sincere or sarcastic. He was within a foot of me now and I needed to look up to meet his gaze.

"What I wanted to know was, why were you spying on me in the cemetery?"

"Oh." I bit my lip. "I don't know why I was there." I thought about it a moment. "Did you know it was me? I mean, did your past self know it was me in the woods or did you always go around threatening people?" I didn't add that from what I knew of him in the afterlife, it was completely believable.

"Do you always snort?" he asked.

He was outrageous, the master of deflection. I could feel a vein pulsing in my temple.

"Me? Did you not hear the snort that came out of your nose?" I demanded.

The chuckle rumbled from someplace down in his gut. It rolled up and out and bounced around me. He was laughing. For the first time, he wasn't hard and angry. My tongue felt dry from the breeze blowing into my gaping mouth. A piece of me wanted to be angry that he was making fun of me, but that smile was like light reflecting off the snow on a crystal clear day. I was hypnotized by it, blinded.

"I'm not a beast," he said, the corner of his mouth twitching.

"Sure acted like one," I fired off without thinking.

"Ha." He threw back his head. "I think I like you better with a backbone."

"Hey, I've always had a backbone." I glared at him, trying to distract myself from the hummingbirds doing loop-the-loops in my stomach. Where did those little birds come from? I tried to concentrate. "I, on the other hand, was just wondering where you've had that smile stashed."

I sucked in some air for fortification and took a step forward. Shoot, he didn't back up. Now we were almost nose-to-nose. Actually it was nose-to-chest. All the breath I'd taken in came rushing back out and piled up against the place on his T-shirt where he displayed his witty slogans. God, I hoped it was minty fresh.

"Fair enough," he said. "I came here angry."

Neither of us budged and the hummingbirds were going all ADHD on me now.

Breaking the spell, he rocked back and knelt down to tie his shoe. I took that moment to remind myself to breathe.

"I emerged from the lake right after you arrived. I could see you, the back of you, heading up to the Haven with Mel and I think I just imprinted my anger on you. I had no idea who you were, but I could barely control it. Then . . ." He tugged the lace of his shoe free and started tying all over again.

I finished the thought for him. "Then I Delved and you discovered that manslaughter was a pretty decent reason to hate me." I plopped myself down on the ground next to him.

"I've got two questions for you," I said.

"Just two, huh? I've got more than that for you." He chuckled. How could I respond? It was just outright weird to be having a semi-pleasant conversation with him.

"Fire away," he said, facing me straight on. The pale blue staring back at me was caught between emotions that I couldn't read or understand.

I fingered my necklace, running the charm swiftly back and forth across the chain. "Okay. I understand why you're so angry with me." I stopped. His arm was tossed casually over his knee and he was chewing on a blade of grass, watching me in a way that made goose bumps run up and down my arms. "But why were the sparks flying between you and Oliver from the start?"

"I don't know. Something ignited when I came face-to-face

with him." His knuckles cracked under the pressure of his fingers. "During this last Delve, the me from the past was flooded with thoughts of him. I think some of the emotions were more complicated than just grief." He picked at the worn threads on the knee of his jeans, causing a hole to appear. "I'm not sure what it meant because the Elliot in the past interrupted me."

I ignored his implication of blame. This was the first truce we'd acquired and I didn't want to crush it.

"So did the past-life Trevor know that it was me in the trees?" I asked, repeating my original question.

"I only knew it was you because I know you now. Back then, the other Trevor had no idea who was stalking him."

"I wouldn't call standing quietly in the trees *stalking!*" I said, my voice getting higher.

"I probably wouldn't have either, but past-life me was thinking that you'd been there every day for a week. I guess you were freaking him out."

I pulled a pen out of my pocket, grateful for the ability to create something to keep my nervous fingers busy. I started tattooing the sole of my shoe.

"I don't know what it all means either," Trevor continued, "but I think that Mel is probably right."

I couldn't help it, another snort snuck out. "Sorry," I said, trying not to do it again.

"As I was saying," Trevor continued, "it might be better if we do this together. I'll try to put my anger aside."

I clicked the top of my pen up and down. "You've been doing a little better while we've been sitting here," I said.

"I can't make any promises."

I could hear the underlying edge in his voice. Mean, angry Trevor—that guy could show up again at any time. I wasn't going to fool myself about that, but there was something about this new Trevor who smiled. He reminded me of the brother he'd been at the Basin. Obviously, we would never be friends, but maybe a truce wasn't out of the realm of possibility.

"Trevor, I have one last question."

"You've used up your allotment for the day, but I'm feeling charitable." He almost grinned as he pushed a thatch of hair out of his face.

"What made you change your mind? Why are you giving me a chance?" I asked. Before I could blink, I was hit with a Delve faster and harder than any I'd experienced previously. I was catapulted into the past.

There was a knock on the door, but there was no waiting.

"Elliot?" Mom called as she walked in. There was concern etched in deep lines all over her face.

For years I'd watched my mother's fantastic rituals in front of the mirror, creams and serums applied to keep her skin looking young. A lifetime of faithful care had been erased in moments. My mistake had aged my mother, hardened her. The weight of it was on her face and she seemed as if she could barely hold it.

My breath caught as my dad followed my mom into my bedroom. I'd hardly uttered a word since that single scream of terror had lodged itself in my throat weeks before. I knew that the silence caused my mom and dad to panic, but I couldn't seem to get control over my voice. I was drowning in my own horror.

It was agonizing to watch my dad pretend to be brave. I was well aware that he always adjusted his face before he walked into my room. I wasn't fooled. At night I could hear him down in the den. When he thought the world was asleep, the sounds of his weeping traveled through the lonely house. Heaving gasps would rise out of him as he realized he couldn't fix things for me, his only child.

I wanted to block it out. Instead I listened to his anguish and watched my mom's torment. It was part of my punishment.

It would never be enough.

My mind had wandered, but I suddenly realized my parents were staring at me. I wondered if they noticed my greasy hair and my pale skeletal remains. The sheets and blankets around me were a nest I'd burrowed in. I sniffed. They smelled like fear and I reeked of it too. Mom and Dad wanted their daughter back. I didn't know where to begin to search for her, and I certainly didn't know the girl who was sitting here in her place.

I just wanted them to leave me alone. Couldn't they see that their daughter had died the same day as Oliver Lowry, one of the most popular kids at school? I scanned their faces, realizing that they couldn't let go of their hope, denial, or both.

I questioned my ability to rouse enough energy to get them to leave me alone. There was only one way they'd let me be; I needed to lie. If I fed the illusion they were clinging to, their denial would have something to nourish it.

My unused voice cracked, but the words fell easily from my lips. "I was thinking of taking a walk, maybe going over to Cari's house." It didn't matter that my BFF hadn't stopped by, hadn't called. It didn't matter that Cari's silence was so loud it hurt my ears. She did know what I had done, but she had nothing to say and that spoke volumes.

Like I'd expected, their hope was a spark, so I blew on it gently.

"Sweetie," said my dad, "would you like me to drive you over to her house?"

"Or I could brush out your hair and curl it for you?" my mom asked. Her fingers trembled. It was as if she longed to touch something familiar.

"I—I would really like to get out and about by myself. Maybe things will feel more normal," I said, pasting a smile on my face. I hoped my cheeks wouldn't crack from the effort. It hurt, knowing for sure that it was so easy to fool them.

I climbed out of bed and headed for the shower. It's amazing what water doesn't wash away. An hour later I gave a reassuring wave to my parents as I walked down the road toward Cari's house. I glanced back over my shoulder once. Mom and Dad pulsated with hope at the appearance of normality. I turned back, unable to get out of their line of vision fast enough. I felt exposed out here in the open. The world was too big.

Avoiding Cari's house, I headed for the trees, my feet falling into a mind-numbing rhythm as I hiked farther and farther into the woods.

I was ready and willing to be lost, and very much surprised to find myself standing on the tree line of the cemetery.

The guy from the cemetery. Oliver's brother. He saw me watching him in the woods. His index finger made contact with my shoulder. It was a concentrated point of accusation and I tried to flee from it. My heel caught a root and down I went. I was vulnerable. This past week I'd witnessed his agony. I'd watched his pain unfold while I sat hidden in the trees. I knew there was nothing he could do to me that I didn't deserve. Yet despite having lost the will to live, I scooted farther away, trying to find protection from the shrapnel of his fury.

"Who are you? Why are you always here watching me?" he asked, his voice tight. He wedged his fingers under my upper arm, trying to yank me up off the ground. I dug in my heels.

Honestly, I hadn't thought it was possible that he didn't know. How ironic, I thought to myself. This boy hated me already and he didn't even know who I was or what I'd done.

"You're hurting me," I whimpered.

He stopped yanking and let go. I rubbed my upper arm, trying to regain the circulation but not actually feeling any better.

"I'm sorry."

He appeared less menacing when he was apologetic. He had the palest blue eyes that I'd ever seen.

"Like I said," he ran his fingers through a mop of jet-black hair, hair the same color as the marble gravestone he'd been sitting on. "I'm sorry. I don't know what I was thinking, it's just that my bro——" He composed his face. "It's just been a hard time lately. You were making me really uncomfortable. I thought you might be one of those reporters or——never mind. I had no right to take my anger out on you."

I should tell him who I am, *I thought*. I must tell him who I am. *But at the exact moment that my mouth opened, his hand shot out toward me. Without a thought, I cringed and scuttled deeper into the woods, pressed my back against a tree.*

"Oh shit, I'm really sorry. I'm just trying to help you up off of the ground. Please . . ." *His hand moved forward, more slowly this time. He opened his fingers, palm up, advertising its innocence.*

Tell him, *my conscience screamed.* Tell him now!

I reached for his hand. His fingers closed warmly around mine.

"You're freezing! Come out here in the sun where it's warm," *he said.*

I felt so embarrassed. He was obviously trying to keep the crazy girl from climbing into the underbrush.

I'll tell him in a minute, *I thought*. He's being so nice and I haven't spoken to a single person besides my parents in weeks, and with them I mostly nod. *It felt good to say words aloud again.*

Everything at home is so unspeakable. I'll tell him in a minute—when I'm done remembering why I can't possibly tell him.

"Hey, anybody there?" It was Oliver's older brother waving his hand in front of my face. "I forgot to ask, what's your name?"

"Elliot," I said, tensing in case he recognized the name after all. While I'd known Oliver—heck, everyone knew Oliver—I hadn't known his brother. Didn't even know he'd had one.

"My name's Trevor. Listen, I don't blame you for having a bad first impression of me. I'm an idiot. Would it be okay if we just talked for a little bit? It feels good not to be alone." He appeared younger and more vulnerable now that the anger wasn't pouring out of him.

Tell him. You have to tell him the truth.

"All right," came the whisper of air passing over my lips. I was hypnotized by the sensation of being innocent again.

"Okay." Trevor gave a shy smile. "Me first. I'll give you something easy, to warm you up. What's your favorite color?"

"Brown."

"Brown? That's a little weird. I've never met anyone who likes brown the best. Care to elaborate?" He chuckled, giving me the once over. "On second thought," he said slowly. "You don't have to explain at all, it's right in front of me. Earth tones suit you with your large brown eyes."

I could feel a wisp of warmth infuse my face.

"My favorite color is green," Trevor rambled on. "I know you thought it would be blue"—he pointed at his eye—"but you would've been wrong. Now what's your question? I need a little bit of a challenge, though. Distract me."

"Favorite bird?" I asked softly, hardly daring to look up. This couldn't be happening, I thought, I shouldn't be feeling like a person again, even for a minute. Not ever. Not in front of this boy and most certainly not because of this boy.

"Hummingbird," he said with a little lift of his shoulders. "They're the only bird that can fly backward. They seem so cute, but in reality, they're badasses." He flapped his hands up and down like rapid little wings. The corners of my mouth twitched with the thought of him admiring such a tiny bird.

"Hey, I thought you were going to give me something hard to answer. Throw one at me. Give me something tough." Trevor threw his arms open wide.

Unlike the hummingbird, I couldn't fly backward, undo it all. So I leapt.

"What would you do if you met the girl who killed your brother?"

14

choices

I felt groggy and disoriented. The left side of my face was sore where it'd been pressed up against a rock for the duration of the Delve. We were both a lot slower coming out of this Delve than the previous one.

"Stop doing that without giving me any warning." Trevor stood up and stretched out his arms.

"I'm not the only one causing Delves, you know." I kicked a rock and it actually skipped four times before sinking. I couldn't have done that if I'd been trying.

"Yeah, I know, but I can't believe you pulled us back out of that Delve before we found out how your big announcement went over."

"I didn't pull us back, we just came back," I huffed.

"I don't think you consciously pulled us back, but maybe you didn't want to know how I reacted to learning who you were."

He was probably right, now that I thought about it. We'd been in my past life, not his.

"I don't want to do this anymore," I announced.

"Do what? Be dead?" There was a sarcastic edge to his voice. "You could've thought of that before you started playing with your cell phone while you were driving. Before you dragged us all here with you."

It was cruel and it reminded me of how fragile this new peace between us really was.

"I didn't kill you! I killed Oliver and it was an accident." I picked up a rock and launched it as far over the pond as I could, wrenching my shoulder with the effort. The irony that I was defending myself by referencing manslaughter was not lost on me.

"How do I know you didn't kill me too?" came Trevor's steady voice.

I gasped.

He shrugged his shoulders with a fake apology. "All I know is that I'm dead and I died right after you did. I know this because I watched you walk away from the lake, to the Haven. Dying that close together—doesn't that make you wonder?"

Trevor scowled. "Maybe I hated you enough to kill you. And then I couldn't live with myself any more than I could live with you. No matter how you slice it—still your fault."

I hadn't made that connection before. I'd been too engrossed in my own death and reemergence at the Obmil. My head was pounding with the revelation. Could he have really done that? I shivered.

"I don't want to do this anymore," I said again. My voice sounded wooden. I stood up and headed through the trees toward the Haven.

"Hey—where are you going?" Trevor asked. Feeling the now-familiar grip of his fingers around my upper arm, I shook him off and put the pond far behind me as quickly as I could. I wished he would storm off like he usually did, but I could hear him snapping the underbrush behind me.

I whirled around. "I just need to get away from you right now." I dug my fingers into my temples. "Why don't you go find Julia? I'm sure she could distract you." It came out harsher than I'd planned and it brought an unexpected flash of confusion across his face. Just as quickly as the vulnerability had illuminated itself, his all-too-familiar stoniness dropped into place.

"I didn't mean it like that," I pleaded. "It's too much right now. I need to get away from it for a little bit."

"Do you know the funny thing about you, Elliot? You never do the expected. When I wanted you far away and out of my very existence, you just kept popping up. I couldn't get away from you, and now that—" Trevor's voice stopped short.

"Now that . . ." I echoed.

His face gave nothing away.

"Now that I know you better, I'm realizing how perceptive you are. I was hoping you'd get the hell out of here and give me some space. Now that you mention it, I think I will go meet Julia." His shirt blazed with the words I'M NOT BEING RUDE, YOU'RE JUST INSIGNIFICANT!

I didn't wait for another attack; instead I turned around and headed home. Let Julia have him.

The sun was high in the sky, baking the back of my neck as I approached the Haven. The air had become humid and felt heavy in my lungs. Mosquitoes pooled around me.

There wasn't a soul in sight as I moved along the path. It was a relief to be alone. I was exhausted from living and reliving so many emotions. The sound of my footsteps bounced off the shadowy portcullis, emphasizing my solitude. In a flash of panic I imagined everyone else enlightened to the meaning of life, all souls having vanished from the Obmil, leaving me here on my own.

I dashed up the stone steps into the Haven. The air wasn't as moist in the lodge, but everything was eerily still inside the cavernous lobby. I wandered past Freddie's empty front desk to the now dark fireplace that was big enough for me to walk into upright. I'd hoped to find Oliver here, telling funny stories or giving piggyback rides to the little kids. I needed my Oliver battery recharged. But of course no one was here—it was midmorning and everyone was at Workshop. I'd left on my hike before breakfast, and because of Trevor and the Delves, I'd completely lost track of time. Mel was going to be finger-tapping annoyed.

Everyone had probably been sitting there for hours, waiting for us to show up and Delve. I pictured the senior citizens playing bingo. The antsy businessmen who paced the floor might be upset, but they'd likely be more annoyed that we caused a deviation in their schedule than that we deprived them of the opportunity for personal development. Then again, maybe they hadn't been waiting for long. I wouldn't put it past Trevor to head straight there after leaving the pond. His motive, of course, would be to show me up. He'd likely Delve and find out something important without me, something even worse to use against me. Then he'd run to Julia so she could comfort him.

With a sigh of resignation I realized there was no way I

could retreat to the quiet of my little upstairs nest. Mel might not be happy that I'd lost track of time, but she would be even less pleased if I made the decision not to come at all.

I spun around, ready to head back up the trail, when I heard a noise. I froze, straining to hear where the faint moan had come from. Then it came again. What first sounded like an exclamation of pain was now a low rumbling sob. My feet moved me through the lobby and down the hall. As I passed the dining room I realized I'd have to branch off into the residential wing. The gut-wrenching noise was coming from one of the rooms.

Part of me wanted to tear through the hall, flinging open doors so that I could help whoever was in need, but I found myself moving forward cautiously. The sobs became louder as I moved farther down the passageway. When I rounded the last corner, it was clear that they were coming from the end room. I inched forward slowly. The door was halfway open and I was afraid to be seen. Curiosity won out and I allowed myself to sneak a glimpse over the threshold.

"Mama," the voice sobbed. I peeked my head ever so slowly around the door.

I wasn't prepared for what I saw. David was lying on a twin bed, curled up in the fetal position. He was half wrapped in and half cuddling a ratty-looking blue cotton blanket.

His room was nothing like I expected. It was a living book of memories, one layer of decoration and talisman tacked on top of another. At the very top of the room, pressed up against the ceiling, was a wallpaper border of airplanes. As I examined it closer, I saw that the blanket that David was clinging to had matching aeronautics on it.

The room was like a giant scrapbook of a boy's life. Airplanes, robots, baseball paraphernalia, music posters. On the desk and bookcase were da Vinci models and anatomy books stacked in piles. This was the room of a child with dreams. Every inch of the place seemed to tell the story of a boy who was nothing like the hard-hearted man I'd encountered.

I couldn't reconcile it and it scared me a little. David must've created all these items and brought them into his room. Everyone did it to a certain degree. If you were bored while sitting out by the dock, you could simply create a book to read. Then, when the sun went down and it got dark during the very best chapter, a book light would appear. Rarely did anyone erase his or her creations. They just brought them home and dropped them in their rooms or passed them on to someone else. Then, once they'd left the Obmil, their belongings left too. Anything that wasn't consciously connected to a remaining soul disappeared along with its creator.

David's room felt different than creating when a need

arose. It was like he was deliberately reconstructing his childhood, collecting objects to fill an emotional void. Were they memories or wishes?

Quietly I pushed the door open further. David was making soft whispered sounds that I couldn't make out, so I leaned closer.

"What are you doing, Elliot?"

The voice behind me was soft, but it was magnified by the adrenaline already coursing through my body. I whipped around, swallowing a high-pitched squeal of fright.

"Oh crap, Freddie, you scared me to death." I clutched my heart, trying to keep it in my chest. "Well, I guess it's impossible to actually scare me to death." I rambled through my nervousness, unable to stop myself from babbling. "I know it's silly, but I keep forgetting that I'm not alive anymore."

"What makes you think you're not alive?" asked Freddie. He leaned his broom against the wall and tucked his hands into the pockets of his overalls.

His unexpected question made me freeze in place while my mind raced. I sucked in a deep breath to give myself a moment, inhaling the scent of root beer.

"Well, I guess I would consider myself not alive because I just died recently. Although . . ." Something was scratching at the back of my mind, but I couldn't get a clear picture of what it was. I moved closer to Freddie, magnetized by his words.

"Yes, there usually is more to think about under the surface." He nodded at the layers of papers, posters, and art scotch-taped to David's walls. "Scratch that surface and there's typically another layer below it. Makes easy explanations a little bit more complicated, huh?" He pulled his fingers out of his frayed pocket and cupped an antique silver pocket watch.

He flipped it open and gazed at the face.

"Time. Now, time, Elliot, is a very interesting thing to think about." Freddie snapped the watch closed and tucked it back into his pocket.

Before I could say or ask another thing, David began to stir behind me. I'd almost forgotten he was there.

"Freddie?" David's voice was sandpaper.

"You want to know what he's doing, huh?" Freddie stared at me, unruffled by David's ascent into awareness.

I looked back at David, who seemed to be close to waking up. The clock ticking in the background was forcing my breathing into a rapid rhythm. I wanted to hear what Freddie knew, but I didn't want to get caught here. I didn't want David to figure out that I'd seen him. But seen him doing what? Having some kind of emotional breakdown? I wiped the sweat from my palms onto my pants, and decided to be risky. I was already one up on that curious cat, being dead and all already.

"Yes. I want to know what he's doing," I said. I sidled closer.

"Can't rightly say for sure, but maybe he's remembering."

"Remembering what? He can't Delve. He's not a Third Timer. He works here," I said, trying to get it all out before I had to flee. My heart accelerated as David became more alert.

"I can only guess at the things I don't understand, but I can tell you what I do know." Freddie placed a steady hand on my shoulder. "We have a choice. We always have a choice and we can pick again any time we want to."

"What's that mean?"

"You gotta go. You know he wouldn't like knowing that you saw him in the middle of his choices." Freddie pushed me away from the door.

It felt as if I'd stepped farther away from some important piece of knowledge, rather than closer. I glanced back over my shoulder, my feet pointing down the hall but my mind glued to the intrigue of the moment.

"Remember you were saying something about not being alive because you had died?" Freddie's voice reached out to me.

I nodded.

"Well, I think David isn't alive, but it's got nothing to do with the fact that he died."

"Fred? That you?" David's words filtered up out of the depths of wherever he had been.

Freddie went inside and closed the door behind him, releasing me. I ran through the halls and launched myself out the front doors of the Haven, my mind whirling with what had just been dumped in my lap. Every time I thought I was beginning to make sense of the afterlife, something else popped up to muddy the waters.

I was never going to make it before the end of Workshop. Mel was going to be worse than angry, she was going to be disappointed. And then there was Oliver. I pictured myself lost in one of his hugs and couldn't imagine a place I'd feel safer right now.

Wait. If everyone was at Workshop, why wasn't David running his group? Where was his group? Where was Julia? Maybe she really was available to hang out with Trevor. My stomach tightened because the truth was, I hadn't been expecting that, even though I'd run my big mouth about it. I'd left him at the pond because I was mentally exhausted, but things were even worse now. Emotions shot around inside me like Pop Rocks followed by a gulp of soda: repulsion and attraction bouncing together in a hyperactive dance.

It didn't take me long to reach the Delving School because I tromped along at a pace that kept time with my busy mind. When I got to Mel's room I couldn't hear anything so I pushed the door open quietly. Trevor was relaxed in the Delving chair and the rest of the room had on their headsets and were just as submerged as Trevor was. That's when I realized Julia was in the room, curled up like a kitten on a giant pillow near Trevor. I couldn't believe that he'd actually gone searching for her, that she'd had the nerve to come back to Mel's Workshop. She had no business knowing about my past. I headed across the room toward her, not sure what I was going to do when I reached her, then growled at my own stupidity. The moment I crossed the threshold, I could feel myself sinking to the floor as Trevor's Delve dictated my life once again.

The good news, if you can call it that, was that I hadn't missed much. Trevor must've just fallen into his Delve. He was staring at the Elliot from his past. From the look of horror on her—my—face, it appeared everyone would get to see exactly what Trevor would do if he met the girl who'd killed his brother.

"What?" The word left his mouth in slow motion, but the rest of him stayed eerily still. I watched Elliot shrink under his gaze.

"I . . ." She had to clear her throat to make the words come out. "I killed your brother." She shuffled her feet and I thought that she was going to run, but instead she dropped to her knees, bowing her head. She appeared sacrificial.

"You? You killed my brother? You're the unidentified teenage girl under protection? It was you who ran my mother off the road and killed Oliver?"

He took a step closer, towering over Elliot kneeling on the ground.

"Answer me." The words were too quiet. A hurricane was about to hit land.

Elliot lifted her head to look Trevor in the face. Her face was shadowed, fragile. Her response darted out between barely parted lips.

"Yes."

Trevor raised his hand, searching for something to destroy. I flinched, but the old Elliot never batted an eye. She watched him in a detached way, like his hand was a natural side effect that she wasn't surprised to see. His anger was an extension of the original impact that she'd created with the accident, a force that had come full circle and was meant to get her in the end. Trevor ripped at the air near the side of her head and then pointed his finger close to the end of her nose.

"I have to leave right now." His face contorted. "You need to meet me here tomorrow. You have to promise."

Elliot stared at him.

"Promise me!"

Elliot nodded.

"Say it." He took a step back and then another.

Elliot bit her lip. "I promise."

Trevor pointed again. "You owe me." Then he turned and ran.

I felt the familiar sensation of leaving a Delve, but before I could find myself back in Mel's Workshop, I was whipped around, tossed by waves I couldn't see. I could smell the scent of freshly mowed grass mingling with the too-sweet smell of carnations. Trevor was unwilling to go back and he was trying to reengage the Delve, by sheer force of will. He wanted his answers. I felt seasick bobbing along on his emotional rapids.

This wasn't over. When he finally settled back into himself, I wondered if I'd stayed with him by choice.

15

optical
illusion

Still in Trevor's Delve, I saw myself close up, sitting on the bench, the grave marker for Oliver. I could almost feel the length of my leg pressed up against Trevor's. It was a different day. Elliot was wearing another outfit, sure, but I didn't need a wardrobe change to know that this wasn't the same moment I'd just left. The biggest indicator of time having passed was my face. I still appeared tense, close to breaking into a million pieces, but there was a subtle change behind the surface.

Of course, I couldn't see Trevor because I was in his Delve, and when he suddenly turned his head, Elliot was no longer in the picture either. As he began to speak, he looked down into his cupped hands, his forearms propped on his thighs. It appeared as if he was trying to give his words a place to land so they wouldn't scatter.

"You were brave, Elliot, telling me about you and Oliver."

His leg brushed up against Elliot's as it moved up and down, as if to discharge whatever excess emotion he was feeling.

"I watched you kneeling there, telling me how you killed Oliver and destroyed my family. I wanted to rip you limb from limb. I came close."

A crow cawed in agreement.

"That's when I saw you, really saw you for the first time. I didn't intend to look at you, it just happened. It was like those pictures, you know, those optical illusions. You can gaze at them forever and see only one thing. Then when you relax your eyes for just a moment, another picture magically appears. The funny thing with that kind of visual trick is that it's really hard to go back to seeing the original picture once you've seen the new one." He sighed. "I realized instantaneously that there wasn't a thing I could do to you that you hadn't already done to yourself. You were already gone, a shell of a person. You stared me in the face and I knew. You wanted the hate and the rage that I was providing. You wanted punishment."

He didn't face me, so I couldn't see myself either, but I could hear my soft sobs and almost feel my shoulder pushing up against him in time with my tears.

After a few minutes Trevor said, "I'll be honest, in that first moment that I backed off, I only did it because I hated you so much. I couldn't give you anything that you wanted. It was empowering to realize that I could get back at you by withdrawing my viciousness, depriving you of punishment."

I could hear myself gulping in more air.

Trevor turned and I was once again in my own line of vision—a horrid, weeping mess.

"That's when it happened. There was a flash of knowledge flitting across your face, an understanding that it was over for you. You couldn't bear to live like this anymore. Without the punishment, there was no way to survive your own pain. Is that about right? Were you contemplating suicide right there in front of me?"

My head nodded in reluctant agreement.

"I needed time to think, to digest my feelings. But I had to know for sure that you'd come back, that you wouldn't do anything stupid. I couldn't have the weight of your life in my hands. That's why I made you promise to meet me back here today.

"Before you start thinking something that's not true," Trevor continued, "you should know I wasn't being selfless." He sucked in a deep breath. "I need to tell someone my horrible secret. Ironically, it occurred to me that you are the only one who would be able to understand."

I was unprepared for Trevor's next words and the shock on my face showed it.

"I'm just as much to blame for Oliver's death as you are."

16

the things

we

don't see

My mind was swimming as I pulled my head up off the floor. My fingers bumped into someone close by. I rolled over onto my stomach, meeting Oliver eye-to-eye on the floor. He had a smudge on the tip of his nose, perhaps from working with Freddie. I reached out to brush away the imperfection and then changed my mind at the last minute. He was almost too beautiful. The streak of dirt grounded him, made his connection to me much easier to believe. My hand was still stalled in front of his nose, so Oliver threaded his fingers through mine, connecting us.

"Keeping watch?"

"Haven't seen you all day. I missed you." He brushed back a lock of hair that was hanging over my eye.

Like a child waking up from a deep sleep, I remembered where I was and who was in the room. Oliver steadied me by the elbow on my way to my feet. The first person I saw was Mel. There were worry lines etched on her forehead and it made me uncomfortable. I wrenched my neck toward the Delving chair, but Trevor was gone.

"Elliot?" I turned around. Julia was standing behind me, nibbling on an apple. I'd forgotten she was there. Everything had fallen out of my head except Oliver and Trevor. Julia hitched her thumb toward the door. "He ran out right after the Delve."

"Seems he's pretty good at storming off." Oliver said it like it was a casual observation, but his right eye twitched ever so slightly.

"He's mad at me. I hurt his feelings earlier this morning. We'd been Delving." I sounded guilty, as if we'd spent the whole time doing something illicit. I felt bad saying it in front of Oliver, but then I thought of Julia entangled in Trevor's arms and felt a little thrill to hear her soft intake of breath.

"We were sitting around waiting," Oliver said. "Lily had already come out of her Delve by the time Trevor and Julia got here."

Color infused my cheeks. I hadn't been present for one of Lily's Delves yet. Talk about being self-centered. I bit my lip and looked at Lily. "Sorry."

"It's okay." She gave a little nod of her head and I was floored by how gracious she was. It was hard to believe that someone like her would be a Third Timer, lumped in with a screwup like me.

I focused on Julia. "What are you doing here, anyway?"

Julia had demolished her apple and moved on to a chunk of cheddar cheese. She swallowed. "Oh, David had a scheduling conflict. He canceled our Workshop, and when I ran into Trevor in the hall, he asked me to join him."

I searched for signs that his fingers had been threaded through her hair again, but who could tell with her helter-skelter curls? I was inundated with dark feelings.

Mel jumped in. "We were delighted to have you join us today, Julia." She hugged her around the shoulders, practically lifting Julia off her feet.

Julia gave me a shy smile and kept nibbling. I didn't understand her intentions. I smiled back anyway. It was an automatic response to her sunshine. She was like Tinkerbell with a tapeworm. I wasn't hungry for food; I just wanted things to be the way they'd always been between us. Then I really thought about why she was in this Workshop. "Maybe you're delighted, but I'm not." I said it to Mel but glared at Julia.

"But—but you said you wanted me in Workshop with you."

"You didn't show up for me."

"Maybe she did," Oliver said.

Oh, no. I couldn't believe it. Now *he* was taking her side. What did she have? A freaking magic wand? "Maybe you're being a little naive," I fired off at Oliver, sick and tired of this whole gallant knight thing that was going on. Oliver looked stunned. I reached for him, thinking to explain myself, but before my fingers could find their target . . .

We were in a dance studio. Julia's Delve. I could see her warming up in the mirror. She was sitting on the floor, stretching her limbs like a contortionist. She wore mismatched leg warmers that added bulk to her legs and a wraparound sweater over her outfit. Her usual mop of curls was piled into a pom-pom at the top of her head. Watching her, it didn't surprise me that she was a dancer. Now that I thought about it, she was always gliding from one place to another, silent and graceful. I drank in the sight of her as she twisted and moved her muscles. I'd been curious as to what her life was like—without me.

"I've got a great idea!"

Who? I wanted to look around but of course I couldn't. Julia's nose was resting into her toes and she wasn't looking up, so I had no idea who was talking. Complete frustration.

"You came up with a possible song?" Julia said, her voice muffled in her fuzzy leg warmers.

"No . . . I came up with the perfect *song." Julia's head shot up. Through*

the mirror, she connected with a girl who was visually her polar opposite. The girl was dark haired with olive skin, but it wasn't just that. She had curves. Voluptuous was the word that came to mind. It was funny because I might not have thought that if I'd seen her walking down the street, but as a dancer, she was unusual.

"Come on, Becks." Julia stopped stretching and hopped to her feet. I could see them both now, as they stood shoulder to shoulder in the mirrored wall.

"I don't know why I didn't think of this before. It's so perfect for us." Becks bounced up and down on her toes. Julia whirled around to face her.

"Just tell me!" She grabbed Becks by the shoulders and pretended to shake her. "Please, tell me."

"Well . . ." Becks teased. You could tell she enjoyed the suspense.

"Becca!" Julia said.

Becks scowled and looked like she couldn't decide whether to be pissed or to cry. She sucked in a deep breath. "I'll tell—just promise not to call me that." She shivered. "You know how I hate it."

"And you know how I hate it when you keep me dangling." Julia's whine was interrupted by Becks's giggle.

Know what I hated? I loathed the fact that they were friends. That should have been me. Would have been me, if things hadn't gotten so screwed up at the Basin.

Becks grabbed Julia's hands and they plopped down on the floor. She flashed Julia a high-wattage smile. "It's the perfect song—not overdone like the one we talked about. The other one is funnier, but in this one they're still best friends, just like us."

My stomach lurched and I didn't know if it was from watching them be so familiar and close with each other, or if it had to do with the sudden shift in the Delve. Time flying forward like the fanning of pages.

Whoa . . .

One minute I was watching the face of BFF-stealer Becks and the next minute I was kissing some guy. Only—too weird—because it wasn't my Delve, I couldn't pick up on any of the emotion or physically feel what was going on. I was in the dark, stuck and smashed up against some guy.

Julia's eyes were closed so I couldn't even see the guy she was sucking face with. For all I knew, he wasn't even cute and had bad breath. I decided I needed to do something like count sheep to distract myself—God knows how long this was going to go on. Then I imagined how much worse it must be for Oliver to be in this Delve and couldn't stop myself from laughing. If only Trevor were still around.

It all happened at once. There was a loud gasp. Julia's eyes flew open. She was angled just enough that she could see the person who made the noise. It was Becks—her face falling like an avalanche. She was the picture of devastation, and then she was gone. Julia flew after her, boy forgotten.

"Becks, it's not what you think . . ."

I cleared my throat. "That's funny, it seemed exactly like what Becks thought it was." I couldn't help it. "You have a way of making your best friends feel really good about themselves." I narrowed my eyes at Julia. Now Oliver had his arm around her.

Oliver shook his head at me, while Julia just appeared horrified. I wanted to be more compassionate, I did—but really, Julia was the one being mean to me. She was the one who'd cut me out of her life.

"Oliver, can you walk Julia over there?" Mel waggled her finger in the direction of her desk. "Have her sit down and get her a drink of water."

"Sure," Oliver said, gently holding Julia up. He turned to look at me, his jaw clenched tight. "You want to help me?" I wasn't falling for that Jedi mind trick. I glared at him. The sensation of being misunderstood was bubbling up and threatening to choke me.

Before I could say anything, Mel shooed Oliver forward. "I need to speak with Elliot. We'll be over in a minute."

Mel turned to me. Her voice was soft and private. "You can't blame them too much. It's not their fault they're unable to see what's going on inside your head. I know how confused you are. First Julia doesn't treat you the way you expected and then Oliver shows up and smothers you with unconditional love. Then to add to the confusion, there's that connection between you and Trevor. No wonder you're flustered."

"I think you're confused, Mel. I don't have a connection

with that asshole—" Mel threw up her hands but I kept going. "It's Julia and Trevor who are connected." Connected at the lips.

"I agree, they do have a link too, but you and Trevor seem bound and determined to be together."

"What?" I said it so loud that the whole room halted mid-sentence and turned to stare at me. I backed up, definitely not making eye contact with Trevor's *girlfriend*. I zeroed in on Mel.

"What's that supposed to mean? I don't want to—ewwww!" I spat out the last part, daring her to contradict me.

"Oh, don't get your panties in a twist," Mel said. She waved me off, which turned my mood extra sour.

"It's not funny."

"I understand. I apologize. Let me clarify. What I meant was that both of your souls are pulling you together. It's as if you need each other to figure out what's going on and understand how to move forward. It seems to me, the more you try to avoid each other, the more entangled your paths become. Right?"

I didn't want to admit it, but it was true. And I really wondered what he had meant in his last Delve, when he announced that *he* was to blame for Oliver's death.

"You don't always have to be so hard on yourself," Mel said gently. "Everything is simply about choices . . ."

Just like Freddie had said.

Screw it.

Everyone was conspiring to make me crazy.

"In that case"—I turned my back on the room—"I choose to get the hell out of here." I stalked off, exiting the building, but came up short—I had no idea where the hell I wanted to go. Needing to move, I started out toward Trevor's pond. After working up a sweat, I changed my mind about going there. That hadn't really worked out so well. Instead I decided it would be better to just go back to my nest. Backtracking, I was about halfway down the hill when I heard the sharp snap of a branch breaking behind me. I whirled around, but I could barely see a thing. I couldn't believe that I hadn't noticed the eerily quiet forest all around me before now. Fog twisted heavily around the trunks of the trees. It draped over the lowest branches of the cool evergreens.

I'd never run across such a place at the Obmil before, so I peered out into the mist to discover whose creation I'd stumbled upon. As I strained to see, a warm light seemed to break up the fog. The harder I looked, the brighter the light became.

This was my creation.

It was a little unnerving to be reminded how my subconscious operated without me. If this reflected my personal level of clarity, I wasn't getting out of the Obmil any time soon.

There was another noise. I turned toward it. Before I could decipher the sound, Oliver broke through the mist and stopped short in front of me. The expression on his face looked just like that girl Becks, when she'd caught Julia kissing someone important. It was a patchwork of hurt and disappointment, sewn together with shock.

I suddenly felt unbalanced, like I'd made a misstep and should realize it, but I couldn't quite figure it out. I'd never seen him like this.

"What's the matter? Are you okay?"

"What the hell was that back there?" Oliver was literally giving off sparks.

"What?" Oliver angry? My mind was spinning.

"You. At Workshop."

Understanding unraveled from the inside out. He'd wanted me to help him with Julia. He was such a good guy and he expected me to be like him. Compassionate. "Hey, she's the one who's always pushing me away." I sniffed and swallowed at the lump in my throat. "But anyway, I'm sorry. You're sweet and kind and I know I really should try to be a bigger person." I shoved my hands in my pockets, not knowing what else to do with myself.

"You're jealous." Oliver's voice had a bit of an edge to it and it took me up short.

"Jealous?"

"Of Trevor and Julia. After everything I've done for you. You want him."

"What?" I asked, but a panic was building inside my chest. I knew who he was talking about and thinking about it made me afraid. It seemed like I was a magnet for trouble—prone to thinking asinine things. Oliver was standing in front of me, once again wearing his heart on his sleeve, and I'd just taken it for granted. Instead of appreciating the love I had, I couldn't stop myself from thinking about someone who didn't make me feel safe and comfortable—how stupid was that? I could see it clearly. I'd hurt him and, even worse, I hadn't even thought of him in the moment I was having my Trevor rant. Seeing the look of betrayal etched across his features felt as bad as the moment I realized I'd killed him.

Apathy and self-absorption should have been a smaller wound than manslaughter, but in some ways, it cut deeper.

"I'm sorry, I wasn't thinking." I started to cry, a sick feeling in my stomach.

"I gave up everything to be here for you. Why do you need more?" Appearing exhausted, he sat down. "I'm supposed to be helping you find your way, and unbelievably, hanging out with you makes me feel lost and in need of intervention."

I'd made things even worse. I should've paid more attention. I'd been lost in my own thoughts and I'd dragged Oliver right along into the abyss with me.

"Can I walk home with you?" I pleaded, wanting a way to make us both feel better.

It stung, watching him flinch at my approach, but he allowed me to pull him off of the carpet of pine needles. As soon as he was on his feet, he let my fingers fall away.

Neither one of us made a sound as we traveled through the woods, scattering the mist that had become more ominous as we both wandered around in our own thoughts.

I was hoping we could talk once we reached the Haven. I didn't want to leave things like this. But Oliver said he'd promised to meet Mel at her room. I followed him there, not wanting to let him out of my sight until things were back to normal between us.

I twisted Mel's art deco silver doorknob and pushed against the heavy dark wood with my shoulder. When the door gave way, I was surprised to see Mel already inside, sitting on her forest-green chenille overstuffed couch. Her feet were tucked up underneath her and she cradled a hot mug of peppermint tea. The steam rising from the hand-thrown pottery mirrored my damp, swirling thoughts. I could feel the heat of shame as if I were the one holding the mug.

Mel met my eyes. Hers were steady but not twinkling like I was used to.

"Elliot, I'm glad Oliver was able to catch up with you. I was concerned."

She appeared both sad and angry at the same time. Was she judging me? She never judged me. She was my constant, my safe place to be.

I wanted to scream at both of them that I was sorry. To explain how I hadn't meant to be cruel, I'd just been distracted with my own trauma. No words could get past the lump in my throat that threatened to gag me.

Standing there completely incapacitated, I felt Oliver bump past me. There they were, my two unconditional loves, and they appeared anything but. I wanted to beg them to love me again, but I didn't have the heart to hear them reject me out loud. I started to follow Oliver into Mel's room, but he began to close the door. He was no longer my safe place to fall. When I looked at him through the narrowing space, what stared back at me was Trevor's Oliver. The guy who lets you know that he disapproves of something you'd done.

I reached out my hand, begging for a lifeline. His hands never left his sides.

There were a million questions I needed to ask him, even more things I wanted to tell him, but I'd lost the right. I could've asked him anything up until then. So why hadn't I? I rubbed my temples. It wasn't an option now anyway.

Still, the questions must have been written on my face. Oliver's usual sunshine sank into the shadows, as if a dark, ugly thought was enveloping him. The moment he opened his mouth to speak, I knew I wasn't ready to hear what he had to say.

the funny

thing about

wishes

"Elliot, I died for you." His shoulders slumped and his voice was just a whisper. "I didn't know what I was doing, but my soul did. Sure, I unbuckled my seat belt to put my little sister back in her car seat, but I also did it for you on some unconscious level. I decided to take that risk in order to force you into an intense examination of yourself. I made a choice and a promise when I was leaving the Basin to do what I needed to do as your Passenger. You picked me. I didn't *know* it in my last life, but I was hardwired to connect with you in the most intense way possible. To be the catalyst for you to realize who you really are. Damn it, I'm still trying to do that."

What? He'd died on purpose? For me? It couldn't be. I felt dirty, stained.

I tore off down the hall, unable to search deeper, afraid of what I might possibly learn about myself if I stayed. I raced straight to my room, ignoring everyone else along the way. I couldn't risk another personal interaction that might end in disappointment, but when I passed by Freddie's desk I couldn't help but pilfer the soft, blue plaid flannel shirt that was hanging on a brass hook. I stuck my nose into the kind of softness that only comes with time and breathed in the scent of apples and cinnamon. It wasn't his aroma; he'd been filching pie from the kitchen again.

My stomach rumbled, but the need to hide away and watch the eagles was stronger than my need for comfort food. I couldn't stand the heaviness of my thoughts anymore. Couldn't they be weightless for a change? I wanted to soar. What would it feel like to leap with abandon and ride the currents? Imagine launching into the unknown. Could falling be only a heartbeat away from flying?

It was nowhere near bedtime, but I pulled off my clothes and dove into Freddie's shirt. I wasn't going anywhere and I wanted to be able to pretend I was asleep when Julia arrived. I didn't know what to say to her. I let my finger trail across the ledge, over to the paper cranes. My heart skipped a beat. There had to be at least fifty cranes in different sizes and colors, standing at attention.

When had she made them and, more important, why?

My head was throbbing. I couldn't think about those delicate origami birds. I perched on my window seat, scanning the sky and waiting. I wanted to see something real, not cleverly folded paper that masqueraded as something true. I rubbed my silver eagle feather charm. It felt familiar and strange at the same time.

I couldn't remember how the necklace had come to me, but I must have acquired it on one of my other visits to the Obmil. Tokens from life don't travel with souls into the afterlife, but gifts made in the afterlife have a way of sticking with a person. Here at the Obmil, the charm was a cool and tangible connection that I could place my fingers on. In my last life it would've been the ghost of a necklace, a niggling feeling that there was something I could tap into if I could only access it. It would have felt like intuition, guiding me, if I was paying attention.

Sighing, I pressed my thumbs into my eye sockets. My headache had deepened from the effort of thinking in spirals. I looked back out across the lake. There they were, the two eagles. They were free and I was envious. Could I fly away from the Obmil? My lids became heavy, exhaustion catching up with me as I wondered how far you really did have to travel to leave limbo.

• • •

I was aware of the cool night air blowing across my face before I registered anything else. I shifted slightly, eyes still closed. I could smell the nightly bonfire from down on the beach. I stretched, rotating my sleepy, stiff muscles, as I snuggled deeper under the warmth of the down comforter.

"What the—ouch!" I sat up in a rush and smacked the top of my head against the inside storm shutter that must've come loose from its hook on the wall. I tried to search the room while extricating myself from the tangle of blankets, but all I could see were stars shooting around in my own head.

"Who's here?" I yelled. The smell that hit me was wrong— it wasn't Julia. Who did I know that smelled like pinecones and jelly beans?

The final indignity was tipping off the window seat into a heap on the floor. My head was half buried in down, and suddenly I didn't care if there was an axe murderer in the room. I just lay there, rubbing the goose egg on my noggin. Damn thing felt more like an ostrich egg.

"How'd you know I was here?" the voice asked. It was soft like the breeze in summer.

Really? Pinecones and jelly beans? Trevor? I must've been quite distracted when I was pinned beneath him at the pond. I didn't remember that at all.

"Elliot?"

The gentleness of his voice ran a finger down my back to the base of my spine, sending goose bumps everywhere. Goose bumps were better than goose eggs.

"Elliot, you okay down there?"

He actually sounded a little concerned, like I might've knocked myself unconscious during my acrobatic fit. I thought about playing dead, but then I realized how ridiculous that was and couldn't stop giggling.

"What's the joke?" he asked, his voice traveling to me from across the room. I flipped over and sat up, gazing out the window. I needed to give myself a moment. No eagles, but lights, similar to the aurora borealis, rippled in the black sky. I turned to look at him.

Trevor was sitting on the floor, his back angled against the door to my room. His knees were propped up but I could see enough of him in the starlight to know that his black T-shirt was absent its usual commentary. He was mindlessly banging his thumb in a rhythmic beat against his thigh.

I stood up, piling my blanket back onto the window seat. I could feel myself growing increasingly warm despite the cool air blowing my oversized flannel shirt around my knees, the very same knees that seemed to no longer be qualified to hold my own weight. I wanted to ask what he was doing in my room, but he was busy mumbling something under his breath.

He stared at me with a steady gaze, but I didn't believe he was relaxed at all. His fingers were making tracks through his hair.

"The comforter," I said.

"Huh?"

"You asked how I knew you were here. It was the comforter. I hadn't been wrapped up when I fell asleep."

"Oh, yeah."

"You covered me?" I asked.

"Your toes were cold."

"How did you know my toes were cold?"

"I accidentally brushed up against them when I checked to see if you were Delving. Julia thought you might be sleeping up here and didn't want to wake you. I said I'd check." He shrugged as if going around and testing people for Delves was an average, everyday occurrence. Like hanging out with Julia was what he always did. He shrugged as if being here with me was completely random. Then I noticed the way he was fiddling with the laces of his boots.

I wanted to feel violated that he'd snuck into my room uninvited while I was sleeping, angry that he was with Julia before he came to see me, but I didn't. I had the unexpected feeling that he was here because he needed me. The fragile tenderness had returned from those moments at the pond. My heart beat like the wings of a baby bird.

"Thank you—for covering me."

"What, no huffing and puffing? No lecture for sneaking up on you even if I had a good reason?" His voice had a scratchiness to it, like he'd been sitting quietly for a long time. He was baiting me. I decided my best bet was to ignore it.

"You said you had a good reason for being here?" Luckily, I sounded calm, but inside I was ready to spring in a million directions. I grabbed at a lock of hair, wrapping and unwrapping it around my finger.

He sighed. "You're twisted, Elliot."

I tried to drop my hand but I'd gotten myself tangled in my own hair. Before I could unknot myself, he was on his feet and moving closer.

"You need to Delve." He was fixed on me like a hawk tracking a baby bunny.

I freed myself just in time to throw my palms up in surrender. "I'll be there in the morning. I'm not hiding from this anymore."

I peeked down at my toes. They were getting cold again now that they were hanging out on the night floor. But pulling on my woolly socks wasn't an option. I didn't need to make my outfit look any more embarrassing than it already was. I added, "Something's been bothering me. I didn't really have time to think about it before, but . . . I don't know how I died."

He moved to within a foot of me. "Not tomorrow. We

need to Delve now. I can't wait, Elliot. I've been thinking about this too and I have to know what happened." He needed me to Delve? Well, that explained why Julia couldn't help him.

"I—I think I might have killed myself," I spat out. The cold in my feet moved upward, freezing my heart so it could barely beat. "Things were so bad and I was feeling so dead inside." I didn't know what else to say.

"Jesus, Elliot. I don't want to hear that." He began pacing the floor like the walls held him here against his will. "There are too many unknowns to start making stupid guesses. Like we need to worry about your eternal damnation when we can't even figure out what I was ready to confess."

"So this is about you? I should have known." Here I was worried that I'd committed a cosmically irreversible offense. I could end up banished to hell and he was only concerned about himself. My fears were more than realistic. Mel had hinted that there were consequences for taking too long to sort out your soul, but I had a feeling there were also ramifications for the really big screwups. It wasn't so hard to believe that certain crimes were unforgivable. I shivered.

"Oh for God's sake, this isn't about who's the biggest drama queen." He rolled his eyes. "Even Julia knows that." I involuntarily reached for my cheek. His harsh words should have left a five-fingered mark on my face.

"Why do you need me? Why can't you go fall into your own Delve, like you did at the pond?"

He mumbled something that I couldn't make out.

"What?"

His head shot up sharply. "Don't you think I would if I could? That I haven't tried? I'd been standing in that spot forever, staring at the stagnant fucking water. I didn't drop into that goddamn Delve until you wound your way up the path."

I sucked in my breath. I hadn't known. And why did it feel like my chest was being crushed, to hear him say that he'd tried to Delve without me? So stupid.

"We just need to Delve so we can find out what happened. I need to know!" He exhaled, pushing his demands in my face.

"What? What do you need to know?"

"Come on, are you going to make me say it? How much are you going to take from me?"

I jumped back as if I'd touched a live wire.

"I don't know why I told you I was just as responsible as you for Oliver's death. We already know you caused that. So what the hell was I talking about?"

God! He was so insensitive. My teeth ground together.

"That's not the only thing, Elliot. The other problem is that I don't know why I followed you here. Obviously, I came to the Obmil because I didn't figure out what I needed to during my life, but why did I come *right* after you? Nothing makes any sense the way we left it. All I know for sure right now is that you killed my brother." His lip started to tremble. "But I think it's my fault too." He took a deep breath. "We also know that Oliver hates me but loves you. So I'm thinking, I did something pretty damn terrible. Elliot, please. You know better than anyone what it feels like to be the walking dead. You saw what your past self looked like when I found you." Tears were running down his face and now his T-shirt glowed softly . . . DON'T FOLLOW ME, I'M LOST TOO.

I couldn't help it; I moved closer and touched the tip of my finger against a tear sliding down his cheek.

"Elliot, I'm just as much to blame for Oliver's death as you are."

Before I realized there was a tear sliding down the side of Trevor's cheek, my finger had already reached out to touch it. His eyes were huge. I'd seen them full of rage and anger, full of hostility. This was different. Now they were bottomless. He was floating through my Delve without an anchor.

"I was fourteen years old when my parents had Abby. That made Oliver lucky number thirteen. We were just a year apart and more like twins. We did everything together, until Abby came along."

I traced that single tear down his jaw line.

"Our sister was a surprise, but my parents were completely thrilled to have a girl, insane with joy, in fact. And she was beautiful—a real charmer.

Had us all wrapped around her little finger in a matter of hours."

Trevor shrugged his shoulders, as if he didn't know how to adequately explain it.

"So what was the problem?" I prodded.

"The problem is that I'm a self-centered jerk and—"

"And . . ."

"And I was jealous. Abby seemed to prefer Oliver to me, just like everyone always did." Trevor's voice dropped even lower. "I—I felt like a third wheel when I was with them. It sounds so goddamn stupid when I say it out loud, but there isn't any other way to say it." He moaned from someplace deep.

"It doesn't make you a bad guy just because you had a selfish thought or two," I said softly.

"But it wasn't just a thought, don't you see?" He pounded his hand into his fist. "I started acting on those thoughts. I avoided Oliver, wanting him to see what it felt like to be left out. But it backfired. He was hurt. He overcompensated, spending more time with Abbs because I was pushing him away. They got closer and I pushed harder. It was so fucking stupid."

Trevor didn't seem able to look at me anymore. I knew about telling the truth and how vulnerable that makes you feel. Suddenly I wondered if you could only be that raw with another person when you have nothing left to lose. My fingers reached for the hollow of my neck, but grasped at nothing—the ghost of a necklace.

When Trevor stood up and moved behind me, I didn't turn around. I just gave him his space, hoping to shelter this thing between us, hoping it would grow. I sensed enough to understand that this truth, no matter how fragile, was the most real thing I'd ever brushed up against.

"I was supposed to be in the car that day. It was my turn to help Mom with the errands. I shoved the job off on Oliver, and that stupid fool unbuckled his damn seat belt while they were driving. If I was there, I never would have done something so idiotic." Trevor's voice sounded crazed. "Shit." He moved right in front of me, so I could see how much he meant what he was saying. "I would have been smart—safe. I would have done the logical thing." He let out a verbal gush of anguish and punched his fist into his palm. "Then when you hit our car, I would have been buckled and instead of me, Abby would have been thrown through the windshield. I would have saved myself, and my sister would have died. Oliver was a hero and I'm—I'm nothing."

My stomach gave a sharp, tight twist. I could feel the impact of the crash all over again. I could see blood in those curls. I knew what Oliver's face looked like when it was empty, vacant. That was horrific enough—I couldn't let my mind even imagine a three-year-old in his place.

Trevor stared at me again. Blue to brown. Sky to earth.

"I've made such a mess." He barely choked out the words. "Because of me, Oliver is dead."

creating

distance

I thought my heart would explode—unable to contain our mutual grief. Without thinking, I launched myself across the bench and engulfed Trevor in my arms. He was racked with sobs and I could barely hold on to him. The truth was tearing him apart from the inside out. I pulled him closer—aware of how painful it was to search within.

Even knowing what I'd done, a part of me was uncomfortable with his confession. As bad as my crime was, it was a careless accident. In a way, his had intent. He hadn't caused anyone's death but he'd shaped his relationships with Abby and Oliver. He'd chosen his own path over and over again. I would have given anything to have a brother or a sister. How could he just close them out?

But I knew what it felt like to have someone see past your worst fears about yourself. He'd given me a thread of something to hold on to and it made him beautiful to me. My hand rubbed slow, even circles of comfort across his back, creating new patterns for us to follow.

We were still standing in my room, cloaked in midnight and wrapped around each other. We stood there, our hearts hammering in unison. I wasn't sure if I would be able to look him in the eye considering how intimate we'd suddenly become. My knees wobbled and I wondered if he was overcome by the same sensation.

"Elliot, I can't go to Workshop anymore. I don't want to do this in front of other people."

"No, we can't."

"I won't go if you don't go. Promise not to expose us?"

It was hard to squeeze him tighter, but I certainly tried. "I vow to avoid the Delving chair at all costs. I won't even buckle if Mel hunts us down and tries to bribe me with chocolate."

A tiny sigh escaped his lips, warming my scalp. For the briefest moment, I thought about telling him what I'd learned about Oliver. How he'd said that he'd died for me. Wouldn't it ease Trevor's mind, to know that there were things in motion that he didn't have any control over? But even if he wasn't really to blame, I was. And then we wouldn't be in this together.

"So, how are we going to do this?" he asked. I could tell

he wanted to Delve again right away and I couldn't blame him. Hope was addictive.

"Hold that thought. And turn around." I didn't know if it would help with finding the answers, but I needed to get out of the Haven. Something was pulling me. I threw on my clothes from before, whipped my hair up into a ponytail, then strode across the room and grabbed his sleeve. I was ready, proactive for a change, and it felt good.

"Let's go."

I pulled him out the door with me, expecting him to resist, but surprisingly he followed.

We walked along the edge of the lake side by side for as long as we could, watching the moon dance on the surface of the water. Eventually the rocky landscape became too much, so we broke apart, concentrating on the moonlit rocks we were navigating.

As the terrain became more difficult to maneuver, I had no choice but to lean on Trevor. My fingers grazed his as I reached for the same handhold he was using. His hand fitted into the small of my back as he boosted me up over a fallen tree. We helped each other over obstacle after obstacle, and each touch was a small electric spark in the night.

"Wow, I don't remember it being this difficult to get up the mountain to the pond earlier today. Do you?" I asked as I blew at a wisp of hair that was tickling my nose.

A rumbling chuckle echoed from behind me.

"What's so funny? It is harder to navigate at night, you know."

He reached across the tree that lay between us and tucked the fallen strand of my hair back behind my ear.

"*We* aren't cocreating," came his voice, huskier than his laugh.

"Huh?"

I had trouble remembering what we'd been talking about. All I could manage to focus on was how close he was to my face and how his hand lingered.

"You're doing the creating, I'm just along for the ride." He waited with his eyebrows raised and a crooked little sideways grin on his face.

"I'm creating this? No, I wouldn't," I said in disbelief.

"I know I'm not creating anything at the moment. I'm having too much fun watching what you're coming up with all on your own."

"Oh." I could feel my face becoming hot. The night air, that moments ago had been so cool, was now uncomfortably warm.

"Maybe you made the route difficult so that I'd have to assist you up over every obstacle?"

"I wasn't thinking at all!" I sputtered.

"I know. That's what I'm enjoying about it the most," said Trevor.

"You what?" My voice sounded high-pitched and screechy. As I finally got myself untangled from Trevor and the tree I was straddling, I stepped back and noticed the new lettering that glowed white against the black of his T-shirt: I REJECT YOUR REALITY AND SUBSTITUTE MY OWN.

I plopped my forehead into my hands. "Okay, Lowry, I get it, you're messing with me. I'm not completely used to this lack of hostility between us." I braved a peek and said, "I don't remember how we—I mean the past-life Elliot and Trevor—were with each other after we learned each other's darkest fears and failures. Even though I don't remember it, I have a strange feeling that things between us got a bit better. Maybe we found some hope to hang on to."

I wondered how big hope could actually grow.

"I don't remember either," he said. "But if we base our assumptions about us on what we actually know, you do realize that it's not pretty."

He kept his tone light as he said this, but I knew he wasn't off the mark.

"You're right." I plopped down next to him. "It's crazy."

I glanced over at Trevor's tousled hair. I impulsively reached up and ran my fingers through the silky black strands and squeezed my eyes shut, internally bracing myself. "It might be possible that I—that I wanted you near me." I didn't dare peek at him as I made the admission.

I felt his warm breath in my ear. "If I promise to be near you, do you think you could create an easier path up to wherever it is that you're taking me?"

My eyes popped open. His face was unreadable.

"I can do that. Yeah, I can definitely do that," I said, grabbing his hand. I had no idea what I was doing, but I decided I didn't have to think about it. Within moments we found ourselves spiraling into another Delve, hand in hand.

My vision came into focus and I found myself staring up into the canopy of a mature maple tree. The sun was directly overhead and the wind was blowing just enough that bits of light danced everywhere, like water bugs shooting across the surface of a pond.

Lying there, I felt calm. I couldn't remember the last time I hadn't felt dead or dying on the inside. It was like finally breathing after being underwater.

I could feel the cool ground supporting the length of my body. Sparse blades of grass tickled the backs of my knees. My head was propped up on Trevor's stomach, slowly rising up and down in time to his breathing.

"Do you like it better over here? Not so hot, huh?" came Trevor's voice.

I turned my head and saw Oliver's bench gleaming in the hot sun.

"Yeah, this is better," I said, remembering how we'd sat in the bright white sun all last week, getting to know the very worst things about each other. It was almost as if we'd let the sun bleach away our personal shortcomings.

"What made you think to come over here?" I asked.

"I'm not sure." He paused long enough that I wasn't positive he would continue, but he did. "It was your face, I think. Your cheeks were so red and flushed; I was worried that you might pass out from heat stroke. Then who would I talk to while hanging out at the local cemetery?"

I'd spent enough time with him now to know that the teasing sound in his voice would correspond to a twisted little smirk near the corner of his mouth. It was thrilling to finally be able to know some of his nuances.

"Thank you," I said, returning to the comfortable silence we'd been sharing. There'd been so many words and tears over the last week. Now it was a quieter time.

The sky was bright blue and the clouds were exquisite. They were billowing and pristine as they rollicked across my line of vision. When they passed across the sun in just the right place, they appeared illuminated from within.

"Do you think it looks like that?" Trevor said.

"Do I think what looks like what?" I asked.

"Heaven."

How could one word invoke so many mysteries?

"It seems just like I always imagined Heaven. These really are the kind of clouds a Heaven would exist in," I said.

"That's what I was thinking, but——" He sucked in a deep breath. "I think that would be too easy. I used to believe that clouds were a fine place for Heaven, until I understood that people could fly above them. It sort of ruined it for me."

"Did you stop believing in the afterlife?" I asked, a hint of reservation in my voice.

"Not sure exactly. I guess I always figured there's a place that you go, but I stopped thinking of it being in the clouds. It seems childish to think that way."

He hadn't asked anything else, so I allowed him to ruminate.

"Where do you think he is?" The questioned ripped raggedly from the depths of him. He wanted to know about Oliver.

"I don't know, Trevor. I don't know the answer to that any more than I know where I'm headed after what I've done." The words skittered shakily, fear catching in my throat.

A cloud passed over the sun, leaving Oliver Lowry's bench cool, black, and lonely.

There was hardly any disorientation as we came out of this Delve. We were getting used to hurtling around on the space-time continuum. I was still holding Trevor's hand. We weren't sprawled across each other on the ground. I wondered if that was significant at all. Were we gaining some control?

"Well, that was interesting," said Trevor.

"It's all interesting, but what do you mean exactly?" I gave him a tiny nudge in the ribs, still unsure if he recognized the humor in my voice when I was teasing him.

"I was thinking about us under the tree."

"Well, it was so much more comfortable under there."

"So you were comfortable, leaning on me?" He gripped my hand a bit more firmly, maybe guessing that I'd yank it back when he teased.

It was becoming harder to separate the way I'd felt about the boy from my past and the way I responded to Trevor now. It didn't seem so strange to be holding his hand and smiling at him when moments ago I'd had my head tucked against his chest. This was getting way too weird. I didn't want to talk about it until I'd had more time to think.

"It was fascinating to watch what was happening from a different perspective," Trevor continued. "We'd put some distance between ourselves and Oliver's death."

"Oh, I hadn't thought of it that way. What do you think it means?"

"I think it means that I'm more confused than I was before," he muttered under his breath. I was ready to second the thought when I heard an out-of-place sound behind me. I whipped my head around in time to see David thundering up the path behind us, the sunrise framing him.

"*Not* an interesting development." I was pleased that my voice sounded snarky instead of terrified, despite the bull that was charging straight for me. Trevor's presence gave me a boost of confidence.

Trevor stepped forward, more diplomatic than I'd expected, probably trying to run interference. "Hey, David." He paused. "You don't seem like the type who goes out for a stroll."

David bent over and gave a wheeze while mopping his drippy forehead with the sleeve of his shirt. "I—I was searching for you." He righted himself and took a deep breath. Then he squinted and a bottle of water appeared in his hand. He motioned for us to wait as he inhaled the contents. David gulped so hard, the plastic walls caved in, making a crunching sound. Looking less like a heart attack in the making, he tossed the bottle over his shoulder.

"Ever hear of recycling?" I popped off. Trevor put a hand on my shoulder.

Before David could get in my face, Trevor inserted himself between us. "You said you were looking for us. Here we are."

"Hmph. I saw the two of you sneaking out of the Haven in the dark and figured you could use a chaperone." His grin was massive. "Fortunately for you, I had a little trouble following you in the dark. Lost you there for a bit, but no matter." He glanced back over his shoulder at the sun, now a pink and orange Jell-O mold in the sky. "I've got you now. Seems to me like we'll have just enough time to get back down for breakfast." I rolled my eyes, but he didn't notice. "Oh, and because we're bonding so nicely up here on this mountain, I'll even personally escort my new best buddies to Workshop this morning." He turned to go and then spun back around. "Follow. Me." He said it slowly, exaggerating his words.

All my anger and frustration bubbled inside like a shaken can of soda. Trevor leaned down and whispered in my ear, "It's not the time, hothead." He gave my elbow a squeeze. "Just remember your promise about Delving and follow my lead at Workshop. And—don't get too close to me in there." He winked. "It seems to bring on the Delves." I nodded. "Tonight, after everyone goes to sleep, we split up and meet back here," he said.

"We have to wait until tonight?" Irritation made my voice prickly.

"Yes. That is, if you're savvy enough to get past him?"

I bit my lip, holding back my amusement. "Is that a challenge, Lowry?"

"NOW!" David bellowed from the path below.

Trevor's mouth twitched. "Damn straight it's a challenge."

19

bellyaches

Just about everyone was gone when we walked in to breakfast, but, lucky me, Julia was still there, waiting for Trevor. She was sitting all alone like that last crumb in a pie pan. I half hoped to find Oliver waiting for me, but if he'd been there he was already gone.

At first I was too strung out to eat, busy thinking about how to avoid Delving in front of the group, but when I saw Julia with a mound of blueberry pancakes swimming in maple syrup, I gave in to my baser instincts and decided to follow her lead. I was four pancakes in when I came up for air in time to find Julia picking at a warm cinnamon bun. Did she have a hollow leg? I leaned back and contemplated popping the button on my pants, then saw David doing exactly that and thought better of it.

"Carb-loading, Elliot?" Trevor appeared amused.

I wasn't sure what he'd eaten, but *he* didn't look like he needed to be rolled to Workshop.

"Julia, I'm heading up to Workshop, you going that way?" Trevor looked pointedly at Julia, who appeared bouncy and not at all held back by the mountain of dough she'd swallowed. I felt like I'd eaten a bowling ball. My stomach twisted as she fell into step next to him. Neither one of them took the time to glance back at me. Everything in my gut turned sour.

"He's got a cute little girlfriend there. She's one of the sweetest Third Timers I've ever had in Workshop." My jaw hung open and David let out a rumbling burp muffled by his fist.

"Excuse me?" I tried to make laser beams shoot out of my eyes. Of course afterlife hocus-pocus didn't work for stuff like that.

He turned his head sharply and my bravado withered as I realized I was alone with him. He pushed back from the table and stood. "Time to go, Miss Turner. We don't want to be late."

I stood up, seething that Trevor had paired up with Julia and left me with this Neanderthal. *Grrrrrrr.*

"Look on the bright side . . ." David said.

I waited. Then he roared with laughter.

"What?"

"I can't think of anything."

"Asshole," I mumbled under my breath, and stalked out of the Haven with David lumbering behind me.

David and I parted ways in the hall of the Delving School. I was relieved to have some significant physical distance between us. I pushed through the door to my classroom and then remembered that I had bigger problems. Mel and Oliver. I'd forgotten how stressful things were between us. I opted for the mature path. I put my head down, high-tailed it to my chair, and immediately put my nose in a book. The maps in the oversized atlas I'd grabbed blurred and I dabbed at my face with my sleeve. At least the mammoth pages made a wonderful defensive barrier.

"Trevor, there you are. We were just getting ready to start," Mel said, spotting Trevor in the hallway. She didn't even give me a hello.

"Hey, Mel," Trevor said as he walked in the door.

He'd left before me and arrived after me. I scowled, suspecting that he'd walked Julia to her Workshop. Above me I could hear the rhythmic creak of Oliver's hammock rocking back and forth. I couldn't bear to look up.

"Interested in being the first to Delve today?" Mel asked Trevor in her usual jovial tone.

"That sounds great."

My eyebrows shot up over the Arctic Circle. Hadn't he said no Delving?

Trevor started toward the swing. About halfway there he leaned over and clutched his midsection. "Uh, Mel. I'm not feeling too good right now." He mimed something involving his gag reflex and then bolted out the door.

"That was attractive," Oliver said. I could almost feel his words dropping down onto the top of my head.

"It must've been something he ate?" I said in a squeaky voice. "Food poisoning?" What a great idea. I was just about to give a convincing moan when Mel interjected.

"Can't be food poisoning—the afterlife, automatic healing. Remember?" When was I going to learn that Trevor was not the ideal person to follow around? There went my cover. I heard Oliver snort. Now I really felt sick. I was covered in a cold sweat and panic was making my pulse race. Mel was going to make me Delve next. I knew I was being selfish, running away from everyone in Workshop when they were all depending on me, but I just hated it. Wasn't it enough that I'd been letting Trevor see my bucket full of ugly? Did I really need to paint the room with it?

I felt like a juicy gazelle on the savannah. I shifted my gaze to avoid contact. It felt like minutes, slow painful minutes, before Mel continued speaking.

170

"Well, I'm sure he'll be fine. I think we're going to let Lily Delve first today. Is that okay with you?" I looked up slowly, but she was directing one of her sunny smiles at Lily. I closed the atlas and rested my forehead against its smooth cool cover.

"Not a problem," Lily said. She quickly moved to the swing and I marveled at how happy she was to be visiting her mistakes. I pulled on my headset, happy to tune it all out. I drifted into Lily's Delve, a long hospital corridor awaiting me . . . *welcoming me to her world.*

I no longer had to fake a stomachache. Witnessing the after-effects of chemo was enough to make me sick. I wasn't any closer to understanding why Lily was a Third Timer, but I'd discovered that I could live without knowing, if it meant that I didn't have to watch her Delves. I pushed my headset out of the way and dashed past Oliver's tree, very aware that he wasn't calling out to stop me.

I gulped in the fresh air and wondered what the heck I was going to do until it was time to meet Trevor. Not that he was high on my list of people to have a rendezvous with. I pictured him *rendezvousing* with Julia and stomped on a tulip. I bit my lip as I looked under my boot. I was mean. I was a flower killer. I longed for Oliver in that moment. If I weren't such a hor-rible person to start with, he would have been out here with me trying to convince me how I was good at heart. But he was nowhere in sight.

I choked back sobs, feeling more alone then I ever had at the Obmil. Only I could alienate a guy who loved me enough to die for me. I squished a little crocus, twisting the ball of my foot until it disappeared into a purple, pulpy mess. The flood of tears was blinding.

I heard voices in the distance and couldn't bear for the lunch crowd to see me like this, surrounded by flower corpses. I took off at a run, searching for a place to get away. I needed to hide. As soon as the word "hide" jumped to the forefront of my brain, enormous boulders popped up all around me, making me feel like I was in a cavern or a rock maze. There was no exit behind me, so I shot through the narrow passages, knowing that if I calmed down I could make this all disappear, but at the same time sickly fascinated to see what was really going on in my own mind. So I ran. A lot.

Damn. My breathing was ragged and sweat poured down my face. It was a dead end. I was full of nothing. No wonder everyone had jumped the Elliot ship. I was going nowhere. The only escape, besides going back, was a seam of light, hundreds of feet above. I didn't want to go back. I just couldn't turn around. I wasn't calloused enough to keep returning for more. I just wanted out. I tipped my head and gasped when a pathetic, makeshift ladder stretched from the ground to the light above. I waved my fist at the sky, yelling out loud, not caring who heard. "Is this some kind of sick joke? Is this the best I can do? A crappy, rickety ladder for a girl who's afraid of heights? It's so obvious—I don't even like myself." I plopped down with my back against the ladder. If I loved me, wouldn't I be able to create a better exit, or even an elevator? I was so sick of this. Screw it. I'd use the ladder.

I stood up, wiped the snot from my nose with the sleeve of my shirt. I no longer cared. It wasn't like I had anybody to impress. I grabbed the wooden rungs, stared straight ahead, and scrambled upward. I went fast and furious and was doing fine until I got a splinter. Until I stopped and looked down. Saliva pooled in my mouth. I was going to fall. I wrapped my arms around the ladder and squinted against the vertigo. I needed to think one good, coherent thought. Focus on a way out, a way to safety. But my mind jumped all over the place like a grasshopper. Very slowly, still not looking, I reached one foot down until I felt the rung below, solid under my foot. Methodically I repeated the same action over and over again until I felt a hard jolt of rock against my sole. I opened my eyes. Right next to my still shaking foot was the bud of a sunflower. I felt my toes twitching in my boot but didn't think it would be wise to stomp out the only sunshine that I had left, even if it made me feel better. No sooner had I decided to let the little flower live, than another sprung up next to it. Then another and another. My eyes followed the thickening trail of sunflowers that were leading to an opening in the rock wall that hadn't been there before. I wasn't sure how or why, but I'd found my own kind of light to guide my way.

Out in the open field of flowers, I could feel the sun and see how every golden blossom faced the light. I tilted my own face in the same direction, trying to discover what it was that was making them content—complete. I felt the warmth on the bridge of my nose but it didn't give me any answers. Very carefully, I thought about one smooth boulder, with all its sharp edges tumbled away with time. It rose out of the ground before me and I scrambled up and stretched out on top. I knew that if I stayed there long enough, the flowers would follow the path of the sun across the sky. It seemed like they knew what they were doing, and at least for a little while, I wanted to be part of that.

I watched the sunflowers dance until the sky turned pink and orange and dusky. I wasn't any smarter than I'd been before I sat down, but I was calmer at least.

When I walked into the dining room to grab something to eat, there were only a few stragglers left. My heart thumped involuntarily when I saw a flash of wavy blond hair, but any hopes I had that Oliver was worried about me were dashed when I realized that it wasn't Oliver at all, but some woman who was kicking butt in Scrabble. I hunched over my pasta and ate alone.

I thought about stopping up in my room for a little while before I was supposed to sneak out and meet Trevor back on the trail, but I didn't want to run into Julia. Or not run into Julia and picture her with Trevor. I decided to curl up in a nook in the library instead.

I couldn't make up my mind about whether I should even sneak out to see Trevor like we'd planned. I felt more than a little torn: different thoughts and feelings paraded through my head like they were on a high-speed conveyor belt, each giving me contradictory advice. When it was near midnight I decided to stop thinking about it and just go. Besides, all this hiding had made me lonely and it hurt to realize that no one had even missed me. Screw it—I'd go. I could decide how I felt about it after I knew what the hell was going on.

Keeping David in mind, I exited the Haven in the most bizarre path I could think of. After twenty minutes of duck and cover, my final escape was a very tight exit through the upper window in the kitchen pantry. I dared David to follow me now.

It wasn't hard to stay quiet as I threaded through the woods and over to the trail. I just imagined several inches of pine needles underfoot to soundproof my steps. When I arrived at the spot where David had interrupted us, I could see Trevor casually leaning against a downed tree. It didn't seem like Julia was with him, but I bit my lip and stayed in recon-mode for a little longer. I squinted, watching him carefully. Every time there was a noise he glanced. Finally I had to sneeze and I didn't want to be discovered spying because I had pansy-ass mucous membranes, so I pinched my nose and powered out into the open.

"Hey." His whole face lit up when he saw me, and like an idiot, I stopped and grinned at him like I was five and just discovered Santa in my living room. I was riddled with idiotic weakness.

"You made it. I was getting worried. Did you get out of Workshop this morning?" Trevor asked.

"Not exactly. After you left, Mel pointed out how food poisoning is incompatible with the afterlife."

"Shit. Guess I didn't think that one through very well." He started to laugh but then stopped short. "You didn't Delve without me, did you?"

I put a hand up to stop further questions. "No, I didn't Delve. For whatever reason, she had Lily hit the chair instead of me." I thought about sharing some of the ugliness that I'd seen, but realized that in order to dump some of it on him, I would have to relive it. I decided it would be better to just not think about it.

"Oh, good. So it worked out."

"If that's what you want to call ditching me for Julia. Then yes, it all worked out just fine," I snapped.

"What? Julia? Oh, you mean my decoy." He was way too calm, perhaps deliberately choosing to ignore my bad attitude. I dialed it up a notch on the off chance he'd missed it the first time.

"Decoy? Is that what we're calling it now?"

"Yeah, I told you we can't be near each other and risk falling into another Delve in public. I figured keeping Julia around would also help keep David off our backs." He was like a puppy, all expectant and waiting for a biscuit.

I sighed and stared at him. Did I believe him, or was it that I *wanted* to believe him? He grabbed my fingers in his hand, and my heart blasted against my rib cage. He'd been holding my hand in the same way yesterday, but that time it had been a slow process of acclimation. This felt like jumping from an icy lake into a hot spring. I could barely breathe. All I could hear was a thundering rush in my ears. I braced myself for a Delve, but then realized foolishly that the noise wasn't just my blood racing through my veins. There was a steady roar of water coming from higher on the trail.

"What's that?" I shouted. "It sounds like a waterfall. I don't remember there being a waterfall up here before."

"No idea," Trevor said.

"Come on, let's check it out." I yanked at his hand, pulling him behind me before he could say a word.

The terrain was easy to navigate, and it was only a few minutes before we rounded a bend in the trail and stood face-to-face with a revolving waterwheel attached to a small wooden building. The cottage was set on a natural stone foundation, with old-fashioned windows and a wood shingled roof. It had a cozy, rustic feel.

"You doing this?" I asked, having witnessed what he could do with a pond.

"Yeah, I think it's me."

"It's beautiful."

He didn't respond, but tugged me closer.

"Did you know you were creating this?" I asked gently.

"Not until the moment you asked me if I was."

"It makes me feel content," I said, pulling him with me as I settled down on a large, flat, moss-covered rock. I found myself unable to tear myself away from the revolving wheel and its hypnotic flow of water.

"There's more to it than that," Trevor said, plopping down next to me, "but it does feel inviting."

"No, it feels safe," I said.

"Okay, I'll give you that, but if it's a piece of my subconscious poking through, doesn't it concern you a little bit?"

"How could creating your own little safe haven be problematic?"

"It's the waterwheel that worries me."

"The waterwheel? It's so beautiful and peaceful the way it goes around and around," I said, swaying back and forth.

"Yeah, but it never gets anywhere. Feels a little bit like what's going on in my head right now."

"I know how you feel," I said. "You don't have a monopoly on dark moments, just stupid T-shirts." I thought that would make him smile, but his brow furrowed instead.

"Seriously," I said, and told him how I'd managed to alienate Oliver earlier, to hurt him in a completely different way; how this time he finally hated me; how the cherry on my sundae was that Mel was now giving me the cold shoulder too.

"I'm sure they don't hate you." Trevor's voice was calm.

"You weren't there," I said, not sure how to explain how awful it had felt. It hurt too much to contemplate.

"Tell me what you're thinking about. What do you believe is

driving the waterwheel?" I asked, wanting to change the subject.

"You really want to get inside my head, Turner?"

I tipped my head to the side and rested it on his upper arm. "Yes."

I waited, knowing that he would tell me when he was ready.

20

go with
the flow

I wouldn't have known we'd entered a Delve except that the waterwheel disappeared. One minute it was there and then it was gone. Instead of sitting in the shade, surrounded by ferns and pines, I was perched high in the air with the sun making everything dazzlingly bright.

I attempted to turn my head, but my eyes stayed glued to the endless blue sky painted across my field of vision. This wasn't my Delve, it was Trevor's.

Without warning, my gaze shot downward to an immense river. I felt a wave of vertigo at the sudden movement. This was uncomfortable. I had no idea where we were and I could feel Trevor's body tense up and my stomach roil as I peeked at the water below.

Just as I thought Trevor would tip over, he turned to look at me, the past-life version of me. The sight was shocking. She was glorious. She was sitting on the edge of a granite outcrop, feet dangling aimlessly over the abyss. Her arms were propped behind her, with her face turned up to the sun. Elliot's eyes were closed and the sun lit up her hair with a warm caramel glow.

I was clearly watching a stranger, not the girl I thought of as myself. I started to sweat, watching her on the edge. A jittering ball of height-induced fear rolled around my stomach, yet this Elliot was in her element.

"So, this is what you do to relax?" There was a mixture of admiration and disbelief in Trevor's voice.

Elliot turned to look at him and I drew in my breath.

"Yeah. This is what I do," she replied with a twitch in the corner of her mouth.

I felt myself wanting to lean toward this strange vision of myself, to discover this new unexpected version of me. Before this, I hadn't discovered anything good about Elliot Turner I wanted to explore. The first memory of Oliver had been the start of a slippery slope, one negative thing after another.

"My dad brought me up here all the time when I was younger." Elliot turned back to stare out over the water, completely at ease sitting on the edge of the world. "The first time, I was nine years old. We brought along a little picnic. While we were sitting here, we watched an eagle soar on the wind."

"That must've been amazing."

"Oh, it was. I was perched in the same piece of sky where an eagle flew. It felt as if I was about as close to heaven as anyone could possibly get."

"Back to heaven in the clouds," Trevor said.

Elliot nodded and continued. "My dad and I would hike up here from time to time, but as I got older I found myself craving this place. So I started to come by myself when I needed to get away from the rest of the world."

Trevor panned the horizon. "It's freakin' amazing. I can see why you come here."

He edged over to the side of the rock, peering down. My stomach did flip-flops in response.

What was she thinking, sitting up here like this? I was really beginning to question my own past-life sanity, yet I couldn't argue with the look of contentment on her face—on my face. What the hell had happened to me? I used to love this and now I was chickenshit when it came to heights.

"The more time I spend up here, the more I find myself," said Elliot. "When I'm down on the ground walking around in my regular life, I can never see anything but the complications. When I'm up here, seeing the world from a different perspective, even the smallest things are meaningful and more interesting."

"How so?"

"Well, one day, when my eagle didn't show up, I found myself captivated by the surface of the water. I couldn't believe it. It appeared as if the river was moving in two different directions."

"Seriously?"

"I know. I thought it was some weird visual trick, but I researched it later and discovered that the Hudson is actually part river and part estuary."

"And that means . . . ?" Trevor asked.

"It means that my eyes weren't actually playing tricks on me. The river can't make up its mind."

I could hear my own laugh as Trevor's focus stayed locked on the water below, probably searching for evidence of the odd behavior of the currents.

Elliot put on her very best flight attendant voice and waved her fingers like she was indicating floor lights. "This intriguing piece of information has been around for generations. The Algonquin people in the Hudson River Valley termed the Hudson estuary Mohicanituk, *"The River That Flows Both Ways." Thank you for flying Elliot Air."*

Her voice returned to its normal cadence. "Every time I come up here now, I flip around the concept in my head. It's like a puzzle. I still can't shake the feeling that there is some nugget of knowledge here." She gave a sigh. "In all seriousness, if I could just get more than a fleeting glimpse of it, I know I'd understand something significant."

Elliot threw up her arms. "But as you can see, I'm still chasing enlightenment." She said it with humor and maybe the faintest longing for something more.

"So, enough about me. We now know that I hike, perch on cliffs, bird watch, and get philosophical for relaxation. What do you do, Lowry? Because you're obviously not super comfortable with heights."

Elliot winked at Trevor and I ever so softly returned to the waterwheel, where everything moved in only one direction over and over again.

"So, you don't want to tell me what you do to unwind? Seems suspicious," I said. He'd pulled us out of his Delve just before he was going to impart some personal information.

Apparently, I wasn't the only one who avoided things.

"I would tell you right now if the me sitting next to you could remember." He tapped his index finger against his temple. "Delving is getting easier though, isn't it?"

"Yeah." I nodded back.

"So where are we going, Elliot?" He searched my face for answers.

"You mean what's out there for us after this? I don't know any more than you." My insides twisted around. "Heaven, hell, a different limbo?" There had to be more Obmils in existence than this one. It wasn't like the whole deceased population of the world was here. I'd have to ask Mel if she knew. Maybe she and the other guides got some kind of special training before they came to the afterlife. Maybe she knew if souls were grouped by need or if everything was completely random.

"I just meant where are we going *now*." Trevor raised his eyebrow at me. "You couldn't have been headed *here*, I just created it. Besides, you seemed like you were climbing this mountain with intent. You do remember yesterday when you dragged me out of your room and halfway up here before David sidetracked us? Call me curious."

I stared at him, mouth half open. "Oh."

He smiled.

"Oh, right," I repeated, getting up and dusting myself off. "The truth is, I didn't really have a destination in mind. I just hoped that we might figure out how to come up with some answers."

He didn't say anything so I continued. "I couldn't Delve in front of everyone anymore either. I know that's what we're supposed to do, but everything is becoming too . . ."

"Personal," Trevor filled in.

"Private," I said at the same time.

Trevor got to his feet. "So you have no idea where we're going?"

"I didn't say that. I said I didn't know earlier, but I do now. Before I tell you, I have a question."

"Shoot."

"Will we ever come back here again? I mean, the waterwheel is your creation, but it's an unconscious one. I guess I like it here and was just wondering if we'll be able to get back some time." I took in the scene, made more amazing because it was a visceral piece of what was deep inside him.

"I have no idea." He sighed. "It's all uncharted territory for me too."

I glanced around one last time. I wanted to clutch this magical place between my fingers but it would have been easier to catch a handful of steam.

"We're off to the top of the mountain," I said, tipping my head in the direction of the eagle's aerie and adding a significant amount of bravado to my voice.

"And why would we do that?" Trevor asked.

"I think we spent a lot of time on a very similar outcrop." I nodded toward the summit. "The thought of going to the top of a mountain scares the heck out of me. It makes my heart race. It's also intriguing. I hate the height, but being close to the eagles . . . What I've started to figure out is that the things I avoid the most seem to have the most importance."

"You've avoided me like the plague," said Trevor.

"You were obnoxious."

Trevor clutched his chest in mock anguish. "I'm wounded by your words."

I couldn't help it; I gave him an exasperated shove. I didn't intend for him to lose his balance. His arms flew round and around like twin waterwheels, trying to keep himself perched on the mossy rock. The last thing I saw before he plopped backward into the small pool of water was his T-shirt . . . SHIT HAPPENS.

This time it was my Delve, which took me off guard. I assumed I'd be back in Trevor's past, considering we transitioned the minute he hit the surface of the water, but I could see him, standing next to a vintage red Ford pickup truck. It was clean and pristine, even on this dusty, tree-lined back road.

187

As I settled into myself, I noticed that my heart was racing and my breathing was shallow. Trevor walked toward me, his face concerned.

"Elliot, are you okay? You don't seem so good. Here, sit down and put your head between your knees," he said.

Now all I could see was the tiny patch of grass between my shoes. Trevor's hand was massaging the tension out of my neck.

"I'm confused," Trevor said. "You took me up to a dangerous mountain peak and laughed at me because my knees were practically knocking together in height-fright. But when I suggest that we take a ride in my truck, a truck so old that it shakes a little when the speedometer hits sixty, you almost pass out."

My head stayed wedged between my knees.

"Come on, Elliot. This is what I do. I drive the back roads in my grandfather's old truck and listen to music. This is how I get lost in myself. I thought you wanted to be a part of that." The vulnerability in his voice was unavoidable now.

My head flew up. Trevor was blurry as tears welled up.

"I haven't been in a c-c-car since . . ." My voice trembled so badly I couldn't continue talking. I wiped my face with the back of my hand.

"Oh, shit. That never even occurred to me. I have no idea what I was thinking. Damn. I wasn't thinking at all." He shook his hair in every direction. "Let's get out of here. We can climb your mountain and go see the eagles. I promise I won't even complain about how scary it is sitting on the tip of that rock." He was suddenly crouched in front of me. "Let's leave Sally parked and get out of here."

That didn't feel right either.

"No." My voice was steady, sure of what it was about to say, although the stiffness in my limbs hadn't managed to catch up with my new attitude. "I don't want to leave. I want to stay here. I don't think I can actually get in your—did you call your truck Sally?" I made a sound that was something between a chuckle and a gulp.

"That's right. Her name is Sally." He puffed up proudly.

Before I could snicker, he leaned in close to my ear and his warm breath rustled the loose hair against my neck.

"Shhh, don't tease her. She's very sensitive. She thinks she's a Mustang, and I don't have the heart to tell her any different." Then he winked.

It was like a lightning strike.

In that moment, I realized I was in love with Trevor. It felt like an instantaneous revelation. In truth there were hundreds of small moments building to it, all in varying degrees of proximity to a tiny little gravestone. This was just the moment when it came together—the tipping point.

"I don't want to leave. I want to hear all about your complicated relationship with Sally." My heart felt like it was leaking golden light and filling up all my empty spaces.

Trevor jumped to his feet like an excited little boy.

"Really?" he asked.

"Really," I confirmed. "I don't think I'm ready to sit in the front, but what about if we sit in the back instead? We wouldn't even be facing in the typical direction; it wouldn't feel like driving at all."

"I've got some of my grandfather's old blankets tucked behind the seat in the cab. I'll go grab them, okay?"

"Okay." I couldn't believe I wasn't close to hysterics.

"Is this change of heart about Sally?" he yelled from behind the backseat. "Are you jealous of another girl?" He popped up with a huge teasing smile and an armful of scratchy wool.

"It seems to me that Sally is formidable competition."

"Here, let me help you up. Put your foot on the back bumper."

"Gee, Trevor, I can get into the back of a pickup truck." I shook my head. "I'm not afraid of Sally, either. She's a bit old for you. Besides, I could take her if I had to."

"Ah, I forgot you're fearless." He patted the pile of blankets next to him and I took a seat. "You're the bravest person I've ever met," Trevor said, putting his arm around my shoulders.

"I don't feel brave. I feel like I'm only surviving because I'm with you. My parents think I'm at Cari's house every day. If they bothered to check up, they would know that she never even called me, that she wants nothing to do with me. But they won't check. They don't want to push too hard on the truth. They're just relieved that I'm not catatonic in bed anymore. They're more than happy to believe the illusion—it's so much better than the reality they were living with. At least now they have a little hope."

"I don't take it back, you know. You can say what you want, but no matter how you look at it, you are the bravest person I know," Trevor said.

"But I'm scared to death most of the time. I still have nightmares."

"Being brave isn't about not being scared. Being brave is what you do despite being scared," Trevor said.

Yes, it was a done deal. I knew for sure that I was in love with this boy who could see past the ugliness in me. I would always be in love with this boy.

He pulled me closer but let his words settle in a moment before he changed the subject back to Sally, music, and winding roads. I decided to relax and be content for the moment.

21

complications

I'd loved him. Ugh! Could things get any more complicated? Well, they probably could. I should be grateful that Trevor hadn't been privy to my private thoughts in the past. We were getting along much better now. We might even be friends, but I couldn't be in love with a guy who could explode at any time. I couldn't be in love with my ex–best friend's possible boyfriend. Just because my heart raced when I got too close to him didn't mean that—

"Time to go," I said, taking control of the situation and my mutinous thoughts. I reached to help Trevor climb out of the pond.

He gripped my hand all the way up to the wrist and with a quick yank I was flying through the air and toppling head first into the water.

I came up sputtering, trying to work myself up into a good huff, but when I saw how pleased he was with himself, I had to appreciate his master plan.

"I should've seen that coming." I dipped my head back under the water, enjoying the sensation of my hair floating and then drying instantly as I broke the surface. Giant beads of water tumbled back to where they'd come from.

"It is a weird sensation," said Trevor, watching me defy water.

"Did you ever play with cornstarch and water when you were a kid?" I asked, suddenly remembering that I had. Hadn't Mel mentioned that once some of the big memories were unlocked, smaller ones would start popping up with little triggers?

"Can't say I did. Why?" Trevor asked.

"When you mix the powdered cornstarch with water it's almost solid, but the minute the heat of your hand makes contact, it softens the goop and it runs through your fingers. You can't hold on to it."

"Like the way we're wet and dry simultaneously," Trevor said.

"Yes and no," I said. "It does have its similarities, I guess, but I was thinking more about Delving."

"Yup, Delving is a weird sensation. *Especially* when I'm in one of your Delves."

"Hey!" I punched him in the arm, but it wasn't very effective, considering that I was treading water.

"Here, let me help you, shorty."

Before I could protest, Trevor had wrapped his arm around my waist and pulled my back against his chest. His chin brushed the top of my head.

"Is that better?"

Oh boy—this qualified as a weird sensation. I didn't know that contentment and electric shock could exist in the same moment of contact.

"What were you saying about Delving?" asked Trevor.

"Um, well . . ." I was having a hard time remembering what I'd been talking about.

Trevor's mouth was so darn close to my ear. "It's fine—I get distracted all the time. I'm sure you'll think of it later."

Before I could come up with a witty retort, he was gliding me toward the rock so we could climb out of the water. With a little boost, I was up and out of the pool. I froze. Julia was standing in the shadow of the waterwheel. How long had she been there? Long enough, I guessed from seeing her shocked face.

Trevor turned and used his arms to pop up into a sitting position next to me on the rock. "So what dangerous paths are you going to lead me down now?" He grabbed my hand, mingling his fingers with mine. Then he looked up.

"Julia?" Trevor said.

She appeared forlorn and I was dumbfounded, unable to think of a single thing to say.

"Julia, what's the matter?" Trevor's fingers untangled themselves from mine, but he still hadn't moved.

"I was searching for you." She sounded shaky. "I had a bad Delve earlier and I can't get it out of my head. I need someone to talk to." Her voice caught at the same time that her face crumpled.

The way she stared at me, it was as if none of the nonsense that had gone on between us had ever occurred. She needed me, finally. And I needed to be needed. My heart swelled and I took a step forward, ready to forgive her. I was all set to cover her with my friendship, like bubble wrap. I'd help to keep her safe.

When Trevor rushed past me, my humiliation was complete. I watched as he pulled her to him, enveloping her in his arms. She didn't need me. She'd been searching for him. I clenched my fists. My teeth were grinding into each other. At first I thought the dizzy sensation had to do with the fact that I was so steamed I was holding my breath, but—

I was in dark shadows and a woman towered over me, framed in bright lights. I disliked her immediately. Her face was shifting plates of harsh lines and her anger drilled into my face or the face of whoever's Delve this was.

"Mama, I don't want to go out there." The voice was whispery and pleading.

Where the hell was I?

"Julia Antonio Going. We have been through this before. You will go out on that stage," the woman hissed, and stepped closer.

Julia—this was Julia's Delve again. She peeked up at the woman. *My stomach sank with the realization that this was her mother. The woman seemed gigantic. All I could think about was Cruella de Vil.*

"But I told you, I don't want to do dancing. It's scary to do a recital. I don't like the people watching me and the lights in my face."

The pieces were starting to fall into place. Julia's mother wasn't overly tall—Julia was little, really young from the sound of it. Then there was music, a swell of notes, and a woman with her hair in a bun and a corsage pinned to her dress popped her head over Mrs. Going's shoulder.

"Everything all right here?" *The woman sounded nervous, but you could tell she was trying to hide it behind her happy preschool voice.*

"Everything's fine." Mrs. Going grabbed Julia by the upper arm, her nails digging into her daughter's skin. *I felt myself flinch. The first time because of the cruelty of the act and the second time because Julia didn't flinch at all, telling me all I needed to know. She was used to this.*

"Are you ready to dance then, Julia? It's time," *the woman with the corsage said. I saw a flock of tiny girls in tutus being herded onto the stage.*

"She's ready to dance. Aren't you, Julia?" *Her mother leaned over and* whispered in her ear, "You're already a disappointment. Don't embarrass me out there."

Julia nodded as she was led away to join the rest of the ballerinas.

I said a little prayer, hoping she'd realize that the stage wasn't such a bad place to be. At least her mother wasn't on it. I was pretty sure that there weren't a lot of things scarier than that woman. Julia found a glow-in-the-dark circle in the row of stickers on the stage floor. She fixed her feet and I took in what she was seeing. We now stood center stage, facing the rich royal blue curtain—watching it slide open. The widening gap, becoming bigger by the second, exposed a sea of bright lights and shadowed faces. The curtains stopped and in the moment just before the audience made its first sound, Julia looked down to see a stream of liquid race down her little leg, fill her pink ballet slipper, and then puddle at her feet.

"Shh," Trevor cooed, rocking her in his arms. "It's okay. She's not really here. You're safe with me."

Julia lifted her head and there was no hiding from what I'd seen. She stood up and faced me, so close I could have reached out and hugged her. Her expression was full of things, some that I understood and some that I didn't have a clue how to decipher, but I wanted to try. I found myself leaning toward her, wanting to be included. In one second I realized that a single horrific event, in my otherwise pretty good life, was less traumatic than her life full of tragedy.

Julia's delicate wrist dabbed at the corners of her leaky eyes. "Elliot, would it be okay if I borrowed Trevor for a little while?"

Of all the things she could've ask for, she picked the one that would wound me the most. This was beyond taking Trevor away from me.

It was utter rejection.

I could feel the anger boiling in my soul. She should understand what rejection feels like and not ever want to hurt someone else that way. And now I couldn't help it—I hated her. It seemed so wrong after what I'd just witnessed, but it was beyond my control. It all roared out of me as a storm—clouds, raindrops, and lightning. Julia stood her ground, even though my feelings were pouring down on her. Of course she had her protector behind her. Another rush of anguish. Trevor, on the other hand, appeared frazzled as he watched my volatile emotions, making God knows what kind of display over my head. A sharp crack of thunder made Trevor tense, which I enjoyed until Julia practically shot back into his arms.

"Please? Please give us a couple minutes. Will you wait for me?" Trevor asked.

I wanted to say no, that I hated him, too, but flashes from our Delves kept going off like fireworks in my brain. I'd fallen in love with him once, but that didn't have to mean anything now.

"I'm heading up," I said, tight-lipped, trying to reel in my emotions.

"Promise me you'll wait up top." He looked dangerous and demanding, but I didn't care. Julia was still folded into his arms like she belonged there.

I remembered when he'd demanded that the suicidal Elliot return to meet him. I threw imaginary daggers at his face, although I was aiming for his heart. "You don't get to use that request twice."

Conveniently, a path opened up in front of me as I turned to stalk off.

I walked until the trees had swallowed me up and then I waited. It was pathetic and I knew it, but I did it anyway. Plopping down, I hugged my knees to my chest and rocked back and forth and cried.

He didn't come. I felt a tiny ache like a small hammer banging in the outer corner of my left eye. Choices were made and I was deemed inconsequential. I wanted to get up and do something productive. Sneak back and see if Trevor was making Julia forget her troubles. But if he was . . .

Another part of me wanted to head up to the top of the mountain and Delve without him. I'd have the answers that he wanted and then I could refuse him when he asked. I wanted to send him back to Julia empty-handed.

I did neither. I sat right where I was and let the beat in my head drown out the sad song in my soul.

It seemed like forever had passed when he finally came tromping through the woods. He stopped short, not expecting me to be so close to the pond. He must've believed that I'd taken off to the top without him.

He sucked in a deep breath and then plopped down next to me. As I continued to rock, I could feel the sleeve of his shirt dance back and forth over my upper arm.

I had a million and one things that I wanted to say, but they were all pushing and shoving to get to the head of the line. I couldn't decide which thought to let out of its cage first.

"She's not my girlfriend." His voice was controlled.

"I didn't ask."

"No, I guess you didn't." There was a frayed spot on the knee of his jeans and he picked at it with his finger.

"She needs a friend."

"She had a friend and she threw me away." I stopped rocking. The silence sat between us like the ghost of Julia.

"It's complicated." We both said it at the same time. How did he always do that? Fall into sync with me when he'd just been—gone.

We studied each other and then we both smirked.

"Everything's complicated." Trevor hopped up and reached out a hand to pull me up.

"I'm here now," Trevor said, his shoulders relaxing. Uncharacteristically, he nibbled at his cuticle. I felt myself wanting to soften at the gesture of insecurity, but I also knew what he looked like when Julia was entangled in his arms, when he was her protector. I understood what it felt like to be chosen last. I was at the bottom of everyone's list lately.

Despite knowing that I was second best, I wanted him to stay. I swallowed the stuff that hurt. I couldn't fix it and I was tired of trying. The best I could do was to worry about the rest later. For once I just wanted to have what *I* wanted.

"Come on, Elliot, we should go." Trevor grabbed my arm. I expected him to pull me toward the summit, so I nearly tipped over as he started downhill toward the Haven.

"Where the hell are you going?" I asked, digging in my heels.

"We're leaving."

"You're going in the wrong direction. We need to head that way." I pulled against him. I got a queasy feeling in my stomach as I watched his emotions clamp down and shut me out.

"I want to go back down." Trevor resumed his tugging.

I poked my finger into his chest. "What about where I want to go? And exactly why do you want to go back now?" But I shouldn't have asked; it was clearly written all over his face.

"I—I told Julia that I would meet her. She needs . . ."

"Really?"

His silence said everything I needed to hear. I wanted to disappear—I felt used and gullible. But I'd learned that closing your eyes doesn't make you vanish, and now I was sick to death of feeling like I was the last to know everything. I felt the tiniest flame of anger ignite, and instead of squelching it, I fed it with the feelings of stupidity that had piled up inside me. I could feel the heat.

"I'm sorry," I said sweetly, too saccharine to go unnoticed.

Trevor's face started to relax when he heard the words, but then froze at the tone.

"Sorry for what?" He sounded leery and I struggled to hide that girl who takes great satisfaction in squishing flowers. I wasn't successful.

"Since you're going back down, you won't get to see the birds, my eagles." I made an exaggerated frown. "Oh, wait—we don't want Julia to interrupt everything—here, you can check this out instead."

I flipped him the bird. It was stupid and spiteful and completely unproductive and yet it made me feel pretty darn good. I hitched my thumb over my shoulder, pointing down the trail. "*Now* I feel like going back to the Haven." The last thing I wanted to do was spend more time with Trevor.

the rain

on

the pain

It had been raining for three days and all I wanted to do was curl up in some cozy corner and have everyone leave me alone. I didn't want drama, excuses, guilt, or responsibility. I just wanted to drink hot chocolate and get lost in the pages of a good book. But every time I tucked myself away in a discreet corner, I was inundated by people trying to steer clear of me. Irony sucks. Julia would stumble into our room and mumble under her breath while trying to avoid coming anywhere near me. Trevor would show up wherever I happened to be and scowl at me. Like I was the one who'd followed him into the room. Hello? I was here first.

Even Mel was a problem. I'd approached her with an excuse for missing Workshop, but before I could open my mouth to suggest a hiatus, she gave me a hard stare and I shriveled up like a raisin. So I'd created some all-weather gear and a heavy-duty umbrella and trudged my way up the trail and back, day after day after day. I never stayed wet for more than a second, but in a strong rain, with each drop hitting me in succession, I felt damp and annoyed until I was out of the storm.

At Workshop, I settled into a defensive position and was ready to dare anyone to make me Delve. I wasn't sure if it was the vibe I was giving off or the ring of barbed wire around my chair, but Mel and everyone else left me alone. The only person I didn't see was Oliver, and asking about him really wasn't an option since I'd started flying my freak flag to keep everyone at bay.

So now it'd been three days and I was tired of defensive machinations. I grabbed my slicker and slipped outside as everyone was settling down for the night. I stopped caring that the rain was beating on my skull. I needed to be in open spaces so I headed to the lake.

"Nice hiding place."

Trevor. Did I have a tracking chip or something? "I'm not hiding, I'm sailing," I shot back. The water was smooth but the unrelenting rain bounced on its surface with a staccato sound. I was surrounded, inundated with water.

"Your dinghy is tied to the dock. I'm not sure you can call that sailing."

I could feel a snort trying to sneak out as I pictured the sides of his mouth curling up. I bit my cheek. I wasn't ready to stop hating him. I fished for a sharp retort but I must have exhausted my supply. "Who are you calling dingy?"

He chuckled in the darkness, and for the first time in days I felt like I could take a deep breath. I turned around. He was in the shadows, barely a silhouette.

"We've been fighting," he said.

"I guess we have."

His voice lowered. "I don't want to fight anymore. I can explain about Jul—. No, wait. I don't even want to talk about our fight. All we ever seem to do around here is rehash the past. I just want to move forward."

"So we can hurry up and relive the past?"

"Funny, huh?"

"A laugh a minute." I adjusted my rain hat. "You've been following me around. It would be my assessment that you didn't want to actually be near me, so, I'm guessing you were only worried that I'd go off and Delve without you."

He looked guilty of my claim but I was feeling like it didn't matter as much anymore. Ten minutes ago I would have submitted to waterboarding before allowing Trevor to be my friend again, but now that he was here, it only mattered that I felt warm again. Things might not be what I wanted when he was around, but they didn't really seem to be any better when he wasn't.

"Hey, the rain stopped." I glanced around, surprised.

He shook his head at me as he grabbed the dinghy rope and started reeling me in.

"What?" I asked.

"It's only been raining in *your* world. Anyone unfortunate enough to be in your vicinity for the last three days has been the victim of Hurricane Elliot." He tapped his temple with his fingers indicating that I was mental.

"Shit."

He reached out his hand to pull me from the boat. "You're developing quite a potty mouth."

I placed my hands on his chest, contemplating a good push into the lake. Just like at the waterwheel, where we'd left off. I dropped my hands and lifted my chin to see him. Rivulets of rain danced down my neck when he tipped back the hood of my raincoat. I shivered. "What do we do now?"

Someone behind me cleared his throat and I tensed, sure David had found us again.

"Kids these days. Gotta tell them everything." I gave a sigh of relief. It was Freddie. I relaxed and rested my forehead against Trevor's chest. His smelled good, woodsy and sweet at the same time.

"Hi, Freddie," Trevor said. I couldn't manage to get my nose out of Trevor's T-shirt. How embarrassing—yet I persisted.

"Hi," Freddie said back. "You were wondering what to do, young lady? I'll tell you what you're going to do."

My head shot up. Even Freddie? He'd been the only one who I thought I hadn't really truly annoyed.

Freddie took two steps closer and leaned in, lowering his voice. "You're going to run. David is on his way down from checking your room. Don't quite know why you get under his skin so much more than everyone else." He turned his head to evaluate Trevor. "I take that back. He doesn't like you much either." Freddie tipped his hat at Trevor, who gave a grunt in return. "So wherever it is that you two are headed, I suggest you be quick about it."

Trevor grabbed my hand and started pulling me off the dock and toward the woods. I yanked back, needing to give Freddie a hug, but Trevor wouldn't loosen his grip.

Freddie winked at me. "Go! I'll send him in the wrong direction."

I opened my trap to at least yell a thank-you and got a mouthful of Trevor's fingers.

"Shhhh—he's coming," Trevor hissed. He removed his hand and we were off.

"Are we going to the——?" My voice was a gasp from the unexpected sprint.

"Yes."

We moved quickly, stopping every so often to listen for David, but everything remained silent once our breathing slowed. With the frantic pace we were keeping, it didn't take long to reach the summit of the mountain and the rock outcrop that looked an awful lot like the one in Trevor's Delve.

"Do you know what I found to be a weird sensation?" Trevor asked as he jumped onto the edge of the rock and plopped down, his feet dangling into space.

It was amazing. He could just drop back into the middle of a discussion we'd been having almost four days ago, the conversation that Julia had interrupted. I felt my chest tighten someplace in the vicinity of my heart. I shook my head when I realized he was waiting for a response: gazing at me like we'd never been in the middle of a storm. Well, if he wanted to pretend that Julia had never interfered, that was fine with me. In fact, it was better than fine.

Trevor was still sitting on the ledge and out of nowhere I was feeling lightheaded. I stayed back a good twenty feet, sweat now dripping at the pace of my racing heart. An overwhelming fear of heights gripped me, making my head spin like a dog chasing his tail. What was my problem? The old me was fear-less, at least when it came to mountains. And the old Trevor would never have perched so casually on the edge of the world.

"Elliot, you gonna come sit down?" He turned to look at me and my face must have given me away. "You okay?"

"Uh-huh," I said while shaking my head left to right.

"Interesting development," Trevor said. He squinted, like it might help him see me clearer.

He hopped back up and joined me farther back.

"So, as we were saying," Trevor continued, possibly attempt-ing not to draw attention to my new weakness. "I find it strange to be in your Delves. It's bizarre enough to be dropped back into my own memories, where I know what I'm thinking and feeling as the memory unfolds. When I'm in your Delve, I'm inside and outside at the same time."

"That's what I was going to say earlier. I mean, the other day."

"Kinda like cornstarch," Trevor said with a sideways glance.

"Exactly," I replied, happy that he'd remembered.

"I need to know more," Trevor said. "I can't be in this half-informed limbo anymore." Trevor paced back and forth between me and the edge of rock that jutted out over the glassy surface of the lake far below. I drew in my breath every time he was out there.

"I don't mean to bring up a slightly embarrassing subject," I said. A picture of Julia danced in front of me, making me hesitate. Maybe I shouldn't be saying what I was about to say. I made a snap decision. I wasn't responsible for her anymore. It was time to clean up my past, and that included Julia. My stomach dropped as I mentally pushed her image over the side of the cliff. For all intents and purposes she was gone.

"Yes?" Trevor examined me like I was an X ray.

I couldn't help it, I was blushing again. This was so frustrating. I couldn't seem to pin down which way the wind was blowing with this guy. He was a lottery.

"Remember when we were walking and you accused me of creating an obstacle course so that we would have to, you know, be near each other?" I ducked my head, unable to look at him. He reached over and grabbed my hand, threading his fingers through mine. His palms weren't even sweaty. Mine were like Niagara Falls. I hoped he didn't notice.

"Refresh my memory," he said. "Near each other like this?"

What was he doing? If I didn't know better, I would think that he was flirting with me, but it couldn't be. It must be mockery. I wiped my other hand on my jeans and couldn't help but gulp in too much air when I noticed his T-shirt. It now read LET'S COMPLICATE THINGS.

"What?" His eyebrows shot up in surrender, a look of

pure innocence on his face. "You make obstacle courses and hurricanes, I make T-shirt slogans."

"Let's not complicate things," I said with the straightest face I could muster. He gave me the stink eye as he realized I'd used his own humor against him. But he didn't let go of my hand.

"Seriously, listen to me. The other day, why were you at the pond? Was that your destination, or did you just not get where you were going because of your Delve and the argument with me?" I asked.

"I don't know," he said slowly. "After walking around for a while, I stopped to think. Before I knew it the pond just materialized. My thoughts were so stagnant and I was standing there thinking about you—"

"Not fondly I'm sure," I said.

"No, not fondly at that moment." He at least seemed apologetic when he said it. "Yes, I was thinking of you and Oliver and that's when the Delve hit and I dropped so hard that I broke my arm." He gave it the once-over, reconfirming the healing powers of the afterlife.

"To answer your original question, no, the pond wasn't my destination, but I couldn't say what was. I guess I was searching, trying to find something. Why? What are you thinking?" he asked.

"Maybe you were unconsciously headed here, the way I was before I even knew I had a past-life penchant for standing on cliffs."

"I can't argue with that, but why do you look so concerned?"

"Don't know." I turned, too antsy to stay in one place. "It just seems significant for some reason." At that exact moment, two eagles shot out of the tree line behind us and launched themselves onto a thermal. For a moment they almost seemed suspended, neither falling nor flying.

"Wow," said Trevor. "I can see why you have a thing for them. They're magnificent. They almost rival a hummingbird."

I elbowed him in the ribs, but I breathed deeply. Seeing the eagles lessened my earlier anxiety, and Trevor's instantaneous awe of them filled me with delight. I turned to face him, feeling hopeful again. That's when I saw his newest T-shirt. NOW CAN WE COMPLICATE THINGS?

I did a head thunk into my hands. "Scraping the bottom of the barrel for slogans?"

"Come here." He wasn't asking.

I wanted to comply. I wanted to run. The look on his face, soft and hard at the same time, seemed to incapacitate me, so I didn't move a muscle.

He was mere inches from me now and I couldn't break

away from his gaze. The shadows of the eagles danced over us.

"It isn't fair." His voice was a groan, deep and gravelly.

He reached behind me and wrapped the end of my pony-tail around his finger until it swirled back over my shoulder.

"What isn't fair?" It sounded more like a squeak.

"It doesn't matter whether it's in life or the afterlife, it seems that Oliver is always getting the things that I want the most."

He leaned down and whispered, his lips almost touching my ear. "Has he been kissing you?"

My heart, moving at full throttle, stopped short like he'd yanked the emergency brake. He only wanted me because he was jealous of his brother. I was tired of being his last resort, something he dallied with when no one else was available to help him. I cocked back my arm, ready to lambast him with a right hook, when we disappeared.

What a stupid time for a Delve.

near

misses

I felt sick, so this had to be my Delve. I could feel bile rising in my throat, but I couldn't see anything. Was it dark or were my eyes closed?

"This wasn't my idea, Elliot," Trevor said with a mix of humor and concern.

"It isn't my fault either." I gasped. "I wasn't thinking straight."

My sweaty palms hid my face, creating the darkness. I felt the wind whipping my hair around. Was I on the rock ledge? No, I was on a seat. That's when it occurred to me that I was sitting in Sally. We were riding in Trevor's truck. No wonder I was a mess.

"You weren't thinking straight? Hmmmm, that's interesting to know," Trevor said with glee.

Why was he so happy?

"I just meant that I was a bit distracted when I decided it would be

a good idea," I said in my best huffy breath. "I was feeling safe there for a moment. You should have known better and talked me out of it."

Trevor's voice was soft and deliberate. "So you feel safe when I'm kissing you? I must be a pretty good kisser to——"

My eyes flew open, and if looks were able to turn a person to dust, Trevor would have been a sandbox.

"You're an arrogant ass!"

"And you're so pretty when your face is all lit up and alive."

He was so charming when he wanted to be. No wonder I'd kissed him.

"You've been baiting me. Distracting me from riding in Sally," I said with a mix of accusation and relief.

Trevor smirked. "It must've worked. You stopped being scared when you had something else to think about."

I ignored him and glanced around. Sure enough we were driving along a winding mountain road. It was mostly tree-lined, but at odd moments the sun poked through, illuminating a scenic view of the Hudson on the other side of a low stone wall.

"Wanna drive?"

"Don't push it, Lowry. I'm never getting behind the wheel of a car again, but maybe——"

I could feel myself peeking over at him. He was like a seat belt for my soul.

I continued, "Maybe I'll be okay if I'm with you."

"Speaking of being safe with me." Trevor's tone lost its playfulness. "Are you ready to talk about going back to school?"

So much for feeling relaxed. I now had rigor mortis.

"They hate me." My stomach knotted up just thinking of reaching out beyond the safe haven of Trevor.

"They don't know you," Trevor said.

"They don't need to know me. They know what I did. Everyone adored Oliver."

"I know what you did and——"

"And what?" I prodded.

He blushed and stammered over his words, "I know you and I love you."

I could barely breathe.

I hadn't dared to hope, or had I?

Oh, the hummingbirds were back, but they'd migrated to my heart.

"I love you too." I could feel my cheeks pulling up at the corners.

He glanced back at me, making me feel special. Things are so much easier when you're only living in a world of two.

I unbuckled, slid over to the middle seat, buckled back up, and leaned into Trevor's side. He wrapped his arm around my shoulder.

"I promise to be there for you. I'll catch you if you fall."

The Delve began to shift . . .

I was now in Trevor's Delve. I was standing outside Sally's open door and could see Elliot sitting in the truck. She was clutching a messenger bag to her chest, her knuckles white against the brown leather. The high school, freshly painted to start the year off right, should have seemed innocent, but

216

the HOME OF THE SCREAMING EAGLES sign gave it a predatory feel. He'd parked Sally in the farthest corner of the school lot, where the ground was littered with cigarette butts and weeds that managed to grow despite the absence of dirt. They'd found a way to thrive even when the odds weren't in their favor.

I watched Elliot through Trevor's eyes. She was pale, fragile, frightened.

"You promised to come to school with me." Trevor held out his hand.

"I thought I could do it. I really did." Elliot's hands shook.

I wanted to turn away from the desperation on her face, but Trevor was strong enough to look, so I had to be too.

His tone dropped lower. "I'll make everyone understand. It's going to be all right."

"You can't promise that. Nobody can promise that. Things happen."

I shouldn't have been able to feel Elliot shiver.

"I'll make them understand." He stood tall, with his arms crossed like Superman.

I couldn't tell whether she believed him or not, but something changed. I wondered, was it determination or resignation?

The Delve was switching again, and I was moving back into my memories. I had mixed emotions about this. I wouldn't have to see myself anymore, but now I could feel everything. And I was battered.

Trevor was holding my hand, but even though there wasn't anyone else in the parking lot, I self-consciously pulled away from his touch.

He reached for my fingers again, but I shook him off.

"I don't care what anyone else thinks. No one's even here yet." He had a little frown on his face.

"Maybe so, but let's do it this way anyway, okay?"

"Sure. Whatever makes this easier for you."

We walked across the empty parking lot. Behind the school, I could see the mountains that I'd used as a refuge over the last couple of months. I could feel their pull. I craved the safety of the trees, the freedom of standing in the sweet space between heaven and earth, the wind whipping away my sins. I stared at the upper peak and saw low dark clouds rolling in. It was going to storm.

Trevor and I walked on and I sucked in my breath as I crossed the threshold of the school. It took a moment to adjust to the dim light in the main hallway. Trevor was silent, most likely letting me get my bearings. When I was ready, we moved side by side down the hall, feet echoing in the quiet.

He checked the slip of paper in his hand. "Let's stop at my locker first, it's right down here." He pointed to the left. "Then we can walk down to your locker, put your things away, and I can take you to your homeroom."

My head nodded in agreement, but it might have done the same thing if Trevor had suggested that we dress like chickens and run through the school clucking at the top of our lungs.

By the time we reached Trevor's locker there was a small trickling of early birds infiltrating the school. Even though they were way down the hall, I noticed he deliberately used his body to shield me, giving me extra moments unseen.

He closed his locker door, jiggling the lock to make sure that everything was shut tight. "All right, I'm set here. Should we head over to your locker now?"

I shrugged.

Trevor deliberately took a cheerful tone and ignored my ambivalence. "Let's get you set up."

He grabbed my fingers, his large hand swallowing mine. This time he didn't give me the option to let go. Instead he guided me through the maze of hallways to my locker.

By now the school was becoming busy, and even though we were connected, I floated behind Trevor like I was riding in his jet stream. If he stopped moving I was sure I would drop like a rock. When we reached our destination, I leaned my forehead against the cool, smooth metal. Voices ricocheted around me and I felt as if I were trapped in the middle of a pinball machine.

"Hey, Trev, good to see ya. How was your summer?"

"Trev!"

"Yo, Lowry. You doin' okay, man? You didn't return my calls."

"Dude, where you been all summer?" came the chorus of voices as people spotted Trevor. Everyone was working extra hard to avoid the tragedy. I was sure everything had been said over and over again at the service anyway. The whole school would have been there because everyone loved Oliver—he was like that. Some kind of golden boy who mesmerized the lot of us. Even Cari and I'd talked about him being the perfect boyfriend, doodled his name next to ours. We'd never talked about Trevor. Knowing him now, it was hard to believe that I hadn't been aware of Trevor, hadn't loved him before. If it wasn't for Oliver, I might not have ever come in contact with him. A chill ran up my spine.

The voices that filled the hall smashed into me like an air bag. If Trevor wasn't popular before, he was certainly in the limelight now. With his brother's death he was now a quasi-public figure. Apparently, no one had noticed me yet. Who would suspect? A bitter laugh bubbled up from deep inside, but I clenched my teeth, restraining it.

I heard the moment when Trevor moved just enough that I became visible. Underneath the shout-outs to Trevor, there'd been a hum—the static of voices, one indistinguishable from the next. In a domino effect, one person after another fell silent, leaving a black hole of sound for us to fall into. I could smell the freshly painted lockers and the newly waxed floors, but in reality it isn't always so easy to clean up the past.

I felt the burning stares, despite the fact that Trevor was trying to physically block me from prying eyes. I managed to get the locker open with trembling fingers and stow my sweater inside. I grabbed a notebook and pen and, after shoving my bag on the floor, continued to stand with my back to the crowd. The smell of mystery meat was already wafting out from the cafeteria and my stomach rolled.

"It's all right," Trevor whispered into my ear. "You can turn around. They're just surprised, but once everyone sees that I want you here, that I need you here, it will be okay. Elliot . . ." He leaned even closer. "We all make mistakes, don't we? You know my mistakes."

He meant it to be reassuring. It wasn't working. The stares were picking off chunks of my soul.

"The only difference," I whispered back to Trevor, "is that they don't know what your mistakes are. And even if they did, they would still blame me." My voice was on edge. There was nothing else to say and my classmates weren't going away, so I turned around.

Everyone was frozen, unreadable. It was as if time had stopped.

Then, like the flip of a switch, the hum clicked back into place, becoming louder and louder with every beat. The frozen faces thawed into various stages of shock and disgust. I would have turned and run if Trevor wasn't holding on to me.

His voice was cautious. "Hey, everyone, you remember Elliot Turner?" His words sucked all the noise back out of the school again. Trevor tried vainly to fill the empty space.

"We—I have—it's hard to explain but things are all right between us. It's—well, I know it seems strange, but we're friends. We've talked. It was an accident." He looked at me with a stiff smile plastered to his face. This wasn't as easy as he'd thought it was going to be.

The warning bell rang.

24

already

gone

Like a Secret Service agent, Trevor reacted quickly and hustled me past the shocked crowd. He didn't give anyone time to respond to what he'd said. Before I could get my bearings, he had me tucked into a seat in my homeroom. People trickled in after us but no one said anything to me. I knew this was disconcerting for everyone—the unwritten rules for hating and judging are pretty clear in high school, and Trevor had just broken a whole bunch of social norms.

I remembered that Cari Taylor, best friend missing in action, would be walking through that door any minute. Alphabetically we always ended up in the same homeroom. Suspecting that someone you love hates you is difficult, but confirmation of it seemed unbearable. I thumbed through the blank pages of my notebook, staring at the empty sheets. Trevor had found a way to love me and he hadn't even known me. The people who know you should—

Trevor interrupted my thoughts. "Bell's gonna ring. Maybe I should just stay here with you?" He scanned the silent room. It seemed as if he would growl at anyone who got too close. Everyone was suspiciously busy, magnetically drawn to anything other than Trevor, but they wanted to peek. I could smell the ugly desire like a stench that hung in the room.

That's when I saw Cari. She was standing in the doorway, face unreadable.

Despite it all—I wanted. I wanted her and I couldn't stop.

No matter what, I couldn't help holding the door to possibility open a crack. If our friendship had died a different death, it might've hurt just as much as it did now, but I'd get over it eventually. After everything that had happened, I knew that this was going to break me. It was the wrong piece pulled out of my house of cards.

Witnessing this pathetic version of myself, I shuddered and thought about Julia, a much bigger loss than this twit that I'd called my best friend. Even hating Julia, I could see that what we had was so much stronger than this sham of a friendship. But the old me didn't have a Julia to compare and contrast. She didn't know about the lives and afterlives we'd spent together. Regardless, the death of a friendship hurts. The death of anything just sucks. All of it breaks you and scars you; it's indiscriminant. There is no easy way to watch something you love die.

"Elliot, do you want me to stay?" Trevor repeated.

Forever, I whispered to myself.

Looking at him I was filled with love. If it eased him, I could pretend I was standing fearlessly on the mountain. I plastered on a mask of confidence. These wheels were already in motion. There was nothing he could do here.

"I'm fine, Trevor. Cari is just coming in now and you don't want to miss your first homeroom." I nodded in the direction of the door.

I watched Trevor search Cari's face for some indication of friend or foe, but she remained blank.

"All right," Trevor said, still examining her carefully while talking to me. "I'll meet you here after first period."

I watched him just as carefully as he dashed out the door.

Seeing him disappear, I knew instantly that I was alone. The last wisp of hope had fled the room. Then Cari sat down in front of me, continuing to pretend that I was already dead.

The bell rang, surprising me. I hadn't realized that the class had even started, let alone ended. I glanced up and there was Trevor.

He hugged me tight. I didn't bother to look around to see what everyone was thinking. I already knew it wouldn't be good.

"Come on, I'll walk you to your next class."

The trek down the hall was peppered with hellos directed at Trevor, but I didn't think he realized that I wasn't included in them. I didn't blame him for not really seeing it. This was at least better than that frozen silence we'd experienced this morning. Near the cafeteria there was a memorial display for Oliver in the glass trophy case. Trevor's grip tightened as we walked by it. I kept my head down and let him lead wherever it was that he thought I might belong.

"Okay, second period." He spewed forced cheerfulness.

I laid my palm on his cheek, just wanting to be close. It would be a relief to get lost in him. He leaned down at the same moment that I broke away from his gaze. I felt his lips press gently onto the top of my head before he headed off to class. I was relieved that he hadn't heard the hiss of disapproval that cut through the air behind me.

I stumbled into second period and saw faces filled with hatred. I couldn't go in. It was easy to turn and leave. What did it matter? Unable to sit there and wait to be sentenced, I changed directions and walked away from my jury. I gave a sigh of relief.

I moved directly to my locker and turned my back to the rest of the world. Fingers shaking uncontrollably, I twirled the combination. Three tries later, it still wouldn't open. It was too much. Did they think I'd killed him on purpose? My fist beat against the door of the locker. I sank to my knees, tears pouring silently down onto the floor.

"Elliot?"

A familiar voice was calling my name.

I wanted.

I wanted her to love me and I couldn't stop.

I whipped my head around, more of me crumbling to pieces. If bits of me kept breaking off and blowing away there'd be nothing left. Maybe then it wouldn't hurt anymore.

Standing a few feet away from me was Cari, and she was flanked by the masses.

"What did you do to him?" There was no denying the accusation in her voice. It dripped with disgust. Was she right or was she righteous?

I could feel the explosion—her words rubbing an already raw place. The barrier holding it all in became too thin. I could no longer contain it.

"I killed him! Is that what you want to hear me say?" The moan ripped out of me, breaking off another piece of my soul and carrying it away.

"I know what you did to Oliver." Cari spat out the words.

She said it like she'd known him, not just known of him. She'd never linked arms with him or grasped his warm, safe hand. She'd never sat and talked with him about how the meaning of life could be found in Yoda's words of wisdom, while at the same time fighting over the cheesiest nachos on the plate. Every living and dead piece of my soul was wrenching itself apart.

"I want to know what you did to Trevor," Cari said. She jutted her head forward, but it wasn't curiosity, it was a malevolent gesture. "Seems like you're bent on destroying the whole Lowry family in one fell swoop."

I couldn't contain the gasp of pain. It was as physical as if she'd kicked me in the stomach. Cari towered over me, as I lay crumpled and broken on the floor, clutching the place where I imagined I used to have a heart.

She shook her head, making her black bob swing back and forth, sharp as a knife. Something was being permanently severed.

My voice was quiet. "We used to be best friends."

I wanted.

I wanted her to love me and I couldn't stop the realization that she'd never really loved me at all.

I got to my feet and felt a twinge of pride when I realized my back didn't have to be to the wall anymore. I could afford to be reckless. It was easy to be dangerous when there was nothing to lose. I now knew that it didn't matter if Trevor and I found a way to get past our own private disaster. No one was going to allow him to forgive me.

It was out of my control. Everyone had a role to play and Trevor's role was victim. Mine was the role of the villain. Everything was white and black, with no room for gray.

Like a lightning strike, the moment was illuminated. Trevor loving me was real but that didn't mean it could ever be more than an illusion.

Cari, done with her glaring, turned to stalk off, a master showman in front of the crowd. It had always been her way, I'd just never chosen to see it.

"Cari." My voice was strong, dangerous. I didn't recognize it, but I liked it.

She whipped around in irritation, her dramatic exit interrupted. I stood straight and took a step in her direction. She wasn't expecting this from me and took a quick step back, perhaps unwilling to be cut by the ragged edges of my broken soul.

"Cari, you are nothing but surface."

I pushed my way past the silent crowd and out the fire exit door, into the rain. I walked slowly with my head up high until I hit the cover of the tree line where no one could see me crumple from the effort. Hunched over in brokenhearted pain, I climbed, heading for the mountain.

• • •

Ding-ding. Delve over. Thank goodness—I'd seen enough. And it was plenty to convince me that I didn't need to see any more. It felt like an eternity, but my fist finally connected with Trevor's face. How dare he make me the prize in his competition with Oliver? A kiss was supposed to mean something.

The satisfaction of landing the punch quickly dissolved into a shock of pain that radiated up my arm.

"What the hell was that for?" Trevor growled at me while walking in circles and holding his jaw in his hand.

"Oh, just heal yourself and shut up!" I shouted. All the pent-up emotion from the back-to-back Delves was releasing itself. My hand hurt. My pride hurt. My heart even hurt. I wasn't going to cry, so I turned my back to him instead.

"Unbelievable!" he bellowed. "Aren't I the one who just got decked? Remind me not to try to kiss you again." He stalked over to the edge of the cliff, where he knew I would be unwilling to follow.

"You didn't really want to kiss me anyway," I shot back over my shoulder.

"How do you know what I wanted to do?"

"You said you only wanted what Oliver had and I know I haven't been going around kissing Oliver." My hand was feeling better so I pointed a finger at him for emphasis.

"That's not what I said. I made a very simple observation

screwed up royally from the start and now I was going to pay the price.

"We have no proof that there even is a hell," he said.

"You also can't prove that there isn't one," I countered.

His face softened ever so slightly, yet it caused a painful tightening in my chest. What if I was doomed one way or another, but Trevor needed *me* in order to find his way out of the Obmil? And what if Oliver was depending on me to finish what I'd started so he could have his own life back? I loved them both. Could I really let them down like that?

"Have you been carrying this around with you the whole time?" Trevor asked, pulling me away from my thoughts.

"No, not originally." I thought back to those early Delves. "It was a likely outcome in the beginning. How do you survive after doing what I did to Oliver? But I was so distracted at first that I just didn't think it through. Then, when I remembered meeting you and saw what you meant to Elliot, I became hopeful. But things have been going downhill rapidly since we went back to school. Cari was sort of the tipping point. I think she just pushed me over the edge."

"Hate her," Trevor said.

Was it wrong that I wanted to hug him for that?

"What do you think it's like? Hell, I mean. I can't get past the image of heat and flames. Or the absence of fluffy white clouds in a perfect blue sky." I could feel myself choking up again.

"You're not going to hell, Elliot," Trevor said. His teeth were clenched tightly together. Under his breath he muttered, "Not without me."

Rah-rah. Go team.

Trevor faced me, palms up, shoulders shrugged.

"We could run away. . . ." I didn't care if I sounded desperate. I *was* desperate.

"Where would we go?" Trevor asked slowly. Was he searching for a loophole?

The memory snuck up on me. Not a Delve, but a memory that I now owned. A broken Elliot standing up to Cari. A high school hallway that was too quiet considering how many living and breathing judgments were standing in it. I'd pulled myself up because there was nothing else left for me to do, nothing left to lose. It was time for me to surrender again. I couldn't control everything. I had to let this be what it was. More important, I had to do it for the two people I loved the most. The moment I decided to let it all go, a strange calm came over me.

Maybe I could just kiss him a little bit more before I was sent to hell and he was ripped away from me for all eternity. It would be the memory that I would hold on to.

"What are you thinking?" His words held a note of suspicion. Some of my calm resignation must have shown on my face.

"We need to Delve again. We need to see this through," I said.

"There's always a chance that what you think happened might not—"

"That's not why I'm going back." I put my finger up to silence him and said, "We've come this far. We've got growth plans to figure out."

"I still think you're beautiful when you're fierce." His voice was gruff.

"I think you're confused. Past-life Trevor thinks that about past-life Elliot. You, on the other hand, think we're 'boldly going nowhere.'"

"I think what?" He sounded incredulous.

I couldn't go into this now or I'd lose my resolve. "You want to know what's in my head? I think you just want me to kiss you again," I teased, trying to distract him. No point in examining a losing situation too carefully.

"Well, now that you mention it." He smiled slowly. My heart raced. I was grateful he was so easy to divert, but the ease of it dug into me like a splinter.

Then it occurred to me, this would be it. Our Delves

always seemed to happen in the midst of some huge, emotional upheaval. Reaching for him would be the charge we would need to drop into a Delve and find out my final, ugly little secret. Thinking of one more kiss with him was making my legs feel like jelly already. We might not even make it to that last kiss.

I ran at him full force and leapt into his arms, determined to outrun time.

falling

or

flying?

This kiss was an electric shock, but something wasn't right. We hadn't Delved. I raggedly pulled away, confused. We were still standing in the same spot. I wriggled myself out of his arms, spun around in disbelief.

"Am I boring you?" asked Trevor.

"No. I just thought we were going to Delve. We didn't go anywhere." Couldn't *anything* about this place be predictable?

"You trying to get rid of me?"

"Nah," I said, still trying to figure out how it was that we could drop into the past without a moment's notice when I was unprepared and now that I was determined to meet my fate—nothing. Nada.

Trevor glanced down. "Unbelievable. Is that the best you could come up with?" he asked.

"What? Best of what?"

"Your T-shirt. Very romantic. Is that your way of telling me you love me? You're quite the tender heart, Turner."

I pulled out the lower corners of my shirt to read the words emblazoned across my chest: I PEE IN POOLS.

"I didn't—that was not me! You did this, T-shirt man. And what do you mean romantic? Love you?" I sputtered indignantly until I caught his playful expression. He was such a goober.

"You . . ." I punched his arm, which he did not find the least bit painful or intimidating. It didn't have the same emotional fuel as my earlier right hook.

"Do you also pee in lakes?" he asked.

"I don't pee in pools or lakes, smartass."

"Well, that's good because it's time to figure out the rest of our story." He pulled me close. "Do you trust me?"

"Why?" I asked with hesitation, thinking that I might be starting to understand where he was going with this.

"We've got to take a leap."

"And how do you think that's going to help?" I asked, feeling dizzy at the thought of going anywhere near the tip of that rock. I grabbed his hand for an anchor even though I wasn't anywhere near the edge.

"It was your idea."

"Are you insane? I would never suggest jumping off a freaking cliff! I'm not the old me any—oh." My voice stopped short, as I pictured the old Elliot standing on a ledge, leaping into the Hudson.

"The good news is that we're already dead. What's the worst thing that can happen? We get a little wet in a weird, unwet kind of way. You'll definitely have to change your shirt, though," Trevor said.

"Change my shirt?"

"You know, from pool to lake. I have a feeling your bladder won't be able to handle a leap like that." He shrugged.

He was deliberately baiting me to buck me up, but I didn't care because it was working. I walked toward the edge of everything, pulling him along behind me. Filled with calm and purpose, I kissed him gently on the lips and then stood to face my past and my future all at the same time.

He stood behind me and I felt his arms lock tightly around my waist, his chin resting on the top of my head. I thought Trevor might say something but he simply breathed in deeply, smelling the scent of my hair, pulling me in tighter.

Locked together like the eagles I'd seen so long ago, we pushed off from the stability of the rock beneath us. It was a leap of faith and he was following me into the unknown. I flung open my arms like I could ride the wind. For one brief second I couldn't tell the difference between falling and flying, then we raced toward the surface of the blue water.

26

remembering

blue

The drop, which should have taken mere seconds, seemed endless, as if we were hanging between earth and sky. We were momentarily suspended between the best and the worst of us. It occurred to me that as scary as this was, falling together was better than falling apart.

I saw shades of blue beneath me and I angled our bodies to enter the water in a dive. There would be no last-minute change of direction for us. I could feel Trevor's breath warm in my ear as he whispered the single word *remember* . . .

I barely noticed the trail or the rain. The only thing that drummed through my head was the need to escape. The calm that had bucked me up moments ago had been replaced by blind panic and rage. I moved along the slippery rocks without a hand to hold, imploding with the realization that I would never be allowed to love Trevor.

I knew that if I stayed in this life, with these people, I would have no hope.

More gut-wrenching sobs racked my body as I stumbled and slid back down five feet of loose rock, scraping my knees and cutting the palms of my hands.

It seemed wrong to welcome the distraction of physical pain, but it also kept me from thinking. I couldn't live this life anymore. I'd had a taste of forgiveness and losing it was like dying twice for the same crime.

Bloody and bruised, I reached the top, my haven. Instead of sitting in my usual place, feet dangling, snuggled up against Trevor, I stood, threw out my arms, and looked to the heavens.

It was a primal scream. An infinite howl of emotion, caught by the slate-gray clouds that thundered toward me. As I screamed, the ugly things that were sitting on my soul hitched a ride out into the storm.

Spent, I stood there, trying to sense what had changed. It wasn't just my voice that was carried away on the wind. Something angry and broken had taken flight, leaving room for something new. A seed of defiance had been planted earlier, but now it had room to grow. In a single breath, I'd decided that Trevor was worth the effort. One Trevor was worth a population of Caris. The wind roared and the rain battered me. The storm bellowed, but for the first time in what seemed like an eternity, I felt a pocket of peace inside my soul. It was mine and no one else could take it away. I was the eye of the storm.

"Oh God, Elliot—don't do it!" screamed a ragged voice from behind me.

I whipped around and spotted Trevor, white as a ghost, pain and fear etched across his face.

I felt such a deep tenderness for him. He'd come for me. The eye of my storm became bigger, but then awareness thundered through me. He thought I was going to jump. It stung to see it written on his face, now that everything had changed in a heartbeat.

That was the moment my foot slipped out from under me. My arms spun like twin waterwheels.

I plummeted downward, twisting and turning, trying to find a way back to him. A rumble of thunder vibrated the air. In a flash of lightning, I realized he would always think that I'd left him on purpose. The thought of it took my breath away. I kept my eyes open, realizing that I was leaving my life behind, but I wasn't out of choices. This was a stark moment of clarity. I'd spent seventeen years looking in the wrong direction and now wasn't the time to be blind. I relaxed and stopped fighting the fall. My soul was gathering speed and catching up to the rest of me. As I twisted around one last time, I found myself looking back up to the ledge I'd never intended to leave. Trevor's eyes locked on to mine . . . and then he jumped.

"Noooooooooo!" I screamed into the wind. My body smacked the water. Thoughts scattered like a handful of beads dropped on a bare wood floor. I gasped for air and the current rushed in. My throat burned. Panic, thrashing, spots of light exploding in my head. Everything went blue. Surrender.

243

27

frozen

in

place

I could still feel Trevor attached to me when my head broke the water. I instinctively wrapped myself tightly around him as we bobbed in the middle of the lake. No sooner was I curled up against him, than I started to worry that my weight would make it impossible for him to tread water. It was deep here, maybe even bottomless. I tried to break away from him, but his arm was like an iron band around my waist.

"The dead don't die, Elliot. When are you going to remember that?" There was a bite to his words.

"Oh." The reality of our unreality sank back in. I was still feeling relief that I hadn't killed myself in a momentous leap, but there'd been consequences for my choices. I'd put myself on the edge, in a place where I had very little control. How far can you push chance before it isn't chance anymore? I swept the thought aside, opting to leave my subconscious out of the thought process. I hadn't jumped. That was all I needed to know.

I pulled myself out of my memories. Something wasn't right. I was suddenly freezing, my teeth chattering. Glancing around I could see why. The Obmil was coated in snow and ice. Everywhere I looked it was as if the White Witch's Narnia had sprung up. I sucked in a shocked breath and the cold air burned my lungs.

I turned my head to see what Trevor thought of this new development but when I saw his face, I knew. He'd created this winter. The pain was frozen on his face and his eyes were ice. I wondered if he was frozen all the way to his heart.

"Trevor?" I asked. I reached up to stroke his face.

"Don't," he growled as he pulled me closer to him.

I didn't understand his intense reaction. We knew everything now. We had the last of our memories back. We had a chance at a fresh start and yet he seemed to be shutting down, while I only felt relief. I wouldn't be carted off to hell, ripped from his arms. It was easy to see what had happened now. I had fallen and then he had jumped . . . "Oh my God—NO!" I shouted. "It was an accident."

"It wasn't an accident." He sounded as cold as the icicles

hanging like daggers from the surrounding trees. "I went after you."

"Then it's fine," I said as soothingly as I could manage with my teeth chattering. "You were trying to save me again, like you saved me when I found you at Oliver's grave. You loved me despite myself. Our time together was short-lived, but it's all right. Now I have you back again. We can move on together."

"Here, let me help you. Put your hands on the ice." Trevor cupped his hands around my foot and helped to elevate me out of the water. When I turned around he was still bobbing in the small hole in the quickly thickening frozen lake.

"Give me your hand." I kept trying to picture a warm front, but nothing was working. Trevor's creation was just too power-ful. "Come on, I'll pull you up," I said as I reached trembling fingers out to him.

"You don't get it, Elliot. I didn't jump after you to save you."

"You slipped too?" I whispered.

"No! I came after you." His words were painfully slow and deliberate. "I remember." His voice was bitter. "I jumped know-ing full well that you would shatter into a million pieces. I knew that there would be nothing left to save. I jumped anyway."

"Then why?" I asked, unable to think straight in the icy cold.

"Do you really want to know the ugly truth?" he barked at me without waiting for an answer. "In those endless moments when I saw you slip and fall, everything stopped. My life flashed before me. I realized that until I'd let you into my heart, I hadn't lived at all. Right before your back hit the water, our eyes met and I knew that I would go to hell and back for you."

I pressed my fingers into my temples. It was beginning to sink in.

"And," he continued, "if everything we suspected is true, I just might be on my way there—without you."

It was like a dam had burst. Wild ideas, things I hadn't allowed myself to investigate, came flying at me from every direction. Horrified, I turned away, not wanting Trevor to see my thoughts. I couldn't make a sound.

"Elliot, I need to get out of here."

I reached for him.

"Not with you," he said, his voice heavy.

My tears burned hot tracks down my frozen face. I tried to suck in enough air to say the words that would keep him here, but I couldn't breathe.

"Don't you realize how hard it is, knowing that I may never . . ."

"It's just rumors," I said. I was shivering uncontrollably now. "That's what you told me. We don't know anything. No one knows what comes after here. Let's go find Mel. She'll be able to help us. This can't be as bad as you think." Prattling on, I tried to keep him close and my fear at bay.

"You find Mel. I've got to get out of here."

As I reached for him, he ducked under the dark gray water. My fingers slammed into the ice, as the hole froze solid over his head. My only consolation was that he was already dead, as he so often reminded me. It didn't make me worry less.

The top of the lake was a thick sheet of ice. I bent down and ran my hand along the surface, thinking about the walls we build when we're scared and vulnerable. I concentrated, thinking the warmest thoughts I could—a kiss from Trevor. The memory made my face flush but his flash-frozen anger was untouchable. When I could no longer feel my hand, I stood up and faced the shore. I tried not to think of Mel keeping her distance and of Oliver, so obviously hurt and angry. I needed them now.

I turned around one more time to see if Trevor had decided to stay with me after all. He hadn't. He must've swum to the other side of the lake, exited the water, and headed up another section of trail. As he moved northward, the previously green landscape was icing over.

Now I understood. Trevor's raw feelings were too strong for me to affect them. I couldn't breach the wall of ice that he'd placed between us. I'd never seen anyone impact the environment so powerfully. It scared me that he was pushing everyone else's thoughts out of the picture. He was such an emotional force right now that I hadn't even been able to cocreate with him.

I moved closer to the shore and felt a subtle thaw. As I ran, the distance between us grew and so did the variation in temperature. The thick ice was now making groaning noises under my weight. Even though I knew nothing would actually happen to me, I shivered at the thought of breaking through the frozen water. Trevor hadn't needed to come up from underneath the ice to breathe, but I still resisted, unable to shake my innate fear of drowning.

I placed one foot on the ladder leading up to the dock, when my other hiking boot crashed through the ice, sending frigid shards under my pant leg and into my sock. I yanked my already dry foot out of the water. The last time I'd come up out of the lake, Mel had been there to greet me. It felt strange and lonely to walk up that path alone.

I stopped short, realizing I wasn't by myself after all. Julia was perched atop a large boulder, sitting all cross-legged and Zen-like. She hadn't said a word, but she was watching every move that I made. How long had she been here? What had she seen?

"He's not here." I bristled, unsure if it was because I suspected she was searching for Trevor or because I didn't have him.

Julia opened her mouth like she wanted to say something, but before she could mess with my head again, I pointed at her. "Do. Not. Say. It."

"But I——" Julia stood up on the boulder. I took a step in her direction.

"I said, don't say a word. I've had enough of your mixed messages." My voice took on a high-pitched imitation of hers. "I don't want to room with you. Or be your friend. But I love you and I'll make you paper cranes to prove it." I was so close now that I had to tilt my head backward in order to stay in her face.

"Is that what you think?" Her face went blank for all of thirty seconds and I expected her to melt into tears. I realized my mistake right as the shock wave of anger hit me, blasting me into a Delve so hard I was blown over on my back.

"Julia, open-this-door-NOW!"

Julia's mother. I could hear her banging her fist against the door and swiveling the knob. The only thing I could see was the ceiling. Julia wasn't moving.

"Fine, I'll get the key. I am coming in, young lady. You are not doing this to me."

250

Mrs. Going's footsteps strode briskly down the hall, changing to a more frantic pace as her feet took to the stairs. My heart raced faster in time with Julia's mother's footfalls. Just when I thought I couldn't stare at the cobweb strung between the blades of the white ceiling fan a minute longer, Julia turned her head. Or maybe it lolled to the side. I gasped at the sight. Julia had a dance barre attached to the wall of her room and it was backed by a full-length mirror. In it, I could see her lying on her bed—what was left of her.

She was probably always petite, but now she was skeletal. Her hair was limp and matted to her head, and the shadows under her eyes combined with her dilated pupils made it seem as if her face was landscaped with two black holes, capable of sucking every emotion out of the room. And yet she still managed to appear empty. I didn't think she was even capable of moving, but she surprised me, swinging herself into an upright position and then onto her feet. She wobbled like a young child on stilts and then, perhaps it was her dance training kicking in, she found her balance and walked to the door. She used her thumb and pointer finger, so small they looked more like tweezers, to turn the lock. She opened the door at the exact moment that her mother was trying to insert the key. Mrs. Going froze, staring at her daughter.

"Do you think you're being funny?" Julia's mother's voice sounded more controlled than any other time I'd heard it.

Julia turned away from her mother, who couldn't have heard the breathy reply, an emotionless mist of sounds resulting in a single word: "No." Mrs. Going also didn't see the sad little half smile that I caught in the mirror before the image of Julia disappeared. . . .

I rolled over onto all fours and threw up. It was mostly water from the lake and it left an earthy taste on my tongue. As I emptied the contents of my stomach I wondered if that's how Julia had died. Did she vomit her soul out of her body, one little piece at a time? Or did she decide that there was nothing in life worth tasting? I cried out—the ugliness of it all was more than I could wordlessly contain.

"Julia?" I whipped my head around, but she was gone. So utterly and completely gone. Just like Trevor. And I didn't know how to get them back. But maybe there was someone who could help me. I needed to hurry.

Setting off, I raced past the Haven and headed toward the school. I was as fractured as the ice that Trevor had left behind when he'd disappeared and taken a piece of me with him. In contrast, Julia had built a wall and closed me out, leaving a void. I wondered if the three of us would ever be able to put our souls back together—to be whole again. I dashed toward Mel's classroom, holding my breath, hoping against hope that I might have a chance to make something right.

A booming voice came from right behind me. "WHAT ARE YOU DOING, MISS TURNER?"

I jumped, pushing my weight against the door, causing it to swing open. I took a quick couple of steps into the room, putting some distance between David and myself. I couldn't believe I hadn't smelled his cheap cologne before he'd snuck up on me.

Mel ignored David and looked at me. "I was hoping you'd show up, Elliot." The smile on her face was genuine and I felt myself relax a little bit. It'd been good to Delve in privacy and close off the rest of the world, but I suddenly found myself craving Mel's mothering. I thought about Hurricane Elliot and the barbed wire I'd erected. Those were physical walls, but the emotional ones were even harder to break through. What if Mel hadn't been giving me the cold shoulder? What if she was responding to the barriers that I'd put up? I shifted my weight from foot to foot, but she still was beaming at me, open and warm.

I turned to Oliver cautiously. "Hi, Oliver." I couldn't believe how much I'd missed him.

"Told 'em you'd come." His voice was gravelly with emotion. He strode toward me and wrapped me up in a big bear hug, lifting me off my feet.

"Where have you been?" I asked, even though it was hard to talk with him squeezing me so tight.

He chuckled. "Mel put me on a project helping Freddie."

I turned to Mel and the lightbulb went off. She'd been protecting Oliver, didn't want him exposed to my dark and hurtful headspace. She'd given me some time to get myself together without causing him further harm. I mouthed a thank-you over Oliver's shoulder and she winked back.

But I still needed to fix things with Oliver. "It broke my heart to think that you'd stopped loving me," I whispered. He'd put my feet back down on the floor, but I was still wrapped in his arms.

Oliver met my gaze and said, "I was out of line."

"No, you had a valid point, and I'm sorry."

"No, I'm the one who's sorry. Do you think we could talk about it"—he cleared his throat—"someplace a little more private?"

When he said that, I realized that I'd been leaning closer and closer to him. Embarrassing heat flooded my face. The whole room was watching like we were forty-seven minutes into a juicy soap opera. I shook my head to clear it, but Oliver wasn't letting go. "I still love you, Elliot," he said.

Clap, clap, clap. David's sausagelike fingers slapped against each other. I whipped around to face him.

"I heard a rumor that you were quite the little actress in your last life. Seems your skill has carried over to the afterlife,"

David jeered. His features were more hostile than I'd ever seen. "What are you doing here, Miss Turner?" I didn't know if he was questioning why I'd been crouched outside Mel's class or my qualifications for being in the afterlife. My head was spinning and suddenly it didn't matter.

"I have a question for you, too," I said. "Why would someone who works here need to be in his room, Delving by himself, and calling for his mommy?" The words were ugly, but I couldn't stop them from pouring out. All my fear and worry over Trevor had found a place to land. All the horror of Julia's last Delve rushed out of me, and the confusion I'd unexpectedly just felt about Oliver was the last bit of zing I needed to launch the attack. Besides, he'd started it. David was a sizable target and I owed him.

David's fleshy face went pale and he took a step back. I should have been grateful and backed off too, but a tidal wave of pent-up frustration and anger had been unleashed and I no longer had control of it.

"I'VE HAD ENOUGH!" I bellowed, moving deliberately toward him. I flew in for the kill. "I cannot fathom why anyone would have you, YOU, here at the Obmil as a guide, as a mentor."

David backed into the hallway, mouth agape and speechless, for once.

"Leave me alone and mind your own damn business for a change!" I slammed the door with all the force I could muster.

I stood and stared at the heavy wooden divider between David and myself. I slowly turned around.

"That was not a very kind way to treat another soul at the Obmil," Mel said.

I hung my head, knowing she was right. That's when I heard small snickers. They sounded uncertain at first, but the laughter was growing in strength and confidence. I jerked my head up and saw Mel had a huge smile on her face.

"But my, how that soul deserved a good dressing down." Mel succumbed to rolling laughter and no one else bothered to hold it in. Chuckles filled the room and my ears. I was as proud as a little kid who'd managed to snag the last cookie. The best part was listening to Oliver. The more everyone else carried on, the more he doubled over chortling and holding his belly.

Everyone began to settle back down, and Mel walked over to the door, peeked her head out, then announced, "Nope, he's really gone."

The room broke out into another roar. While everyone was talking and reliving the moment, I sidled up to Mel.

"I see Trevor's not with you." Mel sounded concerned enough to wash away all the previous hilarity.

"No, he's not with me anymore." Maybe he'd never been with me. My heart tightened at the truth of the statement. He didn't love me. He loved a version of me that no longer existed.

"Do you know where he is?" Mel asked. My heart contracted tighter in my chest.

"No. I was hoping he'd come here to see you, like he did last time we fought."

"What happened since I last saw you?"

"Everything. But still, nothing makes any sense." I blew a dangling piece of hair off of my face. "Julia hasn't stopped in, has she?" The hair floated back down over my eye and Mel reached over to tuck it behind my ear. I felt a searing longing for Trevor in that moment. I needed to find him. I'd wasted too much time here already.

"No, I haven't seen Julia either." I thought she was going to ask more about it, but she held her tongue. Suddenly I didn't want to talk about it.

"We have to do something. We need to find Trevor." Thinking of him made me feel helpless. Intellectually I knew that he couldn't be physically hurt, but it seemed as if there was so much more at risk now. "I don't have time to fill you in on all of it. It's a knotted pile of tangled threads. And David . . ." My voice dropped an octave. My anger was dissipating and now I wondered if David would lurch out of a corner and try to keep me from finding Trevor.

Mel pinched the bridge of her nose. "David's gone, but there is something you should know."

I stepped back, taken off guard by the possibility of information just being handed to me.

Mel took a deep breath. "David doesn't work here, Elliot. He's a Third Timer like you."

the third

time

lacks charm

My head was spinning. David was a Third Timer? I paused at the realization . . . that's what Mel had been talking about. Freddie was David's Passenger. That explained why he was watching over David the other day. Mel had intended to say something else about Freddie earlier, but David had interrupted. Now it was all coming together. He clearly didn't want anyone to know that he was a Third Timer. He had a lot of nerve, making me feel bad when I arrived at the Obmil again. I could feel my temper beginning to flare.

"Elliot!" From Mel's tone, it must not have been the first time she'd called out my name.

"What?" I said, startled to be taken away from my internal detective work. Things were finally starting to make a little sense.

Mel waggled her pen back and forth. "What happened to make Trevor run away?"

I shivered, trying to consolidate what felt like a lifetime into a few brief sentences.

"I was beginning to believe that I ended up here at the Obmil because I killed myself." I dropped my gaze, avoiding her. "We Delved and I figured it out. I fell accidentally, off a cliff and . . ." Oliver walked back over to where we were standing.

"And?" Mel wanted to know.

I wanted to say that Trevor had followed me into the after-life on purpose, that he was the one who'd committed suicide. I should tell her that he was terrified of going to hell, but I remembered how frightening the possibility had been, and I couldn't say it out loud. I was afraid of making it true.

"He left me!" Everything frozen inside me blazed with a fire that had finally sparked. I hadn't realized how furious I was with him. I loved him and he'd left me. He hadn't trusted me enough to help him. I blew on the flames of my anger. It was easier to deal with this emotion than with the sickening fear that something had gone terribly wrong and I couldn't fix it.

He was the one who'd talked me into taking that final Delve. I knew what his fear felt like—it had been my own. A tear slipped past my defenses. I didn't know how long I had left to be with him, to love him. If our deepest fears were true, he was wasting the time we did have together.

Mel let out a soft breath. It felt like sympathy.

"We need to talk, Elliot. I need to explain some things to you, but right now I must try to find Trevor. Will you stay here with Oliver?"

"No way. I'm going with you." What on earth was she thinking?

Oliver swallowed and his Adam's apple bobbed up and down. "I know you want to go after him, but I need to talk to you first." Oliver watched me with a Trevor-like intensity. I was torn. Oliver and I were finally back on the right foot. If I left I'd have blown him off for Trevor once again. I tugged on a cuticle that I'd been too busy to gnaw at before. Time rushed past me.

I eyed Mel in defeat. "He was leaving the lake, heading up into the tree line, on the opposite side of where the eagles nest."

"I can't believe he left you like that." Oliver's caustic tone sent my internal compass spinning.

"Any place else he might be?" Mel asked.

"We created a rock outcrop that hangs over the lake, but I don't think he'll want to go back there." I couldn't help remembering that moment in his arms when we pushed off the edge.

It was a single moment of optimism, hanging between life and death. It seemed that perfection only existed on the edge of a knife, a place too fragile and sharp to find balance for more than an instant. Oliver grabbed my hand.

"Mel?" I had no idea what to ask, but I couldn't stop myself from wanting more.

"Later, Elliot. Go with Oliver." Mel turned quickly and headed out the door.

"I want to go home." Oliver's words wandered out in front of us on the trail and interrupted my thoughts.

"We're headed back to the Haven right now," I said, bumping my shoulder against his arm as we bounced over the packed earth.

"I miss my mom. I miss Abby, too, and my dad. But I really, really miss my mom."

I stopped abruptly, hearing the emotion before I could see it running down his face.

The woods were empty. Never before had the Obmil felt like such a void. I wrapped my arms around him, muffling his sobs against my shoulder. He was always so put together, so purposeful in everything he did. I hadn't known. Shame on me, for once again forgetting to consider beyond myself. I squeezed him tighter and we cried. It felt as if all the words and all the air had been sucked out of existence.

Eventually, we could both breathe again. I smoothed his blond curls, wondering if I would be able to say the right thing.

"Oliver?"

His lip trembled as he stared at me. This was a chance to make him feel better. Thinking that maybe I could give him something for a change gave me the courage to continue.

"I suspect that there is always *missing* that happens. You don't really love someone unless you miss them."

"I know—in my head at least." Oliver tapped his finger to his temple. "But a part of me"—he slid his finger down to rest on his heart—"kind of wonders why, if everyone is so sad, we just don't stay together? Over and over, we die so we can start again. What's the point of the pain—of the missing?"

"Damn, I wish I knew the answer to that." It was killing me to see him so vulnerable—so un-golden boy. I wasn't used to this. "I don't know, but I can take a guess. I think that no one would know how great being together feels, until they knew what being apart feels like too."

Oliver's eyes darkened like a storm rolling in. "Do you miss your mom?"

I nodded. "I miss a lot of people." Julia popped into my head, MIA from my last life, but now I wasn't so sure that things between us were an easy black and white. Stuff with Julia seemed just as gray as the pallor of her skin in that last

Delve. Then I pictured the frozen face of Trevor, a mask about to crumble. God, I missed him. Something must have shown in the expression on my face because Oliver grabbed my face between his hands and pressed his lips against mine. The kiss was slow and warm and I melted into his arms, once again using him as my soft place to fall. I could have stayed, wrapped up in Oliver for all of eternity—but . . .

Oliver broke away and kissed the tip of my nose, then moved on to the space between my eyes and then my forehead. I glanced up at him, not sure what I was going to see on his face.

"It was nice, wasn't it?"

Oh boy.

"But not a single firework. Same for you?" He gave me a sheepish grin.

"Yeah. I mean, no. No fireworks," I mumbled. "Kind of cozy and warm."

Oliver hooted. "Yeah, cozy is exactly how a guy wants to be described when kissing a girl."

I shook my head. "You knew it was going to be that way, didn't you?" I asked.

"I kinda figured." He shrugged. "I don't know, I just thought we should probably try it—just to be sure. Even though it isn't *that way* between us, I'll admit it, it irks me when you have Trevor written all over your face."

"But I—"

"Nah, you don't have to explain. It's been that way since the moment I saw you. We're like brother and sister." He blushed. "Besides, if Trevor and I both felt like that about you, we'd have even more to fight over."

I gave him a giant hug. "About you and Trevor—"

"Hey, listen," Oliver interrupted. "We're almost at the Haven. Walk the rest of the way with me and then you can go off and search for my butt-head brother." He winked. "And just so you know—the way it is between you and me . . ." His finger flicked back and forth between us. "The Passenger thing, and me dying. I wouldn't change a thing. I love you."

I grabbed his hand in mine, tugging him down the path. I looked at him over my shoulder, hoping he could see how much I meant it. "I love you, too."

As we walked through the front door of the Haven, I kept an eye out for David. Luckily, he was nowhere in sight, but Freddie was nursing a mug of coffee at the front desk while sorting through a large pile of keys.

I plopped my elbows on the desk. Oliver immediately began to help Freddie with his task.

I watched how they worked together intuitively, organizing things into groups that I couldn't figure out the pattern for.

"You guys are freaky in your ability to communicate wordlessly." Freddie gave a two-finger salute and Oliver stood up straight.

"It takes special skill to pull off a job like this." Freddie pretended to be serious.

"The kind of job only a Passenger could do?" I asked pointedly.

"Well, now that you mention it, Passengers do tend to be really good at unlocking things." Freddie stared me in the face. "So, you figured out that I don't work here, love." He pulled off his cap and put it right back on.

"You could have told me you were a Passenger." I tried to keep from sounding hurt, but when I said it out loud, I realized I was tired of not knowing things.

"It wasn't your business, Elliot, but even if it had been, I wouldn't have told you anyway."

"Why not?" I pouted.

"The waters. No need to muddy up the waters. You had enough stuff floating around to figure out. Sometimes it's best to let things settle, then you get to them when you get to them." Freddie stopped fiddling with the keys and looked at Oliver. "Son, I forgot all about it, but before we head out to the greenhouse, we're going to have to take a run over to Miz Connolly's room. She's been having a little trouble with her bed again."

"She could tell her grandson that her bed is not a trampoline," Oliver said.

"And you know as well as I that she feels guilty enough about him being here—that ain't gonna happen."

"Yeah, I guess you're right."

"What I need you to do is run down to the basement and grab my toolbox. If you'd be so kind."

"I'll get it right now." Oliver strode around the desk and headed into Freddie's office. He stopped short, turned, then bounded around and gave me a peck on the cheek.

"What was that for?" I asked, my fingers touching the warm spot, trying to keep it from disappearing.

"You'll be gone before I get back."

"How do you know?" I wrinkled my brow.

"I figure you're not going to like what he's going to tell you." Oliver lifted his chin in Freddie's direction. Freddie tossed a rag at his head.

"You know something I don't?" I asked.

"Nah, but how often do you actually find out news that makes life easier around here?"

He had a point.

"And don't let my brother sidetrack you with his grumpy bullshit, okay?" Oliver gave my ponytail a little tug. I nodded, because what else could I say? I watched Oliver disappear into the office and listened as the basement door opened and his feet double-timed it down the stairs.

"So, did you have something else you wanted to know, Elliot?" Freddie asked.

I sighed because I had a million things I wanted to figure out. "Yeah." I cleared my throat. "I understand why you didn't tell me about being a Passenger, but you've been kept here so long. That's incredibly unfair." I was getting pissed all over again. "It's so damn selfish to leave a Passenger stranded indefinitely at the Obmil. You must feel like you've been stuck here for an eternity."

"Thoughtless maybe, but probably not selfish."

I was about to interrupt and point out what a slimeball David was, when Freddie continued.

"Haven't you had a moment or two when you've been so engrossed in your own soul that you forgot to think about Oliver? He's *your* Passenger after all."

My face flooded red, remembering my thoughtless behavior in the woods and even worse, talking to Trevor about running away and never dealing with my past life. I hadn't given Oliver a passing thought in that moment.

"I love Oliver. What I did was impulsive. I never would have allowed him to suffer because of me. I straightened myself out," I said.

"Elliot, my Third Timer loves me too," Freddie said, his voice steady with conviction.

I searched my memory, trying to think of a single moment when I'd witnessed David showing kindness or respect to anyone, but came up short.

"Any person who is forcing you to stay here is on some power trip, and that's just wrong. There is no way that can be called love!"

"Miss Turner, you've a lot to learn."

"Then teach me, for God's sake. I thought I was here to have some help."

"Hasn't Mel been helping you?" he asked.

"Of course she's been helping me. She's the one who told me that you were a Passenger and that David was a Third Timer. By the way, David and I had a little argument at Workshop."

"And?"

"And, Mel didn't have time to explain the rest. She went after Trevor and we came here, but it was easy to put the pieces together. I can't believe that you're David's Passenger. All along I thought he worked here as a guide like Mel."

Freddie had a funny expression on his face.

"Elliot, I'm not David's Passenger."

a twist

of

faith

It was my turn to be confused. "What?"

"I'm not David's Passenger," Freddie repeated. "I'm Mel's." He reached for me, but I pulled away, feeling as if I'd lost my footing yet again and was spinning wildly out of control.

"Mel?" My heart plummeted into my stomach.

"Mel doesn't work here, Elliot. No one works here. This is simply a stopping place for souls. You stay until you go."

I continued to back away. Everything here was an illusion. Nothing was what I thought it was. It seemed so much simpler when I was just a dumb, forgetful dead girl.

"Please tell Oliver I'll meet him later."

"Don't run away again."

"I gotta go find Trevor and Mel." My feet were moving me backward toward an escape.

"She does, you know," Freddie yelled out as I neared the door.

I didn't want to be near him anymore.

"Mel, I mean. She loves me. She really does love me."

I was happy he didn't have the same doubts that I did.

It wasn't long before I was cresting the mountain. It was easier to climb when my subconscious wasn't creating obstacles. Mel was sitting cross-legged in the exact place that Trevor and I had leapt from. It was surprising to see someone besides Trevor in *our* place.

"Hello, Elliot. I was keeping an eye out for you," she said, without getting up. There was a sadness in her voice that I'd never heard before. I wanted to grab her by the shoulders and shake her.

"I didn't figure you'd have too much luck finding Trevor, unless he was ready to be found." I plopped down beside her, my feet dangling out into space. An unexpected calm—or was it numbness?—had taken over. I glanced below and marveled at what a difference a single cliff dive could make in overcoming one's fear of heights.

"Truth?" asked Mel. Like I might choose a lie.

I raised my eyebrow in an imitation of her usual gesture.

"Ouch, I guess I deserved that," she said. "The truth is, I went after Trevor and sent you with Oliver so someone else would break the news."

"Why didn't you just tell me?"

"No good excuse, really. It's just that love happens in layers." She smoothed her skirt over her legs.

"What do you mean, layers?"

"I've known you through three visits to the Obmil, Elliot. Every time you came here, you were someone different. But your soul, that was constant. As I got to know that soul, I loved it a little bit more every day. At what moment do you love and trust someone enough to share everything? The day I realized that I loved you and trusted you that much was the same day I started wondering if you loved and trusted me enough not to think my admission came too late. It was—"

"Like standing on the edge and not knowing if the leap would result in falling or flying," I finished.

"That wasn't my exact thought, but yes, that was the general feeling." She made a little noise in her throat that was hard to interpret.

"I'm sorry," I said.

"For?" Confusion flitted across her features.

"For not being perfect." I realized I was apologizing to myself as much as to Mel.

She reached out and ran her fingers through my hair—not for connection like Oliver and not charged with electricity like when Trevor touched me. This was different. Her bracelets jingled softly in my ear.

Her touch was absolution from my self-imposed sins.

Mel cleared her throat. "So, now you remember everything." It was a statement not a question.

"I thought that when we remembered, it would all be clear, but it's just made me more confused." I sighed and tugged on a loose thread dangling from my shirt.

"Don't go back to being so hard on yourself. You'll make it unbearable for me."

My head whipped around in surprise.

"I've been here, lost in my own confusion, for so much longer than you. I have my own issues of failure to deal with. If you have the right to be so harsh with yourself then what should I feel like about my track record?" She smiled, softening the words, knowing how easily I took on new forms of guilt.

Curiosity nudged at me. "Can you tell me about it?" I asked. I needed something to keep me from leaping off this cliff and retracing what little I knew of where Trevor might have gone.

Mel pulled me back. "No one works at the Obmil."

"I heard," I said. The sarcasm leaked out, but I tried to rein it in. "But you were placed with me."

Mel shook her head.

"But—but I remember it. You were the guide who was assigned to me."

"Everyone is here for a reason. I'm not a guide, Elliot, just a Third Timer like you, except I've been here a lot longer."

"I was so sure," I responded, feeling like a big idiot.

"Your assumption wasn't crazy. You arrived needing someone, and I needed to be wanted."

I nodded, capitulating a little.

"There are plenty of 'guides' around here. The more the assumption happens, the more real it feels. Lots of souls find themselves lingering here."

"Souls like Freddie?" I knew I was baiting her, but I couldn't help myself.

"I'm assuming you know he's my Passenger?"

There I was, standing on the edge again, wanting to sympathize with Mel and at the same time feeling angry that she was holding Freddie captive in the afterlife.

"Yes. He said he knows you love him."

"I really do, but I feel so guilty. He's always telling me to relax because he's got nowhere else to be, but that just makes it worse. He signed on to help my soul grow and he can't move on until I leave here." Mel broke into choking sobs.

I slid closer and gathered her up in my arms. "Oh, sweetie..." I crooned in her ear. "It's okay. We'll do this together. I won't leave you here. You should've let me help you. I had no idea." I felt her begin to relax and calm down with every word I spoke. I squeezed her shoulder, keeping her close to me.

"Elliot, can you tell me how you were able to do it? How were you able to Delve outside the classroom? I've never met anyone who's done that before. I didn't even know that it could happen. Leave it to a bunch of teenagers to push the boundaries."

I thought about it a minute. "It actually was easy. We just kind of let go. Had a giant emotional surge." I created a couple of tissues to hand to her.

She clutched the wad between her fingers.

"I saw David, Delving in his room. So did Freddie. That means even David knows how to do it."

"Oh, I think you misunderstood. David wasn't Delving, he was having a nightmare."

"How do you know?" I asked. It had seemed like he was Delving to me.

"David can't Delve because you have to be a Third Timer to bring up the memories."

"But you told me he was a Third Timer." I couldn't keep the exasperation out of my tone.

"Yes, but there's a catch. David doesn't think that he's a Third Timer. In order to Delve, you have to *be* a Third Timer, aware of your soul. He isn't cognizant."

"So he thinks he really works here?"

"Believes it with a passion, as I'm sure you've witnessed." Mel gave a little humph.

"How long has he been here?"

"Now, that's a good question because I've been here longer than dust, and David greeted me when I arrived."

We both nudged each other at the exact same time.

"Well, that explains it. That first meeting must have stunted your spiritual growth," I said.

Mel smoothed her billowy skirt and stared off into the horizon.

"Gosh, I wish it were that easy. It would be nice to blame someone else for being stuck here at the Obmil, but this has been my choice."

"Even though Freddie's been stuck here with you?"

I regretted the question the moment it flew out of my mouth. Mel's face lost its color.

"Wow. I've always let myself believe that everything was all right as long as Freddie wasn't complaining. He's always seemed content to wait until I was ready to move on. My, that does sound horribly selfish, doesn't it?"

I wanted to say something to make her feel better, but I was afraid of putting my foot in my mouth again. I felt terrible saying something that hurt her.

"It's okay, Elliot. This isn't your fault. These are my issues and I have to find a way to deal with them. But let's change the subject for a minute."

I moved my hand toward her to protest, but she wrapped her fingers around mine and said, "Trust me, helping you is helping me. So, you and Trevor . . ."

"This is so confusing. And weird. But somehow, in the middle of all the damn Delves"—I cracked my knuckles one finger at a time—"I fell in love with him. After that, even when he was rude or mean, it still hurt me, made me unsure of myself, but I never felt the isolation that I felt in the beginning. Once I was connected to him, it was easier to remember my past."

"Does he love you too?" she asked in a whisper.

"I don't know. We have a strong connection but . . ." There were moments when I was so sure that he did love me. But maybe I was confusing him with the Trevor who adored me in our past life. Or maybe it was just the intensity of the things we'd shared. I pictured our leap off the cliff. I felt the tug behind my navel that you get when you ride a roller coaster. I wasn't sure if the pull was a reminder of our flight downward or the simple fact that thinking of Trevor did the strangest things to my insides. It wasn't just those brief, confusing kisses either. It was the way he examined me sometimes, like he could see my soul. Like he believed in me.

"In the moment we leapt off the cliff together I was so sure he loved me, but when we surfaced from the Delve, everything was all wrong." My stomach tightened.

"The instant we leapt, I wasn't afraid of anything. It wasn't like the past, when I fell off the cliff in real life—when I died. The first time, it was intense, especially the moment when I saw Trevor jump. The physical impact of the fall and the emotional impact of my life collided with indescribable force. Then I surrendered and everything became soft and blue and your hand reached for mine."

Mel squeezed my fingers.

"This time . . ." I swallowed past the lump in my throat. "This time when I jumped with Trevor, I did it without expectations. I was ready to just be whatever I was. I longed to move forward, no matter where that took me. This time I wasn't alone—I jumped with Trevor."

"Maybe *you* should work here, Elliot." Mel's voice caught.

"Oh, Mel." I didn't know what to say to make her feel better. "The only thing I know how to do is to share with you what I figured out about myself. Do you want to know what my life lesson was?"

"You know that now?"

"Yes—I'm pretty sure I'm starting to understand it. The patterns of my life, or I guess I should say lives, is all about forgiveness. I had trouble forgiving others, trouble allowing myself to be forgiven, and the biggest one of all was deciding that I was worthy of my own absolution. I was living in a kind of isolation with no real faith in anyone, not even myself. In my last life, I almost figured out the growth plan after meeting Trevor. Over the summer, when we became close, I started to believe that I could have a life and love. I had hope, despite what had occurred. I started to believe that an accident didn't erase a soul . . ."

"So, what happened?"

"We left the shelter of our world of two. We went back to school. He convinced me that together we could open the eyes of everyone else. He believed that if we were together, every-thing would turn out all right. We made a gamble that, deep down inside, people are good."

"Are you saying they really aren't?"

"No." I took a deep breath. "They really are good at heart, but I couldn't hang on until *they* remembered it. I was so fragile, which gave them free rein to steal my hope, but at the last minute I found my stride. I'd like to think it would have been enough if I hadn't fallen, but I'll never know for sure. I'd like to think that I would've made it—that I found something true in myself."

The words floated in the air, swirling around like the eagles. I felt lighter having said things out loud too. I pulled my knees up, hugging them.

"Trevor killed himself. He jumped after me." Maybe if I said this out loud, it would somehow make it easier to bear.

"Maybe he was trying to—"

"No." I shook my head. "He admitted it. He knew I never would have survived a fall from that height. Our eyes connected when I was falling backward, right before I hit the water. He decided to follow."

Mel's face clouded over.

"He heard—well, we've both heard the rumors. People who commit suicide go to hell. Everyone says so." I stopped talking, not knowing what else to say. I felt my old fears pressing back in on me. I couldn't sit here and wait for him any longer. Even if it was hopeless, I needed to be out and moving, trying to find him. "And when I came back this time, you insinuated the same thing. You said that there were consequences to staying here—but wait, *you've* stayed here—"

Before I could finish, Julia came dashing up the path, her

cheeks flushed with exertion. She was panting, and as she got close she hugged her waist and doubled over. Mel and I jumped up simultaneously. I sucked in my breath, flashes of Julia's withered body moving through my mind. She'd been a walking corpse when I'd last seen her in the Delve and it was hard to erase that visual, even though she now stood in front of me, petite but not sickly. I shuddered.

"Are you all right?" Mel asked, fussing like the mother Julia never got to have.

I stood very still, although my insides teetered back and forth like a seesaw. I'd just talked about forgiveness and believing that all souls were ultimately good. And yet, the hurt I felt when I was near Julia was like a bruise. In some ways it had gotten deeper, more layered over time. Then there was the jealousy. I loved Trevor and I had no idea what he felt for Julia—or, for that matter, what he felt for me.

Her breathing slowed and she lifted her head. Her delicate hand slid into the messenger bag strung sideways across her chest. Resting on the palm of her hand was an origami crane. The paper was a wild pattern of blue and black. It made me think of Trevor.

She walked toward me, hand extended with her peace offering floating on her palm. "I don't love Trevor." She blinked rapidly. "What I mean to say is that I do love him, but I'm not *in love* with him."

"Oh."

I extended my palm until my fingertips touched hers.

"I needed him. I was drawn to him." She grasped the fragile crane between her thumb and pointer finger. "There's a weird connection between us. It's not the same as the one you have with him, but there's something that drew us together. It was irresistible, considering that I was so lonely without you." She slid the crane onto my palm and dropped her hand. I was the one left holding everything.

"You didn't have to be lonely or without me." I cradled the delicate folds of paper, feeling tired of flying in the same old circles with her over and over again.

"I know. I mean—I know that now."

My heart skipped several beats. I couldn't speak for fear that I might've heard her wrong.

"I love you, Elliot. You're my very best friend EVER."

A strangled cry escaped from deep inside me and I crossed the space between us, hugging her tightly to me. "I love you, too. I've missed you so much." That was all I could get out before I crumpled into sobs. We both stayed that way for a while, drenched in tears and sunny raindrops. Above us, the light broke through the clouds, giving the moisture a golden glow. It was a sun shower.

Julia grasped my face between her hands. "I have a million

things to tell you, a zillion things to explain and to make right, but—"

Suddenly there was a hideous crunching noise. It sounded like metal in head-to-head combat with something unforgiving. Then, as if the horrific noise was sucked up into a vacuum, everything was silent.

"What was that?" Something jittery scampered down my spine.

"Yes, what was that?" I'd forgotten that Mel was standing next to us.

"I'm afraid that was Trevor." Julia shivered in my arms.

"Can you take me to him?"

"Yes."

She scampered over to the ledge and pointed to the other side of the lake. Directly across from us was a waterfall that hadn't been there before. The spill off the top of the ridge was furious and slapping violently against islands of boulders jutting out of the water below. I searched every which way, seeking Trevor, but there was nothing to indicate his presence except the eerie feeling that the waterfall was his creation.

"Where is he?" I asked, never breaking my line of sight with the precipitous drop and the water below. What was that gash of red on the rocks? Ice flooded my veins.

"Is that blood?" I pointed my finger in the direction of the goliath boulders that were the farthest from the shore. "Someone answer me! Is that blood on the rocks?"

"It couldn't be," Mel said, sounding shaky.

"It isn't," Julia said. "It's paint. He was driving a red truck when I saw him. He was acting crazy. I'd finished my last Delve and found my path and I wanted to find you guys before I left but he was—"

"You finished your Delves? You're leaving? Without me? No, this can't be. You figured things out, but you're not leaving without me. Right? Of course you're going to wait for us. He's driving Sally? Although, it makes sense, he loved that truck. But why is there red paint on the rocks?" My stomach was churning and my mind was flipping back and forth between a zillion thoughts at once.

"Argh! I quit. I can't do this anymore." I plopped down right where I'd been standing. I hugged my knees to my chest. I wanted to be smaller, so that maybe I could have smaller problems: I wanted to disappear. "I hate this." I dropped my forehead onto my knees.

"You're not a turtle." Mel rubbed my shell.

"I may put in for it—you know, in my next life," I grumped at her.

"I highly doubt you could go that long without speaking."

Mel sounded like she found me entertaining. I hated to be amusing. A little snort snuck out like a traitor.

"Elliot?" Julia's face was awash with emotions. Before I could pinpoint what the primary one might be, there was a sucking sound coming from below the falls. The water on the surface of the lake churned and bubbled. Trevor's truck flew backward out of the water, the front end uncrumpling right in front of us as it landed on the top of the cliff right on the edge of the falls—just like an action movie that someone had run in reverse. From this distance, I couldn't tell if Trevor was inside, but I was going to find out.

Mel took one look at my face and said, "We'll follow you."

I thought about creating a bridge and making a beeline for Trevor, but I wasn't convinced that he wouldn't run at the sight of me. I couldn't risk losing him again. I decided that the quickest way to get over there would be to skirt the rim of the lake at our current height. This way I'd be able to keep an eye on him, without him spotting us. We hadn't gone far when I heard Sally rumble to life.

"He's leaving." I was all set to pick up the pace, even if Mel and Julia couldn't keep up. Just then Trevor revved the engine, and Sally shot forward off the cliff. I knew it wouldn't kill him, but the idea of it made me crazy. I covered my face with my hands, not wanting to see the visual.

"What's his problem?" I threw up my hands.

"He's an idiot." Julia was so sweet and matter-of-fact that I giggled. She smiled conspiratorially at me.

"Yes, he's an idiot." I had to agree. "Come on, let's go save him from himself."

Getting around the lake took a lot longer than expected. By the time we were approximately halfway to our destination, Trevor had driven over the falls a grand total of ten times with no end in sight. Each time Sally's engine roared to life, I stopped and checked out what he was doing, but the minute he hit air, I couldn't watch. I just put my head down and continued our insane rescue mission.

It was attempt number eleven that ignited my fury, pushing me over the edge. As Sally's engine started up, I noticed Oliver standing next to the truck. He was talking to Trevor through the window. *Now* they decided to have a conversation. They hadn't said two pleasant words to each other the whole time we'd been here. My palms were sweating like crazy. I squinted, trying to tell if Oliver was trying to stop Trevor too.

Trevor argued with Oliver and then the truck took off. The next time, Trevor walked away from the truck, deep in conversation with Oliver, then turned and made a mad dash for the cab. On the thirteenth attempt, Trevor threw his keys over the edge, Oliver gave him some space, and then Trevor leaned against the truck's rear bumper, giving a push that started Sally rolling. He hopped into the truck bed. Sally and Trevor were gone before Oliver could reach the edge. Oliver did not seem pleased.

When his brother popped back out of the water in reverse, Oliver took the offensive and latched on to Sally's back bumper. My breath caught, afraid that Trevor wouldn't realize that Oliver was there, but the truck door creaked open and I gave a sigh of relief.

"Trevor's a persistent bugger isn't he?" Mel said.

I nodded, watching Trevor gesticulate wildly while talking to Oliver. Oliver's head bobbed in agreement and he let go of the bumper. Finally, it looked like they were going to stop this nonsense. But both of Sally's doors closed, one after the other like an echo. The significance of the sound registered moments too late for my yell to have any effect. There was no common sense between these boys and now both of them were gone.

deeper

understanding

I took off at a sprint. I didn't care that there were rocks below, that the drop would be messy and I didn't have a vehicle to take the brunt of the landing. I was not going to be left behind. The edge of the cliff was in my sights when my feet left the ground. There was a sharp pain and my whole scalp felt as if it was being peeled off of my head. Instead of seeing the water of the lake below, I saw bright blue sky filled with fluffy white clouds. Just as suddenly as I'd taken flight, I'd landed on my back, pulled back down against the hard ground right where I'd been standing. The air was forced from my lungs and all I could do was wheeze. Julia leaned over me, blocking out the sky above.

"Sorry." She held out her hand. It looked as if a good portion of my ponytail was still stuck to her sweaty palm. "I didn't mean to hurt you. It's just that you shouldn't jump. Sometimes you've got to let other people figure out stuff on their own."

I groaned and rolled over.

"Besides if you hurt that much from this landing, then it wouldn't have been pretty down there, even if you healed yourself quickly." Her head started bopping like a bobblehead doll. I pushed up to my knees and jumped to my feet, feeling better already.

"Oh, for God's sake, will you stop that crazy nodding? You convinced me." I straightened my crooked ponytail. "You couldn't have grabbed my shirt instead?" I gave it a little pull for emphasis. She frowned but didn't say anything. "So, when did you turn into Hercules, by the way?"

"Oh." Julia blushed. "I think it was the adrenaline. I was worried about you."

I studied her face. Took my time, really trying to read her. "You love me. You really love me, don't you?"

She radiated light as if she'd eaten the sun and now glowed from within. "Yes!"

She shined brighter, if that was even possible.

"But you're going to leave without me?"

"Yes." Everything about her was peaceful. She must have felt the shift in me and known that the anger and hurt were gone. Those emotions had flown off the cliff without me when she'd yanked me back.

"You're going right now?"

She reached her hand out, palm facing me. I did the same, my thumb interlocking with hers, our two hands creating the shape of a bird. We both wiggled our fingers, flapping our wings. It had been our secret handshake back when we were twins. When we felt like two halves of the same whole.

"Tell everyone I said good-bye, especially your boyfriend." She winked.

"He's not my—"

"We'll discuss that at a later date." She squeezed my hand.

"You don't know that for sure."

"But I believe it." Julia's thumb slowly unwound from mine. "I left you something in our room." She turned, blew Mel a kiss, and then she was gone to the Basin. Before I could digest what it all meant, Trevor's truck landed back on the top of the rock with a thud that gave Sally's shocks a heavy workout.

My heart raced as the engine revved once more. What was he doing? Was he going over again? Suddenly the truck shifted gears and flew backward all the way to the tree line. Then it circled around twice and headed straight for us.

Everything dropped away. All I could see was Trevor.

He was grinning all the way up to his baby blues. It took

me a minute to realize that Oliver was bouncing along in the seat next to him, giving a whoop every time Trevor hit a bump. From the expression on Trevor's face, I would've bet anything that he was hitting every gully he could find, just to hear Oliver's laughter and know he was the cause of it. Finally, something had changed for the better.

Right in front of me, Trevor threw it into park and jumped out. He was different. I couldn't put a finger on it at first but then I realized he appeared lighter. He had on a deep green T-shirt instead of his usual black one, and it was missing his typical commentary. He also wore a pair of jeans and brown leather boots. Before I could tease him about his new look, he strode toward me and crushed me to his chest. He rested his knuckle under my chin, tilting my face to his.

He leaned in close and whispered, "We need to talk, but we only have a minute. *My little brother* wants to speak with you. He's been jabbering about you nonstop in the truck, yapping about this special connection you both have. I love him, but we'd better sort this out before I forget that." He didn't seem mad when he said it, but I was cautious. I'd gotten to know him pretty well lately.

Staring up at him, I knew with certainty that ice could burn. I didn't expect my knees would work much longer if he kept whispering in my ear like that.

As if he could read my thoughts, he wrapped his arm around my waist, pulling me tighter up against the length of him. It was becoming harder and harder to remember how much I'd disliked him when we had first arrived here.

I reached for him, up on tiptoes. A hairsbreadth separated us. I was mere seconds away from melting into a puddle when I felt Oliver tap me on the shoulder. He was lucky that I loved him just as much as his older brother.

"Elliot, tell him that I'm not in love with you."

My gaze stayed locked on Trevor. "He's not in love with me."

"So I've heard. What I want to know is, do you love him?"

"Yes, I do." Trevor's face paled. I hesitated a moment. "I love him like a brother."

Trevor turned to face Oliver. "Are you sure you're not trying to steal my girl?" he asked.

"Do you ever listen when I talk to you?"

"Just answer the question." Trevor was more serious than I'd ever seen him, which was saying a lot.

Oliver sighed. "You're just as pigheaded as when—never mind. No, I am not trying to steal your girl."

I interjected, "I'm standing right here. I'm not your favorite skateboard, guys." Both of them were starting to get on my nerves with the whole possessive cowboy routine. "Do I get a say in this?"

Trevor cleared his throat. "Good." His shoulders visibly relaxed.

"But you have to share." Oliver gestured first at his brother, then at me. "We're best buds, right, Elliot?"

They were impossible. If I was smart I'd run and catch up with Julia, but I couldn't leave them. After eyeballing each other for over a minute and sniffing the air, checking out each other's testosterone, they both stuck out their hands and shook on it—whatever *it* was. I stepped back and all of a sudden they were back to being kids, wrestling with each other and goofing around. I turned to Mel for a little help.

"Don't look at me, you picked 'em." She chuckled and I groaned, jumping between the two of them like some kind of referee. They were still playfully jabbing at each other as I grabbed their hands and yanked them toward the truck.

"Where we going?" they both asked at the same time.

I nodded at Sally and glanced sharply at Trevor. "I need to know what happened after you left me, literally treading on thin ice. Where did you go? You seem different . . ."

Trevor threw his leg over the side of the pickup, climbing into the truck bed, and extended a hand to pull up Mel. Oliver and I followed.

"Well, that is easily answered," said Trevor. "I went to hell and back."

hell

and

back

"You did what?" I asked, glaring at Trevor from across the truck. He looked amused and I noticed his shirt. BY THE TIME YOU'VE READ THIS, YOU'VE ALREADY READ THIS. I bit the inside of my cheek to keep from smiling. Then I leaned back against the tire well, using Oliver's arm as a pillow.

"Well, after I stalked off and left you on *thin ice*"—he shrugged—"I was half crazed."

"H—" I'd started to say "Half?" when I saw Mel shake her head. My jaw reluctantly banged shut.

"As I was saying, I was not in my right mind. I'd picked a fight with you. I was trying to push you away before you were taken from me. When I came up out of the middle of the lake, with my memory intact and you in my arms, it was heaven.

Then I realized the implications of what I'd done. That I might lose you. It was worse than never having you at all. I just had to get out of there. I'm sorry for hurting you."

"I didn't help either," I whispered, wishing he were sitting next to me. "I was stupidly wrapped up in my own absolution. I was overjoyed that I hadn't jumped on purpose. It was so thoughtless of me." Oliver grabbed my hand and gave it a squeeze. I was waiting for Mel to chastise me for interrupting again, but she just listened.

"Well, I got about halfway up the mountain, on the other side of the lake, and I got really mad at you. You wouldn't have liked the things that were running across my shirt." Trevor swallowed another laugh. "Anyway, long story longer—I was mad at you because I wasn't a hiker."

"You were mad at me for what?" I was flabbergasted. "You hiked with me all the time in our last life and you certainly hiked with me here at the Obmil."

"And I enjoyed it, but it's *your* thing. Remember that first time we left Oliver's grave and went up the mountain together?"

I nodded. It was hard to believe I'd ever forgotten.

"You said that we were going to the place where you went to think. The climb cleared your head. Do you remember what I told you I liked to do?"

"You drive," I said.

"Well, I was so upset and angry to start with, that I didn't know what to do with myself. I became focused on wanting to drive *my* truck. Then I got even angrier when I realized that I'd never seen a single vehicle here at the Obmil. I was murderous as I thought of everyone hoofing it all over the place. That's when I decided to quit."

"Quit what?" I asked, unable to stay quiet either.

"Quit hiking," Trevor said. "I decided that if I wasn't moving on to something better, then I was going to drive to hell in the truck of my dreams with the radio blaring." He reached his arm over the side and gave Sally's fender a good rub with the sleeve of his shirt.

"I focused everything I had on visualizing my red truck. I was at the frog pond sitting in the little gazebo, concentrating like crazy, when the tree line opened up. Out of nowhere, a packed dirt road and my truck emerged. I suppose I shouldn't have been surprised, but I'd never created anything at the Obmil that didn't seem organic to the place. Everyone creates weather and helps to create the buildings. We all create other little characteristics that make the place feel right for us. This seemed different, like it was a sign that I really was on my way to—"

He broke off when he saw the hurt in my face.

"So then what? You drove to hell? And you decided to take Oliver along for the ride. You left without saying good-bye to me." I would have murdered him if he weren't already dead. I thought I was done yelling at him, but I got a second wind. "What if you hadn't come back?" I said, feeling the loss of him all over again.

He hopped to his feet and gave Oliver a look that very nicely asked him to scram. Oliver leaned in my direction. "Just remember, you picked him." His voice was playful and he ruffled my hair as he stood up and moved over to Mel. I leaned back, ready to settle back against the tire well when— *whoosh*—Trevor grabbed me up onto his lap, tucking my head beneath his chin, arms wrapped around me tight.

"I'm sorry, sweetheart. I didn't mean it that way, I swear. I tried to picture saying good-bye to you for good. I couldn't believe that it might be possible for me to die when I was already dead."

I didn't want to admit it, but he was right. It would have been excruciating.

Trevor continued when he felt me relax in his arms. "So I had my truck and I had my destination, and I just needed a way to get from point A to point B. I figured if leaping off a cliff worked to go back in time, maybe it would push me forward into hell."

"So I got in the car and started driving. There was only about a driveway's length of road in front of me at any given time and when I checked the rearview mirror, the trees fell back into place, erasing where I'd just been. It was kind of weird, because I couldn't *see* where I was going. All I could do was picture where I wanted to be. I definitely didn't want it to be on our cliff—that place had become special. So I created the waterfall."

I sucked in my breath. "Did it hurt to hit the rocks?" I tried to block out the hideous images, but my imagination ratcheted everything up another couple degrees. "You're reckless!" I spat, jumping out of his arms so I could see him better.

"Shhhhhhh—it didn't really hurt. It was kind of like taking a metal crowbar to a light post. It was a very intense vibration. I also made sure to start thinking about healing myself on the way down. I anticipated," he said sheepishly.

"I went over the cliff fourteen times, but I only would have had to do it once if I was paying attention. I hadn't realized that I'd landed straight in the middle of hell on my first launch."

"Please explain," Mel asked quietly.

"Well, the first time I sped off the cliff, I reflexively closed my eyes. I didn't open them again until the vibrations had settled down. I realized I wasn't knocked into a Delve, so I just floated there for a while. Down in the depths below Sally, there were bubbles and a deep iridescent blue glow. It reminded me of what it felt like to die and come to the Obmil through the lake. My mind was made up. I was going to see it through. I was determined to find my way to hell. So I kicked my feet and headed downward."

"I can't stand this, Trevor, spit it out! Was it hell? If it was, why didn't you know it was hell the first thirteen times you were down there?" I asked.

"Every single time I came close to reaching the light in the depths of the lake, I couldn't quite make it. I didn't need to worry about running out of breath, so I strained against this force, a gravitational pull toward the surface that wouldn't let me get too close. I swam down with everything I had and that's when I saw it."

I held my breath, imagining a zillion different things. "What did you see?" I asked in a whisper.

"It was you."

My head began to spin. Me? It couldn't have been me. I'd been with Mel the whole time.

"As I moved closer to the blue light and the bubbles, I could see you floating in the water. I don't remember what you looked like when you fell from the cliff and died. Everything happened so fast. Yet somehow, I knew without a doubt, that you must have looked like this. Your hair was seaweed dancing in the river current.

"I went after you. I struggled and came close enough to almost reach you, and then you reached for me, as if you had something so important to say. I yelled out in frustration, unable to understand, and then—*BAM!*—I was transported out of the lake. I found myself standing back up on the cliff, right in my truck, as if it had never happened. I was insane the first time. Nothing was going to make me leave you, so I jumped back in my truck, revved the engine and did it all over again."

"Fourteen times," I said.

"Yeah, fourteen times, but it probably would have been more if Oliver hadn't shown up." He stared across the truck bed, his face lit with adoration for his younger brother.

My arms got goose bumps.

"I materialized back on the ledge after try number seven and there was Oliver standing next to my truck. If you thought that I was an ass to him earlier, you should have seen me then. I was hell-bent, literally, and he wouldn't get out of the way until I told him what I was doing. I wasn't very polite about my irritation.

"When being mean didn't get him to budge—I lied. I told him I wasn't going to drive off again," Trevor said. "It worked the first time, but he's kind of wily. It got progressively more difficult to sidetrack him, then race back to the truck quick enough to get back to you. I was more exhausted from dealing with Oliver than I was from repeatedly dashing myself against the rocks. By the end of my thirteenth trip, he'd figured out that if he held on to the back bumper, I wouldn't have enough time to get away.

"I only had one option left," continued Trevor. "I slowed down, caught my breath, and told him what was going on."

My heart lurched. I could see how important this was to him.

"It felt good to tell someone, didn't it?" Mel's voice got Trevor's attention. He nodded.

"I know the feeling." She dipped her chin in my direction.

Trevor continued. "It was incredible to have a connection with Oliver. It was actually a bit surreal. By fixing the here-and-now I apparently mended something from further back between us."

"Awwwww," I squealed, seriously delighted that they were finally on the same team. This wasn't just a superficial fix, it felt deeper.

Trevor continued. "I had nothing left after that. I didn't know how to fix any of it. Opening up to Oliver took the fight right out of me. I decided to drive Oliver and myself back to the Haven, but . . ."

"I wouldn't even consider it," Oliver said.

I crinkled up my forehead, knowing what was coming.

"Aw, Elliot, don't look at me like that." Trevor hopped out of the truck bed and started moving around. "He's a big boy and he wanted to. He's already dead anyway." His face begged me to understand. "Besides, I knew from experience that it wasn't going to hurt." Trevor took a step back as I got to my feet.

I was mad. I threw a leg over the back of the truck and jumped down, moving toward him. Somewhere deep inside, I knew I was overreacting, but I didn't care. I felt like throttling Trevor, so I kept my focus. "You should have known better. After what he's been through, what I did to him. The car accident!" My words shot out in an angry hiss.

"Oh, for God's sake, Elliot, he's over that. Everyone is over that—everyone but you, anyway. No one is blaming you for what happened to Oliver." Trevor threw up his hands in exasperation.

"It was my job, Elliot. I'm a Passenger." Oliver spoke gently. "It's what I chose."

I couldn't digest the info quick enough for a comeback so I sat and stewed. No one said anything for at least a full minute.

"Okay, then . . ." Trevor cleared his throat. "We decided that Oliver would drive off the cliff with me."

"He made sure I buckled up," Oliver said in a ridiculous attempt to defend his brother.

"For safety reasons," Trevor finished. "When we hit the water and the rocks—it didn't hurt at all."

"It was fun," added Oliver.

Acid churned in my stomach, burning its way out into the air. I hadn't known I was even thinking about it, let alone going to say it out loud. Seconds before I was calm and understanding, now the words sped past my teeth.

"Tell me, Oliver, was it fun the first time you unbuckled your seat belt?"

rubber

band

"What the hell?" Trevor barked at me. He was finally his brother's keeper.

I held my ground. This I needed to know. I needed to understand why Oliver had compounded my wrong, making everything so unbearable. What purpose had it served?

Oliver grabbed me by the shoulders and turned me so that I had to see his face. I fought the ugly urge to push him away.

"It wasn't fun." Oliver's hands trembled where they gripped my shoulders. "It hurt bad, not the being killed, but the leaving people I loved."

Trevor punched Sally with enough force to make me cringe, but I stayed focused on Oliver. "Then why did you do it?"

"I did it because you needed me to, Elliot. Your soul didn't

believe in itself after its first two visits at the Obmil. That"—
he glanced back at Trevor—"what did you call it earlier? God-
damn-stupid-big-superhero heart of mine? It's who I had to
be. You picked me to be your Passenger and we made promises." Tears ran down his face. "I promised to help you grow."

We were both sobbing now.

"You were so young. You had everything going for you."
My moan was guttural. "How could I make such an amazing
person die?"

"Perhaps I was only amazing because you gave me the
opportunity to be. Maybe I was only a superstar because of
you. Perhaps I died so young because you loved me, Elliot."
He grabbed my face between his palms. "You told me, right
before we jumped streams at the Basin, that you didn't want
me wasting a whole life on you. You knew that when I finished
being your Passenger, I could start a new growth plan for my
own soul. You made me promise not to drag it out because you
loved me too."

I pulled him fiercely to me. In an unromantic way, he was
a perfect match for me.

Somehow the four of us shook off the weighty emotions and
settled back into Trevor's story.

"So we hit the water with no problem." Trevor and Oliver

glanced conspiratorially at each other and then looked at me to gauge my reaction. I purposely yawned.

"Just like before, everything cleared, and the bubbling blue light glowed beneath me. I grabbed Oliver's hand and we started to swim to the place I'd last seen you."

"Can I interrupt you for a minute, Trevor? I have a question." Mel waited for Trevor's nod. "The Elliot floating in the water—was she alive or was she dead?"

"I think she was dead. That's why it freaked me out so much when she reached for me, like she was trying to communicate." Trevor touched my arm, as if to make sure I was still really there.

"Like I expected, you were floating where I'd left you the first thirteen times. I pulled Oliver with me to try to get to you. I thought that maybe with the two of us, we would be strong enough to get you out, to rescue you." I heard the catch in his voice.

"So, what happened?" I felt oddly disconnected from my racing heart.

"Oliver got one glimpse of you and hightailed it out of there. He was like an Olympic swimmer."

"Finally, a male with some sense," I mumbled under my breath. "What did you do?"

"I was disappointed," he said, "but I went after Oliver."

310

The expression on his face told the deeper truth . . . it had been so much more than disappointment.

"The moment I made the move to follow Oliver, we both materialized back up on the ledge. Sally was no worse for wear again so . . ."

"So you would have gone right back out again." Mel tsked and Trevor had the grace to look embarrassed. "Isn't there a famous quote about insanity?"

"I know, I know, the one about doing the same thing over and over and believing you'll get a different result. Oh, trust me, Mel, it's a harder lesson to learn when it's pointed out to you by your younger brother."

"So, what changed?" I said.

"Oliver told me it wasn't you. He was right, of course. When I checked, there you were, standing right in front of me. The moment I saw you alive and right there, something jiggled loose in my brain and everything made sense."

"Wish it made sense to me," I said grumpily.

"There is no hell or heaven."

I heard Mel suck in her breath.

"Not in the traditional sense anyway," Trevor said quickly. "There's no destination hell, no location for heaven. There's life and afterlife, which translates into—just more life." His head bobbed as if he had made perfect sense. And in a way, he had.

It was weird, the idea seemed so logical—a complete no-brainer. I found it hard to believe that it had eluded me for so long.

"You'd created your own hell down there in the water."

Trevor nodded.

"You could have stayed there an eternity, punishing yourself."

"I almost did," he said softly, glancing at his brother.

"So, you're telling me that the worst punishment that you could come up with was . . ."

"The most awful thing I could imagine was being unable to reach you."

I breathed in the moment, memorizing it so I would know how to find it again. I hadn't known heaven would feel like this.

What was happening between us was so much more than just touching the surface.

"Oliver, I could use an escort back to the Haven," Mel announced. "Do you think you could come with me? I have a few people I need to talk to." Oliver tucked her fingers into the crook of his arm. Together they headed down the path.

Trevor grabbed my hand and pulled me toward Sally's cab.

We reached the passenger-side door.

"Julia's gone," I blurted out. He didn't say anything.

I waited, everything inside me on pause.

"I'll miss her," he said. "We had a connection."

"A connection?"

"You."

I felt overexposed. I turned around to give myself a moment to think.

"Oh, I forgot," he said.

I pulled the handle of the truck, but it wouldn't budge. His hand was propped up against the top of the door.

"Forgot what?" I asked, turning my back to the sun-warmed metal.

Trevor leaned in closer and whispered in my ear. "I forgot how worked up you get about kissing." From the look in his eye, he hadn't forgotten any such thing. "You want me to kiss you." He twirled a strand of my hair around his fingertip and said, "This isn't the first time I've been to heaven, I just didn't know I was there before. There were moments in my last life and in this one that would qualify. I've loved you in both worlds, but it doesn't really count if you don't know it's heaven, does it?"

I knew exactly what he meant. All the different times in my last life, and here at the Obmil, that I would have considered myself to be in heaven—if I'd only looked at things that way. It was the moments of learning to trust and love Trevor, but not only those: hanging out with Oliver, being hugged by Mel, having a best friend in Julia, wearing Freddie's scented flannel. They were bits and pieces of heaven too. Even the night that I starred in the school play was a moment of heavenly bliss. How strange that it was so quickly followed by a complete immersion into hell. Maybe life was designed to be a seesaw, back and forth.

"Trevor?" I glanced up quickly, forgetting how close he was. The top of my head smashed into his nose.

"Damn it, Elliot, do you ever make kissing easy?" he said, cupping his nose.

"Maybe you should learn not to be such a tease and get to it a little quicker," I shot back.

"So, I've got to get to the kissing before you start thinking too hard about something else?"

"Something like that," I said, reaching to check his nose. He winced.

"You'll heal in a minute," I said with a smirk.

"You're impossible," he groaned. "What have you got for me?" He winced again, but I could tell he was faking it, searching for sympathy points. If he could recover quickly from numerous truck dives, I doubted the top of my head would do any lasting damage.

"Heaven and hell, a state of mind? Is that what we're agreeing to?" I asked, getting serious again.

"That's the word floating around the cosmos," Trevor said.

"It makes sense, when you think about it," I said, "but what happens when you're not thinking about it?"

"What do you mean?"

"A life experience is designed to help a soul grow, to learn. It's a role-play without you knowing you're playing a role. When you're in a life, it's almost impossible to internalize that all events happen perfectly, no matter how imperfect they feel at the time."

"So you think there's no free choice? That doesn't feel right to me. I made a ton of choices, some good and some bad. I had to live with the consequences, remember?" Trevor said.

"Imagine that the premise is wrong. What if there is endless free choice and not a single choice is right or wrong? Could every choice be a possibility? What if every option feels good or bad based only on our perception of it? Or if all the 'rules' aren't really rules? What would happen if just being in the moment was an option?"

I knew I was onto something, because he ran his fingers through his hair.

I took it a step further. "The moment I killed Oliver was the moment I discovered hell on earth, but what would've happened if I hadn't let it be a hell?"

"I don't know if that's possible, Elliot. How can you not be traumatized by that kind of thing?"

"I'm not talking about eliminating the emotional turmoil. That's a big part of the learning. What I want to know is what would happen if"—I struggled to find the right words—"we all did what you did?"

"What did I do?"

"There was that moment, at Oliver's grave, where you let it all go. I saw it in your eyes. From that point on, I wasn't the Elliot who had done something bad. I was just Elliot, the girl who had the experience. You saw *me*."

"You mean, what if the judgments stopped?"

"What if we stopped reacting to everything as if fear was God?" It was right at that moment that the elastic band of my spiritual consciousness snapped. I wasn't capable of reaching out any further into the unknown. I was back to a more realistic state of enlightenment.

"I think you might be right, but it's hard to wrap my mind around it," Trevor said.

"My vision is obscured by all that smoke coming out of your ears," I teased.

"Enough talk."

He took a step closer, pushing me back up against his truck.

"There will be no Delves, no sudden movements that require medical attention. There will be no misinterpreted conversations resulting in someone stalking off in anger." He towered over me, arms braced against the side of his truck, his mouth inches from my ear. "There will be no rescuing Oliver and there will be no spiritually enlightening discussions."

"Uh-huh."

"I'm going to kiss you."

"I . . ."

He touched his finger to my lips. "And there will be no requests for the chocolate bar in the glove department."

My stomach growled. So embarrassing.

"And there will be no beating me to the punch. I love you, Elliot."

His lips replaced his finger and I wound my arms around his neck, unable to get close enough.

"Trevor?"

He gave a low growl, reminding me of his long list of things I was not to do in this moment, but I couldn't help it—this had to be done.

"I love you, too."

He groaned loudly, but for once it was for all the right reasons.

3 4

the be

present

As Trevor's truck bounced toward the Haven, I saw a crowd of familiar people on the large front porch. Mel, Oliver, Freddie, and David were all gesticulating at each other.

Trevor slid Sally under a large oak tree on the side lawn and we both hopped out. I figured this might be my first test, to see if I could keep that heavenly feeling, even under stress. One look at David, spittle flying out of his mouth onto Mel, confirmed that I was nowhere near my goal of enlightenment.

"David, no one here is against you. We are not trying to get you transferred. What Freddie said was true. You don't work here." Mel tried to keep her voice light, but her hands anchored on her hips told a different story.

Trevor shot me a wide-eyed look. I would have filled him

in, but that whole kissing thing . . . I shrugged and took his hand. He was going to have to pick this up on the fly.

"You want me out of here so you can run the whole place by yourself." David had a defensive stance, but he squinted with determination.

"I don't work here either!" Mel's bangles slid from wrists to elbows as she threw up her hands. She scowled at Freddie. "I don't know what else to say to him." She turned to stalk away when she saw Trevor and me coming up the steps of the porch.

I stepped forward. David stared at me and something ignited. The last time we'd met, I'd humiliated him. I should have known that his retreat would only last long enough for him to regroup.

As he powered toward me, ready to put me in my place, one word popped into my head: *heaven*.

"Shit," I said.

Trevor stepped up, ready to defend me. I put my hand on his forearm and shook my head.

"I've got this," I said.

Trevor seemed skeptical, but I caught Freddie out of the corner of my eye. Freddie held up his watch, pointed at it. I was back on the edge again, teetering between understanding and limbo.

"ELLIOT TURNER!" David was almost on me.

I focused in on Freddie's face. He was mouthing the words *be present.*

The answer exploded inside my head. It was all so simple.

Be present.

Be present in the moment.

Be present in time.

Time is a present.

Be the moment.

Nothing before, nothing after . . . just be.

Be a present.

I met David's eye and smiled. He glowered at me and suspicion poured off of him like cologne. I couldn't blame him.

For the first time, instead of seeing all his repulsive characteristics, I saw his armor, his turtle shell. He was coated in protective layers. It dawned on me that living defensively isn't really living—it's simply surviving.

"David." I stared him straight in the face, realizing I didn't even know the color of his eyes until now. They were a warm brown, not so different from mine. "I killed someone and I've been living with that for what feels like an eternity."

David stood stock-still. I couldn't read him, which I took as a good sign.

"One of the worst things is remembering the look on the

face of Oliver's mom when she realized he was gone." I thought about David lying in his bed, more little boy than man, calling for his mother in his nightmares. I reached for his meaty hand. His ring and watch made it feel even heavier in my palm.

"My mom haunts me too. What I did ripped my parents apart, and before they even had a chance to recover, I died. I suspect they think I jumped and killed myself." I couldn't keep the quiver out of my voice.

Trevor squeezed my shoulder.

I wanted to say more, but the tear that was softly sliding down David's face took my breath away.

"I miss my mom too. I'm so sad." He choked out the words. That one tear turned into a flood.

Now I understood . . . surviving life simply wasn't enough.

epilogue

I sat on the wooden rocking chair, feet planted on the railing of the porch that overlooked the lake. I rocked back and forth, the breeze making a soft rustling in the autumn-hued leaves. I was musing about the effects of fall, a season that seemed to encompass both beginnings and endings at the same time.

I'd never seen the Obmil so stable: tranquil, even. Someone somewhere always had a patch or two of autumn, but the other seasons were equally present too. For the first time in my memory, everyone was on the same page, poised between the end of something old and the start of something new.

Julia's letter was in my lap. I'd read it a dozen times. It had been on my pillow, folded in the shape of a giant paper crane and surrounded by hundreds and hundreds of little cranes. I counted them—nine hundred and ninety-nine. At first I thought it was a sick joke until I realized that the last crane Julia had given me was in my pocket. One thousand paper cranes. It was a good sign.

I smoothed the folds of the letter and started reading. I wanted to memorize and internalize the words, so I would never again doubt someone I loved that much.

Dear Elliot,

By the time you read this, I'll be gone. My hope is that we've already fixed things between us, but I still owe you an apology. I'm not sure what drove me to need more; I only know that there was more need and I couldn't seem to find a way to fill it. I was trying to search my soul, and every time I looked, all I could see was you.

Remember our last stop at the Basin, where you wanted me to be your Passenger and I refused? I think you now realize that it wasn't because I didn't want to do that for you, it was because I wanted you to do that for me. But I didn't know how to ask. If I was your Passenger, then who would be mine after you'd figured out the growth plan for your soul, the purpose of your life? I was afraid that you'd move on without me, so I thought it might be better to leave you first.

It was a stupid mistake. I realize now that, like heaven

and hell, invisibility is a choice too. I chose to never be seen and to never be heard. Then I blamed you for that. I also blamed my mother in my last life. She was strong-willed and abusive, and even if I'd stood up to her, it might not have changed anything. She would have worked even harder to dominate me. But it doesn't matter whether I would have won that fight. In the end I didn't even try to fly free. Instead I starved myself until no one could see me. I used anorexia to help me disappear, and I had the odd satisfaction of finally controlling something in the process. It felt good in the moment, but I starved my soul the same way I starved my body.

When I arrived at the Obmil for the third time, a failure once again, something snapped. All I could think about was breaking habits and changing patterns. I didn't want to be stuck and invisible anymore. I wanted more than what was on the surface. Determined to make sweeping change, I turned everything upside down. I wasn't going to leave any stone unturned. It all had to change: even you.

I now know that like Dorothy and her ruby slippers, I had the power all along. I just needed to look inside.

There are lots of things I did that hurt you—like kissing Trevor. We were both so needy. I just want you to know, it was never like that with us. There was a connection, and

I suspect maybe it was because we'd both been suicides. Taking your own life, quickly or slowly, leaves a bruise. We recognized that, even though we weren't sure what made us so protective of each other. And, of course, we both loved you. He's got a good heart. You're perfect for each other.

There are worse things I want to regret about what happened between us, but I'm not going to do it. Part of being visible is showing the bad along with the good and trusting that the people who love you will still love you after they've seen it all. No more regrets.

I'm already starting to feel the pull. My time here is over and I can't stop myself from needing to go. How do I explain it so you'll understand?

I've always felt dominated. It's been my issue, but I'm learning that the things that challenge us have a purpose. I've been controlled and now I've finally discovered how to be in control, but I've never lost control. I've never trusted my instincts, abandoned my head, and followed my heart. I've never stepped foot into that place between falling and flying. My gut tells me that we don't soar in a straight line. Like your eagles, we fly in gorgeous loops. Sometimes it will appear like I'm flying out ahead of you, too far to reach. But all it takes is one small change in perspective and then I'm following you instead. We're a circle, you and I—no, better yet, we're a Mobius strip. One side, one edge—and if you try to separate us, cut us into two, we don't fall apart, we simply make a bigger version of what we already are.

I have faith that the time I've spent with you has only touched the surface. I'll see you soon.

Love~

Julia

I clutched the note to my heart and turned my attention to Sally, now parked in the front driveway. David was helping pack Oliver's favorite tools in a container in the truck's bed, and Freddie was checking the oil under the hood. The very act of it was just silly—neither Oliver's tools nor Sally would be traveling far, since objects don't transfer across time and space.

I fingered my eagle charm, knowing that it, too, would disappear when I moved on to the next leg of my journey, at the Basin. It was daunting to know that I'd acquired so much here, and, like my talisman, all I would eventually have left would be an echo of what I'd learned. I wasn't even sure if I would have the people I loved. Julia was sure, so maybe she was right to go first. I could ride in her tailwind.

I rocked faster. It didn't make sense that in my next life I would be forced to rediscover my old enlightenments and tack on an extra few for good measure.

"Now you can see why I stayed here so long—too long," Mel said as she slipped into the rocker next to me, her chair quickly matching my pace.

But I didn't see. "Why *did* you stay here so long? You still haven't told me, and it's been weeks since we convinced David that he was really an out-of-work, middle-aged man in denial."

I couldn't help but feel the greatest affection for him now. The change had been miraculous. It hadn't been an easy transition. He had so many insecurities and emotional walls to breach, but like an abused animal, he had slowly begun to trust again.

"You did wonders with him," Mel commented, moving her gaze to David and Oliver joking around together in the back of Trevor's truck.

"I think Oliver's been the key, not me. The golden boy just has that effect on people."

"No denying it, Oliver has been a gift to him, but without you, it never would have happened. You figured out that David's ugliness was just a manifestation of his pain." Mel reached over and squeezed my hand.

"It was the most obvious thing I've ever figured out. I don't know why it took me so long to understand."

"You figured it out before me," Mel said, releasing my hand and smoothing out her skirt.

"At least you've always been kind. My behavior was ugly and mean."

"I've been kind because it benefited me. It was my crutch."

"What's wrong with that? Kindness is good no matter how you arrive at it."

"I don't think you're wrong, but my helpfulness here at the Obmil was a kind of selfishness. I had motives for my actions."

"Can you tell me?" I asked again.

"No."

It was hard to keep the hurt from my voice. "Why not? I've shared everything with you. You can trust me."

"I know I can trust you, Elliot. It's not that at all."

"Then why won't you tell me?"

"I just don't know the answer. I've never Delved. I have no idea why I'm here, what I'm avoiding."

The wide wood floor planks creaked. Our rocking chairs were no longer in perfect synchronicity. I stared out over the calm water, feeling my heart sink. So it was for sure. Mel and Freddie would not be leaving the Obmil with Trevor, Oliver, and me today. I had been hoping that Mel would secretly be ready to walk away from here.

"I'm going to do it. After you kids leave, I'm going to

start Delving. I'm finally going to engage with my past. I'll get Freddie out of here."

I could see she meant her words but there was a tinge of something else in her face that made me wonder.

"Listen, I'll go tell Trevor that we're going to delay our exit. We can stay while you Delve and help get you through it, and then we can all take off together. The pull hasn't been that bad up until now."

Mel shook her head, tucking wild curls out of the way as she did so.

"Elliot, please don't take this the wrong way, but I don't want you here."

It was like a fist to the gut.

"Oh, don't look at me like that. I can't do it, sweetie. I can't have another soul held up because I've been incapacitated by my own fears."

I started to protest, to say how much I didn't mind, but Mel put up her finger to stop me.

"It's more than that. I have to do this by myself. I need to start fresh. I'm going to disappear for a little bit, so that I can reinvent myself. When I get back, the people who thought of me as a guide will have moved on. I'll be free to come back here as a Third Timer. A real Third Timer, ready to engage in what I've avoided for so long."

I understood it perfectly, but the idea of it seemed to burn me from the inside out.

"When will I see you again?" I choked out. "I don't want to lose you." The tears came freely now.

"My sweet girl, you can't lose me. That is the one thing I am sure of. I know that my love for you can and will travel through time and space."

"Are you sure you don't want me to stay?"

"I *want* you to stay. I *need* you to leave."

I nodded.

"Besides, you'll still be with me—just like you'll still have your necklace—even when you can't hold it in your hand. You know, I gave you that shortly before you exited the Obmil as a First Timer."

I grabbed for the charm and tried to mask my surprise. I'd been too preoccupied with other things to figure out that mystery.

"It's all right." Mel snorted. "Trevor was a distraction."

"I was a what?" He was close behind me. Knowing he was there sent a shiver up my spine.

"None of your business, Lowry," I said, giving him a playful swat.

"Everything about you is my business, Turner."

I blushed twice, knowing Mel had heard.

"I'm going to check on Freddie," she answered. "Someone has to do an intervention. If he gives Oliver another tool to pack, you'll need to be towed out of the Obmil."

I felt my heart tighten, knowing I was going to be leaving someone else I loved behind.

"I'll see you kids in a little bit," Mel said as she walked lightly across the porch and out into the sun. Her hair glowed with the same vibrancy as the autumn leaves.

I stood and Trevor wrapped me in a big bear hug.

"It'll be okay."

"How do you know?" My words were muffled in his shirt.

"I know because that's what you taught me."

"Me?" I pulled my head back. I couldn't believe I used to despise him.

He kissed the top of my head. "If you could just see yourself you'd understand."

I wanted more tangible proof but I knew he wouldn't give it to me.

"We could stay?" he offered.

"No, we can't," I said, knowing that Julia and Mel had been right all along. For the first time, a small thrill of anticipation washed over me. I had no idea what was out there, no one here did, but it didn't matter. I was acting on faith, and for the first time, it wasn't faith in some unknown entity, it was faith in myself. I could almost feel my inner compass stop spinning wildly and start pointing to my true north. I had grown, and much to my surprise, I was really starting to like this new me.

Trevor cleared his throat and I glanced up at him again. He hesitated, seeming as if he had something to ask.

"What?"

He fiddled around with the belt loop on his jeans.

"After all we've been through together, now you get shy?" I grabbed the loop and pulled him closer.

"Do you remember that Delve when you had picked Oliver instead of me to be your Passenger?"

I was unsure of what he wanted to know.

His face was serious. "Why do you think you didn't pick me? I would have given everything to you too."

I opened my mouth and closed it again. It sounded so superficial to say that one look from him made my pulse race, and I was gambling that I might have more of that.

"I know it's stupid to ask. I was just wondering why I came up short—compared to Oliver."

He was breaking my heart.

I hugged him tight and whispered, "Maybe you can't kiss a Passenger?"

"But you did kiss him."

"Not for very long . . ."

I could feel him relax, melt into me.

"Then I'm not signing up to be your Passenger in our next life either," he said, his lips catching mine.

We walked slowly over to the truck. Mel was hugging Oliver, and David had started helping Freddie with the vehicle maintenance. It was bittersweet seeing them like this. I walked up to Freddie and grabbed him around the middle, not even trying to come up with the words. I inhaled his mix of root beer and motor oil that was so oddly comforting.

"Well, I'll be." Freddie spoke with a mixture of awe and authority.

He was staring off across the lake. I turned, following his gaze. A lone eagle circled the exact spot where I had exited the water as a new Third Timer. It seemed like an eternity ago. It was hard to recall the girl I'd been back then. I wondered if I appeared as different on the outside as I felt on the inside.

"She's beautiful," I whispered.

"Yes, she is."

I felt his broad fingers brush the top of my head.

We piled into the truck. I was wedged between the Lowry boys. Trevor's hand lay across the back of the seat and I felt his arm resting against my neck. I peered out the window and was hit by a wave of panic.

"What if I mess it up again?" I asked.

"What if you can't mess it up?" Mel said through the window.

"What if I can't remember that I can't mess it up? Which means that I'm completely capable of messing up something that's unable to be messed up." The corners of my mouth crept up. It sounded dumb even to me.

"It's just your nerves talking. The unknown is scary for everyone. Why do you think I've stayed here so long?"

I nodded. The unknown was disconcerting; I didn't even know how we'd leave the Obmil. Most souls avoid their fear of the unknown by wrapping it in the familiar. They exit the Obmil the same way they came in.

I'd thought about it, but too much had happened in that water. I wanted a clean break. It wouldn't have mattered anyway. Trevor and Oliver had outvoted me. It seemed that they both had a passion for the road. Neither one of them was giving up their relationship with Sally until they were forced to. My consolation prize was supreme authority over the radio.

Mel leaned in, stretching over Oliver and moving her head close to mine. I thought she was going to whisper something in my ear, but she reached around my neck, unhooking the necklace she had once given me. Stepping back, she smiled and gently dropped the charm, followed by the spirals of chain, into her palm.

I wanted to ask why, but Trevor had shifted the truck into gear and we began to roll across the crunching gravel drive. Maybe she needed the necklace more than me now. Maybe she was trying to tell me that I was ready to fly on my own. Maybe, as I kept being reminded, it didn't matter either way. I watched her in the side-view mirror until the trees ate up the manicured lawn.

The three of us bumped along in silence for several minutes.

I reached over and pushed the button on the radio. The sounds of Annie Lennox filled the cab.

"My my where do I go?
My my what do I know?
My my we reap what we sow.
They always said that you knew best,
But this little bird's fallen out of that nest now.
I've got a feeling that it might have been blessed,
So I've just got to put these wings to test."

Trevor looked at me and winked, while Oliver stuck his head out the window like a big yellow dog. I watched the road up ahead, creating itself as we drove forward. A quick peek over my shoulder confirmed that it ceased to exist once we'd moved on.

"So, where we going?" Oliver was bouncy with anticipation.

I wanted to say something profound, worthy of this big step we were taking, but I couldn't put the feeling of serenity, anticipation, and fear together coherently.

I turned to Trevor for support and nearly choked when I saw his T-shirt slogan. GOING NOWHERE FAST!

"Really?" I asked.

"You never know," he said, full of mischief.

"You never know," I repeated, knowing there was truth behind his playfulness. I leaned my head back to rest on Trevor's arm. The breeze from the open windows washed over me. "I don't think it really matters where we go, I think it's just important to go."

"Together," added Trevor.

"Together," repeated Oliver.

I didn't say it aloud, but the words "you never know" still lingered on the surface of my thoughts. . . .

acknowledgments

To my agent, Michelle Wolfson, and my editor, Anica Rissi—before I started the search for agent and editor, I thought very carefully about what I truly wanted out of those two relationships. I believe in the power of intentions—the magic of words let loose into the universe. Looking inside myself, I realized that what I wanted more than anything in the world were two people I could be myself with. I repeated that wish over and over until you came into my life. Michelle and Anica, you are everything I ever dreamed of and more than I could've imagined. Together, we make a bigger version of what we already are. This is our book.

My deepest thanks to everyone at Simon Pulse who took *Surface* under their wing and helped it to fly. Especially

Bethany Buck, Mara Anastas, Jessica Handelman, Katherine Devendorf, Michael Strother, Guillian Helm, Jen Klonsky, Carolyn Swerdloff, and Virginia Herrick. This newbie-goober is indebted to you. I must also give a howl to Michelle Wolfson's Wolf Pack. My thanks to Tawna Fenske, Linda Grimes, and Kiersten White for the warm welcome; Monica Bustamante-Wagner for being a new pup with me; and Kasie West, Daisy Whitney, and Alyssa Schwartz for giving me someone to haze. Once you go Pack . . . you never go back.

Thanks to Laurie Halse Anderson for being the very first person to ever treat me like a writer—it made all the difference. And to K. L. (Kelly) Going, my "Writer Mama"—you encouraged me to tell the world. I hope I've made you proud. Thank you for believing in me.

Thank you to Heather McElduff for the author luncheon and the driveway. It was pivotal. Much appreciation goes to Chris Shave for sitting next to me at my first conference. I might have left if you hadn't. And much love to the rest of C'RAP—Children's 'Riters Always Procrastinate—especially Linda Hanlon, Michelle Mead, Dean Pacchiana, and Roxanne Werner. I'm also grateful to everyone who's been such a big part of my life through my local Shop Talk and SCBWI (Society of Children's Book Writers & Illustrators) Eastern NY. You have all become such wonderful friends. Additionally, I must give a shout-out to everyone at SCBWI Eastern PA for making me an "honorary" Pennsylvanian.

I would also like to give hugs to all those friends and beta readers who have given me feedback and support. The whole crew of District 14, Rachel Houston, Jessie Harrell, Haley Burns, Lindsay Pologe, Alicia Rowell, Erin Sine, Phyllis Garella, Lisa Koosis, Amber Klemann, Susan Sanchez, and Ida Pearce. And to my Critters—Megan Gilpin, Mindy Weiss, and Jodi Moore—I don't know what I'd do without you. You've taught me so much. I adore you. And it must be said: Jodi, thank you for sitting in the golf bag holder with me.

To everyone at Blodgett Memorial Library—it has meant so much to me that you've been cheering me on from the moment I began to write. And to Merritt Bookstore and Oblong Books & Music, my local independent bookstores, you made me a part of your communities long before I had a book to put on your shelves. To my girls at Workshop and everyone at Yanarella—dancing with you makes me a better writer. Cheers and hugs to Taylor Longenberger and Rebecca Britt, future authors who are teaching me how to be a mentor. And to Amy Miccio, boy-watcher extraordinaire, you are important to me. I also have to thank the SCBWI, Verla Kay and her Blue Boards, the gang at YA Lit Chat, and everyone in the Apocalypsies and the Class of 2k12. Being a part of this tribe has made all the difference. You guys are a bucketful of awesome. And to my homeopath and friend, Melissa Sgroi, my safe place to fall—I'm thinking of you. And I also must thank Dawn Turcy Sela of Dawn Sela Photography for my beautiful author photos. I love that two small-town girls, working as cashiers at the Grand Union, have found themselves in their art.

I would like to thank my family—which is a whole lot of people. If you are, or ever have been, a Urbanak, Stanulwich, or Sabatini, then you know how much I love you. A special Kimmiepoppins thank-you to Lorayne Pulcastro for giving me Trevor's waterwheel. To Joanne Sabatini, the Lanes, and the Pierantozzi family for being my personal fan club. I want to thank my brother, Terry Stanulwich, for saying that he's proud of me. It means everything to have the admiration of someone I adore. I'd also like to thank my mom, Jean Stanulwich. You taught me everything I need to know about being strong. And just so you know—every little note in my lunch box mattered.

And finally, I must give my love and thanks to the four men in my life who are stuck living with me. I know it isn't easy—partially because I'm a writer and partially because I'm just me. First, my thanks to my three smart, amazing, and talented boys—Jamison, Ty, and Aidan. I forget to do your laundry, I "cook" takeout more than I should, and I'm often scatterbrained, grouchy, and late . . . but I always have time to read to you. I love you more than anything—even this book. Never let anyone (even me) tell you who or what you're going to be . . . you get to choose. And last, but never least, I'd like to thank my husband, John, who has always been my biggest fan. I'm your biggest fan too. I can't do the hard times without you, and the good stuff isn't real unless I've shared it with you. I love you.

KIMBERLY SABATINI is a former special education teacher who is now a full-time mom and a part-time dance instructor. She lives in New York's Hudson Valley with her husband and three sons. *Touching the Surface* is her first novel. Find out more at kimberlysabatini.com.

SiMON TEEN

Simon & Schuster's **Simon Teen**
e-newsletter delivers current updates on
the hottest titles, exciting sweepstakes, and
exclusive content from your favorite authors.

Visit **TEEN.SimonandSchuster.com** to
sign up, post your thoughts, and find out what
every avid reader is talking about!

ATHENEUM FICTION

Margaret K. McElderry Books

SIMON & SCHUSTER BFYR

SIMON PULSE